Desperate Betrayal

Hildie McQueen

www.crescentmoonpress.com

Desperate Betrayal
Hildie McQueen

ISBN: 978-1-937254-08-7
E-ISBN: 978-1-937254-09-4

Cover Art: Jeannie Rush
Editor: Donna O'Brien
Layout/Typesetting: jimandzetta.com

Crescent Moon Press
1385 Highway 35
Box 269
Middletown, NJ 07748

Crescent Moon Press electronic publication/print publication: September 2011 www.crescentmoonpress.com

For Kurt, the best husband ever.

CHAPTER ONE

Shadows.

Emma Blake always felt at home in the shadows. It was where she lived, always concealing the truth from those around her.

Now as she hid in the doorway of an abandoned building, she couldn't help but compare the current situation to her life. The dampness of the brick wall behind her seeped through to her skin, as she pushed further into the dark to avoid being noticed. The putrid smell of trash and urine barely registered, as she was mesmerized by the scene unfolding before her.

The scene evoked images of the endless battle forces of dark and light had been waging since the dawn of time.

Although beautiful to behold, the warrior who fought before her wasn't exactly an angel, but he was as close to one as she would ever get. She took a big chance sticking around because once he caught her there were only two possibilities for her.

He would either help her or kill her.

The air blew chilly on this damp drizzly day in Atlanta, a city that for some unknown reason, in the last few years, had become a hotbed for demons. With such an influx of demons, human assaults were on the rise.

Emma continued to watch from the shelter of the doorway, as the Protector fought his aggressors. Ten huge low-level demons armed with medieval-type swords.

She tensed, but didn't flinch as a demon's severed arm flew past her and hit the ground next to her foot with a sickening thud.

Emma had no doubt as to who the victor would be in the end. The fluidity of the Protector's movements and the speed of the fight enthralled her. Her gaze locked on his biceps. Muscles bulged on his right arm, as he swung his sword in seemingly effortless motion. Impressive, for the weapon he wielded had to weigh at least twenty pounds.

He dodged a blow and struck out with his sword to slash through one demon's chest. A dagger flew from his left hand and found its target in another's heart.

He already fought the next opponent as both demons fell.

The Protector was magnificent —she had to give him that. He was one of an army of immortal warriors trained for battle against demons. They kept a low profile, from humans, to avoid discovery. Anyone who happened upon them in battle would most likely mistake them for angels.

Avenging angels.

As she watched the Protector now, Emma could understand why people would make that assumption. He was not an angel, but a warrior that fought for good. His golden skin glistened from the rain as he fought, his long blonde hair, held back with a weathered leather strap, flew around him like a halo as he swung his sword.

His face was a masterpiece that God surely had enjoyed creating. Perfectly arched eyebrows framed his ice-blue eyes. A shallow cleft softened his strong jaw. The sensuality of his full lips was not diminished by the snarl that remained constant as he battled.

Two demons left.

~ ☾ ~

One of them looked in her direction. Did he see her? *No. I'm well hidden in this doorway.*

Emma didn't panic. The demon was more worried about his survival at this point, than feeding on her blood. The best option for him would be to run and save himself, while the Protector was distracted fighting another.

He chose self-preservation. Scant seconds later, the scent of the demon's fear assaulted her nostrils as he raced past her.

The demon disappeared around the corner, and she debated the advantages of running as well. Once enraged, only a fool would stick around and try to talk to a Protector. They were slow to calm.

She was one of the few that could see both Protectors and demons in their true forms.

Because of her demon heritage, she was also the Protector's mortal enemy.

The soft plop of droplets from the overhang splashed into puddles, alerted her to the sudden silence. Emma froze and held her breath. The thumps of her heart echoed in her ears, yet she chanced a peek.

The Protector stood very still. He no longer fought. The body of the last demon lay at his feet, its blue blood pooled around his boots. The body evaporated into a translucent vapor and swirled around the magnificent male.

Emma swallowed hard as the Protector raised his head to sniff the air. His actions slow and steady, as if he knew someone stood nearby. His frosty stare began to scan the alley, his eyes narrowed in her direction. She let out a breath of relief when he peered down at his left shoulder. He grimaced as he rotated it. One of the demons had gotten lucky. A blood stain seeped through his gray t-shirt. He lifted the sleeve up and studied the wound, as if oblivious to her presence. He applied pressure with his right hand for a few moments. When he moved his hand away, the bleeding had stopped.

Emma shrank back when he raised his head and glanced in her direction again.

All air left her lungs, when he stalked toward her with an alert expression, as if he expected her to flee in terror before he reached her. The thought did cross her mind.

As the Protector came closer, Emma gritted her teeth and balled up her fists, to keep from running in the opposite direction. Her heart thumped inside her chest.

His face remained expressionless. He kept his hands relaxed at his sides, his movements smooth but methodical. His sword, no longer drawn was sheathed in a scabbard and slung across his broad back.

His body loomed much larger now that he was up close. Fear surged again when the Protector stopped a few feet from her. Her blood ran cold and she could not suppress a tremble when his ice-blue eyes locked with her own and his nostrils flared. Narrowed eyes skimmed over her.

If he sensed demon first, she was dead.

At this distance, the male was magnificent. He towered over her, at least six four and he exuded power.

Emma remained tense and cursed in silence as fear seized her while she waited for his reaction. This was it, time to confront the man she'd been seeking for so long.

Protectors had more strength than demons and although her demon half made her stronger than most humans, no way in hell could she hope to defend herself if he decided to fight.

Cyn pushed fury aside, and took a deep breath to calm. He wasn't in the mood for more surprises. The low-levels that attacked him were less than a threat to him. What infuriated him the most was that he allowed the ambush.

Now a female waited for him, a small one at that. Just what he needed, another annoyance to deal with.

He'd taken his time pretending to inspect the cut to his shoulder, giving her time to run away.

She hadn't.

Interesting.

At this point, he didn't care if she'd seen him fight demons. Who would believe her anyway? As he stalked towards her, her eyes widened and she shuddered, but then squared her shoulders and held her ground.

Even more interesting, the petite woman barely flinched when Cyn stopped just a couple feet away from her and studied her.

Who was she?

The longer he watched her, the more she frightened she appeared. Her heartbeat picked up, her lips parted, and her breathing accelerated. He inhaled the familiar scent of fear. Could she have witnessed what had just transpired between him and the low-level demons?

Regardless, she was afraid of him.

His inner voice urged him to erase her memory and move on. Curiosity stopped him.

He tried to determine what she was. She didn't seem like a demon. Her skin lacked the telltale blue tinge visible to Protectors.

Fully human? Perhaps, but he doubted it.

Cyn leaned forward and peered into her honey-brown eyes, as he tried to read her thoughts.

But he could not.

She could be one of the few humans that were difficult to read, or did she intentionally block him?

This is trouble. Move on.

Once again, he ignored the voice in his head.

The woman swallowed, but didn't budge; as if afraid

he'd attack at her slightest move. Not a bad assumption on her part.

He took advantage of her stillness, Cyn's eyes traveled over her body again. In her gray business suit, she looked like she'd just stepped away from an office. Certainly, there were better places for her to be, than this alley on such a damp dreary day. Almost as if in response to his thoughts, a rumble of thunder boomed over them.

Both ignored it.

The woman became increasingly nervous as he continued to study her. Her breaths now came in small pants as she shuffled, putting weight on one leg and then the other. Her hand shook slightly when she raised it to brush several strands of golden brown hair away from her flushed, heart shaped face.

Pretty was not an adequate word to describe her. She was exquisite. His eyes lingered on her lips.

How would her lips feel under mine?

The fact that she took his breath away gave Cyn pause. After hundreds of years and many attractive women in his bed, it was rare that beauty affected him so intensely.

The female narrowed her eyes at him and her nostrils flared. She interrupted his thoughts. "I know this is probably not the best time, but I need to talk to you. There's no one else who can do what you do. I need your help."

Cyn's interest spiked as she spoke. No accent, so that didn't help him.

He didn't answer her. Instead, he inhaled deeply and concentrated on isolating her scent that floated in the air. She smelled of tropical islands, a hint of coconut mixed with her natural essence. The heady fragrance forced him to take a step back. His entire body reacted to her.

Definitely time to leave.

~ ☾ ~

Like any normal male, it wasn't unusual for him to become aroused in the presence of an attractive female. But this reaction was different. It was intoxicating. Unlike any other he could remember.

His heartbeat quickened, his hands tingled urging him to reach out and touch her. A rush of heat coursed through his body. A feeling not too different from what he experienced in battle, but this time lust, not rage caused it. He couldn't tear his eyes away from her.

The female appeared normal. Yet something about her that he couldn't quite explain, pulled at him.

A witch? He didn't believe so.

Another type of immortal? He hoped not. He'd have to kill her if she posed a threat to humans.

She seemed to sense his thoughts, and took a step back. "Can we go somewhere to talk?" She asked him in a confident voice.

When he reached out to touch her, she held her hands up defensively. "Wait, don't kill me. Just give me a couple minutes to explain...."

"Believe me, sweetheart killing you is not exactly what I have in mind right now." His fingers curled around her forearm and he drew her to him.

She yelped as if his touch burned her. She tried to yank her arm from his hold and glared at him. Her eyes flickered to his hand. "Let go of me, I am not going anywhere, it's very important that I talk to you."

The woman was either crazy or very brave to stand up to him. He released her forearm but kept his hand on her shoulder, to make sure she didn't bolt. "Alright, talk."

Before speaking, she eyed the hand on her shoulder. "My.... my sister, she's been taken, I need your help to save her. Demons took her hostage. I know you can help her. You're sworn to protect innocents." Her bottom lip quivered, it made him wonder if she acted a part, but the plea in her eyes gave him a jolt.

He hated how she fogged his ability to think. He shook his head to clear it.

"I don't do rescues," He snapped. "Why are you really here? Who are you?"

"I just told you, I'm a woman who's desperate enough to come to you for help," She replied.

He studied her for a moment longer before her eyes slid away from his and focused on his lips.

All of a sudden he was able to hear her thoughts. *"His mouth, it's so nice..."*

His gaze fell to hers.

Thunder clapped simultaneously as he gave in to the powerful connection and drew her to him, ignoring her surprised yelp.

He mouth crushed hers. Caught off guard, she parted her lips and he dove in allowing his tongue to explore. She responded almost immediately. The woman clutched his arms and leaned into him. He hardened, aroused at the lush pliant body pressed against him.

With strength that belied her size, she ran her hands up from his forearms to his shoulders and drew him closer. Her lips were as soft as the rest of her. The woman's entire body molded into his now, and the warmth of it enveloped him. He closed his eyes and allowed the wonderful feel of her to consume him. He deepened the kiss as his hands traveled down her back and cupped her butt. When he ground his hardness into her, he was rewarded by a soft moan.

Time seemed to stop as his lips traveled over her mouth. Aroused beyond thought, his fangs dropped and he used the tips to tease her bottom lip.

The tingling on the back of his neck, alerted him of demon presence nearby. The defensive warning jolted him back to reality. He broke the kiss and raised his head to look around while he held her against him. The sound of their heavy breathing filled the quiet of the alley until a growl came from deep in his throat.

More Demons and they were headed for them.

"Damn it," He said, reluctant to move away from her.

When he released her, the woman swayed blinking repeatedly. An expression of shock and disgust crossed her face. Her upper lip curled and she covered her mouth with her hands. "Oh God! I can't believe I let you kiss me."

Cyn ignored her comment at first. "Demons are headed this way. You gotta go," he told her and then narrowed his eyes at her and added, "And for the record, you not only let me kiss you, but you kissed me back."

Putting her hands on his chest she shoved him away. A light blush confirming that she heard his words.

She narrowed those beautiful golden eyes at him. "What did you expect? You killed a bunch of demons. They are going to send an army after you now."

He shrugged, "So, what else is new."

This female was spunky.

Too bad he'd never see her again.

He bowed his head at her. "Nice meeting you."

Turning away, he rushed towards his Harley.

"Wait!" Emma held up both hands and shouted as the Protector ran toward a massive black and chrome motorcycle. He hesitated for a second and she thought he'd heard her.

But, without a backward glance, he straddled the seat and sped off.

"Damn it! Now I have to find him all over again." She jerked around and scanned the alleyway. He'd said demons were headed there. It wouldn't be good to be there alone when they arrived. She hurried out of the alley.

~ ☾ ~

She felt foolish. After all that work to find the Protector and getting up the nerve to talk to him, she didn't even get the chance to tell him the rest of the information. It'd taken her almost a week to find him. Night after entire night spent skulking through shadowy alleys and streets, following demons all over Atlanta.

Now she was forced to start all over again. She dropped her head, and allowed exhaustion to take over.

It began to rain harder so she hurried across the street toward her office.

# # #

Minutes later, Emma sat at her functional wooden desk at Georgia Bank and Trust with her face in her hands and stared at the bleary words on the papers in front of her. Her thoughts were far away.

When she found him again, she would not allow her attraction to the Protector to hinder her. Her priority was to find her sister.

Emma opened her eyes and scanned the almost empty bank lobby through the glass office walls. The wet weather kept most customers home this day.

It was her last day at the bank. She'd requested an extended leave of absence. With no appointments scheduled, the rest of her afternoon loomed ahead.

Since Briana's kidnapping, the days had been unbearable for her. It was hard to concentrate at work while demons held Briana. She didn't want to imagine what her sister went through at the hands of the evil beings.

Hostage, until she brought the *ransom*.

Now, after she'd failed to convince Cyn to help her, a heavy sense of hopelessness engulfed her.

"What happened?" Wendy, her friend and coworker

asked from the doorway. She didn't wait for an answer and walked in closing the door behind her. Wendy plopped down on a chair with hopeful expression on her face. Wendy leaned forward her vivid green eyes searched Emma's face, as she waited for her answer. Emma's mood lightened.

Wendy was the one of a handful of humans Emma had ever met, that knew about demons and Protectors. Wendy was attacked by a demon one night and a Protector rescued her. Although she'd never seen the Protector again, Wendy could describe him in great detail, which she did every chance she got. By Wendy's description, the Protector who rescued her had an uncanny resemblance to Cyn, except for the eye color. She swore her rescuer had clear green eyes. Cyn's eyes were a very definite shade of blue.

It was very strange that Wendy could remember in great detail what happened to her almost two years earlier. As a rule, Protectors were careful after a rescue to erase the human's memories of the demon attack. Although Emma didn't understand why Wendy's memory remained intact, she was grateful to have a friend to confide in.

As their friendship grew, Emma shared more and more about the Protectors. When she confessed her own demon bloodline, Wendy accepted her disclosure without judgment and their friendship became stronger.

Head still in her hands, Emma answered Wendy's question. "I found Cyn, the Protector. But he refused to help me."

"Really? You gotta be kidding me. I thought they're supposed to rescue humans, or, er innocent beings, from demons." Wendy frowned and bit her bottom lip in thought before she continued. "What did you say? What did he say?"

~ ☾ ~

"I told him that my sister is being held hostage by demons and that I needed his help. He said," she deepened her voice, 'I don't do rescues,' and left before I could say anymore. Now I have to find him all over again."

Eyes stinging with tears, Emma threw her hands up in exasperation. "Every day that passes can only be more torturous for poor Briana."

"You'll find him again Emma. I'll help you," Wendy said. Then she stilled and studied Emma, her brow crinkled. "Good thing you don't have any customers, you're a mess."

Emma's hands flew to her hair, she hadn't even thought about straightening herself up after the encounter with the Protector. "It's windy and drizzling out there," she replied, hoping her discomfort wasn't obvious.

She could feel her friend's stare as she took out a compact mirror to check her hair and make-up. Her lipstick smudged from one side of her mouth to her cheek and her hair was disheveled.

"I'm sorry. I'm sure your makeup is the last thing on your mind right now," Wendy said.

Emma's cheeks warmed as she thought about Cyn's kiss. She grabbed for a tissue wiped at her stained mouth harder than necessary. Wendy didn't seem to notice her discomfort and continued to talk, "Don't worry, we'll find him again and explain everything. Then I'm sure he'll agree to help to you. I'll even help you search for him." Remind him that he is supposed to help. He took an oath."

Emma couldn't help but smile at Wendy's stern expression. "I'll do that."

Wendy's face softened as she gave Emma a reassuring smile. "Briana is in all probability doing okay. You told me yourself, she'd been hanging out with demons lately. She might even know some of the demons that took her."

"These demons are not the BFF type, and it's Gerard, a Master demon that has Briana." Emma replied, but she hoped more than anything Wendy was right.

The lobby doors opened and a pair of customers shuffled in and shook rain off their coats and umbrellas. Both headed to the tellers.

Although she and Briana were like night and day, Emma adored her sister.

Just months earlier, Emma suspected that Briana was going to Inferno, a local nightclub, and known demon hangout. She'd tried on several occasions to talk to her sister about the danger of being around too many demons, but Briana laughed off her concerns and called her a bore.

The fact that being in the company of full-blooded demons presented the possibility of her demon side taking over was a thrill Briana couldn't resist.

Now Briana was in trouble. Big trouble.

Hostage, until Emma lured Cyn to the demons.

~ ☾ ~

CHAPTER TWO

In a clearing behind Cyn's house, two teenage boys went through their sword practice routines. The teens stood side-by-side and swung swords up, down, and across. They grunted dramatically as they completed the exercises. Amused at their antics, Cyn struggled to keep a stern expression and watched them with his arms crossed over his chest.

It still amazed him how much his life had changed since he'd moved to Atlanta twelve years earlier. He'd gone from being a single man, to a father, and an uncle of sorts.

Cyn, one of three Protectors assigned to Atlanta, felt settled. His life was pretty much complete. Well, as complete as possible for him.

He concentrated on the boys' efforts and then stepped closer and pushed one of their elbows up. He waited as the boy adjusted his stance.

"Ten more."

Once they completed the ten repetitions, he took his sword out of the scabbard and demonstrated another move. "Put your left foot in front, swing across, draw back and thrust forward. It's best to practice beheading and piercing the heart at the same time —the two sure ways to kill a demon."

"Don't you think it's kinda sick to be training me to do this Dad?" One of the teenagers, a young half-demon, frowned at Cyn. "I mean that's just wrong."

"Blue, you have to know how to defend yourself." Cyn answered him. "Plus, you are half-demon. Full-blood demons are not your friends. Brock, hold your elbows up!" He corrected the other boy, fellow Protector Roderick's son.

Cyn held his sword up. "Okay, watch me and let's go through the moves again."

The boys grumbled but were instantly quiet when Cyn's sword made a swooshing sound as it flew past them with such swiftness that a soft breeze brushed their faces. They stared up at him awestruck.

"Do twenty repetitions, then come inside for dinner."

As he walked toward his house, Cyn's thoughts went back to the woman he'd kissed earlier that day. Her honey-brown eyes flashed in his mind. At over three hundred years old, he'd been with many women. Memories of some lingered. For the most part however, his brief encounters were forgotten almost as soon as he left their bed.

It was rare that he sought out a woman more than a couple of times; for a Protector, it was best to keep relationships short and casual. He tried to remember the last time he'd had sex. Nothing memorable stood out, so he gave up.

The female back in the alley had been so different. He'd felt a strong attraction toward her. The probable cause — the length of time he'd been without a woman. Good thing he didn't know anything about her. She was already a distraction.

Besides his son, his focus in life was to uphold the oath he'd given upon joining the Protector force.

He was sworn to protect and defend innocents from those out to hurt or kill them.

Once in the kitchen, he gathered everything the boys would need to fix sandwiches and placed the items on the counter. He reached for a bag of potato chips. Before he could open it, the boys came in through the back door. He left them to fix a sandwich.

With a soft drink in hand, he headed back outside to sit on the deck. He glanced back to see the boys piling chips on their plates. Perhaps he should have provided a healthier meal for the boys. Things would be so different for Blue if he had a mother. But no, he accepted long ago that he would be single his entire existence.

Julian, their leader, would arrange a marriage if Cyn wished it. The idea of an arranged marriage wasn't very appealing. So unless he met his life-mate on his own, which amounted to finding the proverbial needle in the haystack, the likelihood of a wife for him was pretty slim. No, he did all right on his own.

He felt better now that he'd sorted his thoughts. With his feet propped on the side railing he contemplated the fluffy clouds that drifted by on the bright blue canvas.

The sound of the boys' laughter got his attention. They ate while sharing a private joke. Catching his attention, Blue gave him a thumbs-up.

Yes, all was well.

# # #

A few days later at dusk, Cyn relaxed at his favorite deli in downtown Atlanta, eating a Rueben sandwich and drinking a glass of cold sweet tea. The familiar sounds of pots banging and conversation at Mae's deli were as comfortable as his favorite pair of jeans. He didn't usually see any demon activity this early, so he took the time to eat before a night of patrolling the streets and alleyways of Atlanta.

Two women, who sat at a nearby booth glanced over at him and whispered to each other. The sideways glances and giggles made him clench his jaw in annoyance. He pretended not to notice their attempts to get his attention.

His line of vision shifted to the deli's large window. He'd parked his motorcycle in front of the building where he could keep an eye on it. By itself, the huge black chrome-laden Harley cruiser intimidated well enough to keep most thieves away. However, when people spotted the hilt of his sword that stuck out from one of the saddlebags, they gave it wide berth.

Cyn took a deep frustrated breath when he saw that one of the women had decided to approach him. A blonde, about thirty, wearing too much makeup, wove her way around the tables between them. Before she reached the table, her excessive flowery perfume burned his nostrils.

She stopped by his booth, and leaned over, a welcome mat wearing a smile. "I'm sorry to bother you Hon," her southern accent strong. "But my friend Marlene and I swear we've seen you on television. Aren't you that actor?"

"No Ma'am." Cyn replied glancing up at her, then away. "Just got out of prison, didn't get to do much acting there," He proceeded to take a healthy bite of the sandwich, before he lifted his eyes to meet hers.

The woman jerked upright and jumped back. Her hand flew to her heart, as she attempted a weak smile while she stepped away from the table. All signs of flirting gone, she turned and scurried back to her companion. Several patrons glanced over at him with uncertainty.

The deli owner, Mae, shuffled over and refilled his sweet tea. "That line works every time," she tsked and shook her head in disapproval. The older women patted the net holding her gray hair in place and raised both eyebrows at him. It became obvious by her hesitation to return to the counter that Mae was about to lecture him. Her pretty brown face scrunched in a frown. "You need to be nicer to the ladies, Cyn. That boy of yours could use a momma," she said with a hand on one of her ample hips. "I'm just saying."

"I keep trying to get you to marry me, Mae and you won't," Cyn replied, as he studied a French fry before popping it in his mouth. Even though his expression remained serious, he winked at her. "I'm waiting for you to get tired of Harold."

"I don't know what's wrong with you young men these days," Mae went on. "It's the men playing hard to get now. I'm glad I'm married. Harold chased me, not the other way around! I ain't chasing after no man," Mae shook her head at him and walked away mumbling under her breath, her sizeable hips swaying.

Cyn chuckled at their familiar banter.

A few minutes later, he left the diner and mounted his motorcycle. He stilled when a sharp tingle radiated up his neck.

A demon, a strong one, must be near.

He ripped open the saddlebag yanked out his sword and scabbard and slung it across his back. The sounds and surroundings all became dull to him. He focused on the demon's location as he crept around to the back of Mae's deli.

A bulky demon, dressed entirely in black, held a woman up against the wall with his fangs burrowed deep into her neck while he fed. The demon's long hair blocked Cyn's view of the woman's features. But he could see her feeble attempts to struggle against him. Her weakened fists hit the demon without effect.

The woman's low moan coincided with the lolling of her head. As the streetlight washed over her face, Cyn noted the all too familiar unfocused eyes and blood starved skin.

By the deep tone of the demons' skin, Cyn could tell he was a high-level, capable of draining the woman dry. He drew his sword and growled in an attempt to draw the demon away and save the woman's life.

The demon withdrew from the woman's throat, crimson rivulets ran down his chin as he turned and snarled in anger. Quick as lightning, the demon yanked out his sword and held it at the ready prepared to exchange blows. With his canines fully extended, dripping blood and his red-rimmed eyes, the demon made for a nightmarish sight.

The woman slid to a limp pile on the ground and neither Protector nor demon paid any attention.

Adrenaline rushed through him, this was what he lived for — battle. Cyn's own fangs snapped down in response as he lunged forward.

Swords clashed. The ring of metal against metal echoed off the walls of the buildings in the alleyway, as the two males faced off.

The alley disappeared to Cyn as he focused solely on the demon. All he could see, hear, and sense was his target. Each movement became clear and distinct for him. He grunted and bent backward to avoid the slash of the demon's sword at his throat.

Cyn raised his sword and brought it down with dizzying speed. The demon blocked it effectively, but stumbled back. Snarling he regained his stance and wielded his sword with both hands.

When his opponent's sword descended, Cyn sprung back out of the blade's reach.

The demon proved to be a worthy adversary, their skills almost evenly matched. Low-levels were aggressive, but sloppy. This demon's style was methodical, a telltale sign of his age and elevated status. Cyn forced the demon to block several times, but he also had to defend from several too near assaults.

As they continued in battle, the demon's sword arm began to tremble.

"Didn't feed enough, blood-breath?" Cyn asked with a cocky smile.

The reply was a loud growl, and a two handed swing of the sword.

Cyn parried and faked to the left hoping the demon would advance.

It did.

Cyn shoved his sword through the demon's heart. The demon's shock widened eyes met his. With one last snarl, he fell to the ground and evaporated.

A woman's gasp caught Cyn off guard. "Oh my God, is she dead?!"

Although her hair fell forward and blocked her face from him, his stomach flipped when the female knelt over the unconscious woman

What the hell?

It was the same woman he'd kissed, days earlier.

His gut tightened.

What was she doing here, and why did his body instantly react to her?

She felt the victim's throat for a pulse while she fumbled in her purse.

"I have a cell phone. I'm calling 9-1-1." She shouted back to him.

Cyn ran to her, grabbed her arm and yanked her to her feet. "Get the fuck out of here. I'll take care of this. Leave now!" He gave her a shove toward the street. Not realizing his own strength, he pushed her too hard and she fell to the pavement on all fours.

She glared at him for a moment before she got up and

scrambled back toward him.

Cyn considered apologizing, but instead crouched down by the unconscious woman and reached out to check her for a pulse. It surprised him to find she had a strong one and he breathed a sigh of relief. She would be all right.

He started to push on his earpiece to call into the Protector's network for an ambulance, when the infuriating woman tapped him on the shoulder.

"Is she alright?"

He took a deep breath, but it did little to calm him. He turned to her, his furious gaze meeting her anxious one. He'd forgotten how stunning her eyes were.

He calmed.

"Look, you have to leave. We've been here too long already. I'll call for help then I'll stay a short distance away and ensure she's all right. I won't leave until after the medics pick her up, okay?"

Both jumped at a voice behind them. "Keep your hands where I can see them and step away from the victim."

"This just keeps getting better and better." Cyn grumbled under his breath as he held his hands up and glared at the intrusive woman. She pressed her lips together, obviously trying hard not to say something else.

"Turn toward me nice and slow." When they did, the police officer motioned for Cyn to move away from the women.

Out of the corner of his eye he saw her eyes shift from him to the officer. She wrinkled her brow in thought then spoke to the policeman. "Officer, it's not what you think. You see we just walked up and found this poor woman lying here. We were checking to make sure she's alright." She gave Cyn a triumphant look, who in return returned a droll stare.

"Then why does he have a sword, and why is your leg bleeding ma'am?" without waiting for her to answer the cop waved his gun at them. "Never mind, we'll sort this out at the station." The police officer clicked on his radio, it crackled but didn't work. Cyn used his powers to block the device. The officer frowned at his radio, and then tried again while he walked toward them.

Cyn waited for him to get closer. The police officer met his eyes and froze.

"Go to the end of the building and wait for me." Cyn snapped at the meddling woman, his eyes not leaving the officer's face.

"You're not going to hurt him are you?" She asked him, not moving. When Cyn growled, she jerked back and scurried to the corner of the building.

Cyn waited for her to be out of the way. He connected with the police officer's mind. The man remained frozen as Cyn spoke in a low monotone. "In one minute you will regain full consciousness and realize you came upon this woman who needs assistance. You did not see anyone else here."

Seconds later, Cyn mounted his motorcycle and glided to where the woman stood waiting. Without a word, he lifted her onto the bike behind him. The motorcycle roared to life and they sped down a maze of narrow alleyways and streets at break neck speed.

~ ☾ ~

CHAPTER THREE

The motorcycle's rumble cut through the warm Georgia night as they rode. Scared but excited at the same time, Emma clutched onto his waist, her arms wrapped around him. She'd never ridden on a motorcycle before, but by the speed by which they passed by buildings and cars, and the harshness of the wind beating on her face it felt like they were flying.

They rode for a while in what felt like circles. *Was he trying to lose a pursuer?* She looked around frantically to see if someone followed. For such an early hour, the streets were almost deserted.

Finally, she gave up trying to look around him to see where they went and since he'd not responded to her earlier requests. She also decided it was useless to scream in his ear for him to slow down. Instead, Emma laid her head on the center of the Protector's muscular back.

Better to face death this way, to die while she held on to his hard body, and not be aware of when they were about to slam into a brick wall, or wrap around a light post.

The intensity of the moment did not stop her from appreciating his strong broad back and trim waist. She'd never placed her arms around such an amazing male. When he shifted and turned the bike around sharp corners his hard muscles flexed under her arms. She closed her eyes and inhaled his scent, an incredible mixture of musk and spices. Just as she began to relax, he tensed again, she held on tighter as they took a curve.

There were worse ways to die.

They took another razor-sharp curve, the motorcycle almost laid down as they turned. Her eyes widened as she stared at the rising blacktop. She gulped forcing her heart from her throat.

But she really didn't want to go yet.

"Please slow down," she yelled into his ear and shoved her face back between his shoulder blades. The bike finally came to a screeching halt a few minutes later.

Emma lifted her head and looked around tentatively. They were in a deserted narrow alleyway that barely allowed room for the motorcycle in between the rows of buildings. It was very dark — the only light, a feeble glow from a lone streetlight.

She dragged her arms from around the Protector and scrambled off the bike. Emma tugged her fingers through her tangled hair to hide her nervousness as she waited for him to dismount.

Hands still on the handlebars, as if composing his thoughts, he sat on the motorcycle and stared straight ahead for a few moments. Enthralled, she watched as he yanked off the thick leather strap that held his hair back and shook his head allowing the golden tresses to fall past his broad shoulders. He swung one long leg over the bike and stood up slowly. When he glared at her, his ice blue eyes practically glowed.

The man was definitely angry and no doubt she was in for a show of his temper.

He didn't disappoint.

"You are annoying the shit out of me," he bellowed while he paced in front of her. He jammed his hands into his pockets and then took them out again in exasperation. "I told you already, I am not going to help you. So why are you stalking me?" He yanked a hand through his hair. The entire time she noticed that he scanned the surrounding buildings, taking inventory of the area.

Always alert.

"How did you find me?" He asked turning on her, his brow pinched. The slight glow of his eyes was a bit disconcerting. Emma had never seen eyes like his. He seemed discomfited by her intense scrutiny and his gaze shifted away from her for a moment. Gorgeous or not, his anger scared her.

"I've been driving around every night for the last f-four days searching for you." Emma stuttered. "I can sense demons —it's a gift of sorts. So I kept an eye out for them, hoping one would lead me to you." He didn't reply, just continued to stare at her, his lips pressed into a straight line.

"That demon you killed earlier, was a high-level demon wasn't he? They are really going to come after you this time." She gave him a stern look and continued on, not waiting for him to answer. "I suppose he would have killed that poor woman."

She remembered the people back at the alley. One or both were dead. Emma stepped closer to him and without thinking she hit him in the chest, hard. He barely moved. Then realizing what she had done she jumped back and mumbled "sorry".

He lowered his head his eyes trained on her. It made her feel like a child. "Why did you hit me?"

"What happened to her?? Did you call an ambulance after you killed the officer?" Emma asked ignoring his question.

Cyn tried his best to stay angry with her, but couldn't. Why did he feel the need to reassure her?

He clenched his jaw.

~ ☾ ~

She wasn't even his type. Very small, he guessed about five-four with a curvy figure. Tall athletic women were more to his liking. Although she did have shapely legs, a slim waist and her breasts would overflow in his palms, and she was gorgeous. Gorgeous was definitely his type.

Irritated at the direction of his thoughts, he snapped at her. "I didn't kill the cop. I just rearranged his memory of what happened. I'm sure once he got his bearings he ensured the woman was cared for."

He took a step closer taking in her scent. For some insane reason, he wanted to know if she still smelled of tropical beaches. She did.

Her puzzled eyes met his. Those honey-brown beauties were definitely a window to her emotions. Right now they told him she was anxious and desperate.

His eyes roamed down to her lips. He'd enjoyed the kiss before, the feel of her body against his.

"I say we finish where we left off the other day, and then I can drop your pretty little ass back where I found you. The demons have a hard-on for me right now, so we don't have much time." Cyn reached for her. She didn't move as he slid his hand down the side of her face and touched her hair.

Puzzled by such a strong tug toward her, he told himself to step away. It was sheer nonsense how much he wanted to kiss her at this moment.

The fact that she did not move away, but maintained eye contact encouraged him, drew him in.

Did she feel the same draw toward him? He lowered his head to kiss her.

"They have Roderick," She croaked, her voice hoarse, her fearful eyes wide.

Cyn froze.

Roderick. His friend. Alive?

He'd crossed paths with the Spartan many times in

the three hundred years since he became a Protector, but after he moved to Atlanta, they'd grown close, even lived together until Roderick married.

When Roderick met Rachel, an Atlanta native, theirs was a classic love at first sight. They married without Julian's permission and Roderick was forced to resign as a Protector. He'd found a renewed purpose in working as a doctor at a local hospital, until he'd disappeared ten days earlier.

Although the Spartan was a fierce warrior, without a sword he was tempting prey for the high-level demons.

Enraged, he glared at the woman, his words clipped as he spoke to her. "If they had Roderick, he is long dead by now." He stepped away from her, fisting his hands at his sides.

Was she part of a trap set up by the demons?

"He is alive. I saw him." Her voice laced with desperation. "Please, my sister Briana will not survive long with the demons."

Cyn backed down. "Look ..."

"Emma."

He ignored her. "You may as well accept it; both Roderick and your sister are dead. End of story." He turned to go, no longer interested in kissing her. He was leaving. She could find her own way back.

When he felt her hand on his arm, the jolt of her touch stopped him in his tracks. He turned and waited to see what other lie she would tell him.

Instead, she just looked at him, the plea in her gaze as evident as the golden specks in her irises. "She's alive, I know it. I feel it. She's my sister, the only family I've got left. Please help me, I beg you. She's all I have. I swear to you, my sister and your friend are both alive. Go ahead see for yourself." She told him as she tilted her head back. Then she closed her eyes and opened her mind to him.

He read her thoughts and narrowed his eyes. "Who sent you?"

"What?" Her eyes flew open and she started to deny, but stopped when he held his hand over her mouth.

"Don't lie to me," he hissed at her. "I just read your mind. A demon sent you. Right? They may or may not have your sister. But a fucking demon sent you."

Emma squared her shoulders and stared straight at him. "No one sent me. All I know is that demons came and grabbed me from my bed one night last week. They took me to their coven. I'm not quite sure where it is. They kept me there all night to wait for Gerard, the Master Demon, to speak to me.

When Cyn didn't speak she continued, her speech faster. "I was forced to stand for hours and watch while the demons fed from humans and did all kinds of horrible things to them. I watched them feed and have sex. They were absolutely brutal. I was so repulsed I got sick. When I crumpled to the floor from exhaustion, they yanked me back up." Her voice shook.

Cyn didn't know why, but his gut clenched as he thought about demons doing who-knew-what to her. He waited for her to finish, not sure he wanted to hear the rest of it.

"I was exhausted and so extremely thirsty...I asked for water, but they wouldn't let me have anything to drink. Finally, Gerard decided to speak to me. He told me he had my sister and wanted both of us to join him. I didn't believe him so they dragged me to see her for myself. I could see her through a one-way mirror. She was alive."

Cyn scanned the area and waited for her to finish.

"On my way to see my sister, I saw your friend, Roderick. He was chained to a wall. They told me who he was. He has long silver hair and lightning bolt tattoos on his biceps. I'm not sure he was conscious, but he was definitely breathing. He had been beaten; one of his eyes completely swollen shut." Her voice hitched as she continued. "I don't know of anyone else who can help me. I am begging you. Please, I need your help."

"And just how did you manage to escape?" He asked her, his voice flat, emotionless.

"I didn't. After I agreed to his terms, Gerard touched the back of my neck and I passed out. I woke up back in my bedroom. I thought Briana would be there too, but she wasn't."

It didn't make any sense. Why would they allow her to go and not her sister? He was torn, but didn't want to take a chance; maybe she could lead him to Roderick.

If he was really alive.

"I'm probably going to be sorry for this." Without another word, he blindfolded her with the leather strap he'd been using to hold his hair back. He picked her up and put her back on the bike, jammed a helmet on her head and they took off again.

~ ☾ ~

CHAPTER FOUR

With the helmet on, the wind did not hammer her as hard. It felt like they rode slower this time. Emma relaxed into Cyn's broad back and she did not try to remove the blindfold. She didn't want to take a chance that if he felt her try anything, he would change his mind and not help her. They rode for a short while before stopping. The sound of mechanical gears, like those of an automatic garage door let her know they'd arrived at their destination. The motorcycle glided forward, and then stopped.

A distinctive odor of oil and gasoline permeated the air. The silence was sudden as Cyn turned off the motor and the motorcycle tipped to the side. The motion caused her to lose her balance. Emma clung tighter to Cyn's waist.

His hands were warm when they covered hers to remove them from his mid-section.

"You won't fall. I'll help you off," he told her.

Emma tensed when his hands wrapped around her and lifted her from the bike. He didn't let go of her until she gained her balance, then he took the helmet. Not able to see a thing, Emma put her hands out to steady herself. She was relieved when he took one of her hands in his and gently guided her ahead.

"Come, I will remove your blindfold in a couple of minutes." She felt self-conscious; having to walk around blindfolded and suppressed the urge to kick at him.

~ ☾ ~

"I have a terrible sense of direction, you could have left off the blindfold and I promise you, I would never find my way here again," she mumbled unhappily.

Without answering her, Cyn led her up some steps and told her to stand still while he placed his hands on her shoulders and held her in place. An electrical hum surrounded her. She tried to move away but couldn't since he still held her.

"Relax, I'm scanning you for weapons and tracers." He stood right behind her, his deep voice too close to her ear.

Her heart fluttered and she tried to let out a shaky breath without calling attention to herself. What was wrong with her? When the humming stopped, Cyn guided her again. She shuffled behind him, trying to make sense of her surroundings. Cyn's blindfold worked perfectly and she couldn't see a damn thing. He continued wordlessly and led her by the hand.

When his hand released hers, she waited listening intently, but all she could hear was her own heartbeat. Finally, he removed her blindfold and she squinted at the brightly lit room.

"Damn! You brought a girl home. Who is she?" A teenage boy stared at her, his mouth forming an "O". He got up from an oversized leather couch and ambled toward them. By the light blue tinge of his skin, she could tell he was part demon. He stood a few inches taller than her, was lean and in very good shape, with well-defined arms. His shoulder length brown hair was messy, as if he hadn't bothered to comb it in days. The teen's deep blue eyes darted between her and Cyn as he waited for a response.

Cyn brushed past the youth and nudged him with his shoulder playfully. "Shut up Blue."

The immense living room flowed into a pristine

kitchen. With its openness and the high ceilings, the home fit Cyn perfectly.

Eyebrows raised, Blue's eyes swept over Emma, from head to toe. Then he smiled and glanced over his shoulder at Cyn. "Super hot. Is she your girlfriend?"

Cyn didn't answer him, but continued to a large stainless steel refrigerator and took out two bottles of water. He held one out to her.

Emma smiled at the boy as she walked around him to grab the drink.

After taking a few sips, she rolled the bottle between her hands and waited, unsure what to do. Both males studied her for several moments, not speaking. She felt awkward under their scrutiny and self-consciously swept a stray strand of hair behind her ear.

"Nice kitchen," She made an attempt at conversation.

Cyn gave a noncommittal grunt in response.

He leaned against the kitchen island and gulped down the water. He propped an elbow on the countertop and crossed his ankles. By his relaxed pose, one would think if it was the most natural thing in the world to bring home a complete stranger.

Maybe it was.

Blue held up a finger to the Protector and began to dig in his jeans pocket, then walked over and handed Cyn some wrinkled pieces of paper he'd dug out.

"Two calls from Uncle Kieran, he's pissed. Another one is from some asshole who called about hiring you to kill his wife. He said he owns Universal Blood Banking, I think. Said she was a demon-bitch. Oh and Aunt Rachel called." Cyn's eyes flashed to Emma, but he waited patiently for Blue to finish. "She said we were supposed to come over for dinner tonight."

All she could do was stare at them, amazed at how comfortable the boy was around the deadly Protector.

~ ☾ ~

"Oh and I need a raise on my allowance. I'm not your damn secretary."

Cyn looked up at the ceiling and then back to Blue. Emma held her breath, hoping he wasn't about to strike the boy. Surprisingly, Cyn answered Blue good-naturedly. "Thank you for the messages Blue. Stop cussing so much. No on the allowance increase because you swear too much. I will take you to Rachel's for dinner, even though I should ground you for... "

"Yeah, yeah, I know too much swearing. Okay deal," Blue replied with a wide smile while bobbing his head. Cyn cocked an eyebrow at the boy and motioned toward Emma with his head.

Blue turned to Emma, with a sheepish grin. "Sorry for cussing in front of you."

Emma smiled and nodded at him. She had a hard time believing the scenario before her. Was Cyn a father? Was he married? Who was this deadly warrior who exercised such patience with the half-demon teenager? Who was Rachel? His sister?

Cyn started to leave the kitchen, and then turned back as though she was an afterthought. He barely glanced at her "Blue, please show Emma where the spare bedroom is and don't touch her."

So he remembered her name.

Blue huffed. "Yes my Lord and Master Cyn. Anything else I can do for you."

Cyn's lips curved into a smile as he shook his head at the boy. His face transformed. His eyes sparkled, bright white even teeth competed with deep dimples for her attention. He took her breath away and she couldn't help but stare with her mouth gaping wide open. How was that possible that he appeared more attractive every time she saw him?

"Smart Alec. Just do it Blue." Cyn glanced over at her,

still smiling and she snapped her mouth shut. "Emma, we'll talk later after I return some calls," He told her before he turned to walk away.

Emma frowned at Cyn's retreating back, and then directed her attention to Blue. "Is that your real name? Blue?"

"Nope, my name is Argos. I keep telling Dad to call me Skyn."

Her eyes widened. *Oh my God. Did he just call Cyn "Dad"!*

Blue continued to talk, not noticing her wide-eyed reaction, "but he won't do it. I think it will make a good team name, when I become a Protector. Don't you? Cyn and Skyn."

Her heart began to pound, but she didn't want Blue to see her distress. She couldn't help but like the boy. "I think I can understand why he won't call you Skyn, it's kind of silly. But I will call you Argos if you want?"

Blue scrunched his handsome face. He was going to be a hunk when he got older. "Nah, that's my birthfather's name and I hate his guts. So Blue works for me."

"I'm Emma." She held out her hand.

He put his hands up, as if in surrender and pointed at a small camera on the wall. "Can't touch remember?" He made a face at the camera and motioned for her to follow. "I'll show you to your room and then we can have a snack."

Emma held back, she was dying to ask what his actual relationship was to Cyn and how he came to live with him. Emma could relate to alternative family lifestyle, since she grew up in foster care.

But this was way past alternative.

A Protector living with a half-demon teenager?

Cyn's a father.

Regardless of how it came to be, it was a fact.

~ ☾ ~

The fact slammed into her gut, and twisted her stomach with guilt over what she had to do. She followed Blue's slim figure, as he walked down a short hallway and showed her into a small bedroom.

"This is where you crash. If you want to freshen up or whatever, there's the bathroom." Blue motioned to a doorway just past the bed. "I'll be in the kitchen. I'm making some grilled cheese sandwiches. I can really grill the cheese," He patted his stomach. "They are sooo good. Want one?"

Emma smiled at him. "Sure that sounds great. I'll be there in a few."

Blue nodded at her and left the room, whistling as he walked back toward the kitchen.

She tried to remember when she'd eaten last. Her stomach growled at the thought of food, confirming that she was, in fact, starving. A grilled cheese sandwich sounded perfect. And, now she wanted to talk to Blue, curious to know how it came to be that he lived with Cyn.

The bedroom was a good size, but sparsely furnished, with only a full size bed, a nightstand and a dresser to complete the room. Emma walked to the bed and threw her purse on it. She sat down on the edge, a myriad of emotions churned through her. What was she going to do now? Her sister's life depended on her. Could she follow through and save her only family member?

What about this family?

Hard as it was to accept, it seemed that Cyn was a father.

Yet, she couldn't allow what she found out about Cyn to distract her. She had a mission to accomplish; she wouldn't let anything stop her from freeing Briana. The more she got to know him the harder it would be to accomplish it.

She hadn't expected this. Protectors were lone

warriors that lived alone and died alone. Her father, a high-level demon, taught her all about the Protectors. He wanted his daughters to be aware of their existence, in case one ever confronted them. He told them Protectors took an oath, to slay demons that posed a threat to humans and that they weren't allowed to marry and couldn't have children.

As the thoughts tumbled through her mind, she ran her fingers through her hair and grimaced when they got stuck in the tangles.

I must be a wreck.

She peered into the bathroom. It was a small bright room, with a toilet and a pedestal sink next to a glass-enclosed shower. On a clear shelf over the sink, some toiletries were scattered. Two plush beige towels hung on a chrome bar attached to the shower door.

Emma studied the disheveled woman in the bathroom mirror, and cringed. Her hair was a tangled mess from the wind and helmet, her mascara was smeared and her clothes were crumpled.

She took a brush out of her bag and combed the knots out, then swept it into a long ponytail. After she splashed water on her face, Emma brushed her teeth. Critically, she assessed her blouse and jeans and smoothed them down with her damp hands. Not much more could be done to remedy her appearance, so she gave up and went to find Blue.

And, to find out more about the Protector she was to betray.

~ ☾ ~

CHAPTER FIVE

Cyn lay back on his bed. His legs hung over the edge as he listened to his brother's Scottish burr over the computer speakers. "Damn it Cyn, what in the bloody hell were you doing? Julian heard about you fighting demons the other day in an alleyway. I can't believe you risked a brawl with demons before dark. Anyone could have seen you. We don't need this shit right now. I know you're pissed about Roderick. Believe me, I know how you feel. But, exposing us will not help. Julian is going to rip you a new one."

Kieran's strong Scottish accent was a remnant of his prolonged stay and subsequent returns to their homeland.

"Okay, Okay. Are you finished?" Cyn snapped. Everything Kieran said was true. Kieran didn't reply. "I didn't go out to fight the damn demons on purpose. I was supposed to meet Argos. He said he wanted to talk to me. He wants custody of Blue. Obviously, it was a set up. Demons were waiting to attack me." Cyn sat up and shoved his hair away from his face.

Mental note - get a haircut.

"Shit I left you a message and told you about the meet." Cyn said.

On the monitor, Kieran's eyes narrowed in thought. The more analytical of the two brothers and although born after Cyn, Kieran was older in human years. Kieran did not become a Protector until his thirties. The stubborn Highlander fought tooth and nail against his calling, choosing to remain in Scotland with his wife, Catarina.

To this day, Kieran always analyzed everything to death before he made a decision. One thing he could never be accused of was being impulsive.

Cyn knew that Kieran, like him, would do anything to protect Blue. Blue, was family, an important part of their life.

His son.

He recalled the night he first laid on eyes on Blue, just as easily as if it had happened yesterday. One night while out on patrol, Cyn sensed the presence of a strong demon and went to investigate. He walked up just as the demon struck a little child. The child began to wail, trying to keep away from the demon's reach. The demon spat at the child. "Worthless little half-blood, no better than the bitch that birthed and left you."

At the time Cyn didn't realize that Blue was half-demon, not that it would have mattered. He couldn't stand by and watch an innocent be harmed. He'd drawn his sword and ran at the demon, a feral growl of anger resonating. The demon picked up the child and threw it at him. Cyn dropped his sword and caught the baby with both hands.

"Take Argos, he's worthless to me. I have no use for a damn kid." The demon yelled, while he backed away at the same time.

Taking advantage of Cyn's distraction, Blue's father took off.

Blue, about two years old at the time, must have sensed safety in Cyn's arms. He promptly stuck his thumb in his mouth, leaned against Cyn's chest and let out a shaky sigh. For reasons he could never explain, Cyn knew at that moment he was meant to raise the boy himself.

At first, it was a difficult transition for him, from bachelor to single parent. The other Protectors were extremely supportive. Roderick and Rachel's son, Brock, was about the same age as Blue, so Rachel kept Blue most nights while Cyn worked.

Roderick, who was already retired from the Protector force, stepped in many times and covered patrols for Cyn if Blue was sick.

His brother was a huge help as well. From the beginning, Kieran never complained when Cyn switched nights with him so that he could be home with Blue as much as possible. The last twelve years passed by swiftly and Blue grew up to be a healthy, well-adjusted young man. Cyn would protect his son with his life.

Kieran's angry voice snapped Cyn's attention back from his thoughts. "You trusted Argos to meet you? I doubt that asshole wants Blue back. He is just using him to get to you. Probably wants money," Kieran shook his head, "When I get back I will find Argos myself and when I do, I will cut off his balls."

Kieran always wanted to cut someone's balls off. He hadn't yet, not that Cyn knew of anyway, but he wouldn't put anything past his angry and sullen brother.

Cyn waited before he spoke. "I brought a woman here tonight." He got up from the bed and faced his brother's stern face on the computer screen. "She says she needs my help. That demons have her sister." Kieran's eyes narrowed. "She also told me she saw Roderick and that he's alive. I read her thoughts and it rang true. She believed it anyway. Said her sister's being held hostage by Gerard."

Kieran crinkled his brow and bent his head as he began to analyze the situation. Cyn continued, "I don't fully trust her, but I'm going to keep her close"

~ ☾ ~

Kieran grunted. "Keeping her close huh? Is she attractive?"

Cyn just glared at him. "I'm keeping her close to get information out of her."

Kieran continued undaunted. "You brought her to your house, and you seem uncomfortable." His brother's sly expression annoyed him. "Hasn't it been a while since you've been with a woman? If she's pretty, enjoy. Just don't let your guard down. Did you scan her for tracers?"

"Yes, the security system didn't find anything. The one thing that bothers me the most is... ," Cyn said, "that she mentioned Gerard by name. Most people don't know the Master demon's name. That, in itself, makes me suspicious of her. I blindfolded her as a preventative measure since I can't erase her memories yet. I don't want to chance that she knows the locations of this house."

"So what are you going to do now?" Kieran asked

"Ask her a lot of questions. Keep trying to read her mind, which is hard. We're going over to Rachel's for dinner. I'll ask Rachel to try to read her as well. Are you coming?"

Kieran's face hardened as he shoved a damp lock of hair out of his eyes. "I can't. I'm asshole deep in this assignment. I have been chasing LeBlanc, through two states, now the damn demon is hiding in the middle of the Louisiana swamps. Why do I always get the ones that like to hide in swamps? I can't stand this foul place." Kieran glanced around, a snarl on his lips.

"Watch your back," Cyn cautioned his brother.

Kieran gave a droll look. "Yeah, I'll be back tomorrow and as far as watching my back, I would say your backside will be more exposed than mine tonight big brother. Call Julian." He abruptly ended the transmission.

~ ☾ ~

Cyn lowered the soundproofing shields in his bedroom and office. Julian could wait. He didn't feel like hearing his boss go off right now. The man had almost as much power as God and none of the Protectors liked to make him angry.

Rich as Midas too, he paid the Protectors very well for their services.

As far as they knew, their Roman commander was one of, if not the first of the Protectors. Julian was also the most powerful of them. He constantly traveled around the world helping out the Protectors in each city. Julian also kept track of higher-level demon's movements and activities. Although he was centuries old, Julian appeared to be about twenty-five and was a force to be reckoned with.

Cyn walked down the hall toward the kitchen and stopped at the end of the hallway to listen. Blue and Emma were in the kitchen. Emma sat across the table from Blue and ate a grilled cheese sandwich while she listened to him describe his latest gaming program. He rarely saw Blue so animated with strangers. The kid waved his hands in the air as he described the different levels of the world he'd created.

Finally, Emma raised her hand, and laughed. "Whoa Blue, I think you lost me there after the second level of the thirty-eighth realm. How do you expect gamers to keep track?"

Blue stared at her, with a look of disbelief and then shook his head. "You're probably too old to get it." Emma gasped, and then threw a piece of cheese at him. It stuck to the middle of his forehead.

Blue grunted as if he'd been shot, and after a dramatic wave of his hand across his brow, he fell out of his chair onto the floor.

Emma giggled and shook her head at his antics.

~ ☾ ~

Blue was a charmer, already well on his way to winning Emma over.

When he spotted Cyn in the hallway, Blue jumped up. “Hey Dad, I didn’t hear you,” he sat back in the chair and picked up a half eaten sandwich, his eyes darting between Cyn and Emma.

The urge to hug his son was strong, but he refrained, knowing Blue would be mortified with any display of affection in front of Emma. “I suggest you work as hard on your school work, as you are on that gaming program.”

Blue frowned and took a bite before replying. “Yes Sir.”

Cyn spoke to Emma, “When you’re done eating, we need to talk.”

Blue was already leaving the room. “I’ll be in my room...um studying.”

~ ☾ ~

CHAPTER SIX

Apprehension gripped Emma at being alone with the Protector. He made her feel things she didn't understand and wasn't prepared to deal with. Enough was going on in her life right now. Too many emotions already battled without adding attraction to the mix.

She picked up her cup and took it to the sink.

Cyn didn't move from the doorway, she could sense his eyes on her as she grabbed a small dishtowel and dried off the sink area and faucet to stall for time, and attempt to try to get her emotions under control.

Not able to prolong it any longer, Emma turned around and faced him. His too intense gaze followed her every movement, a total contrast to the casual picture he portrayed leaning against the doorjamb with his hands in his pockets. "Did you come up with a plan to rescue my sister and your friend?"

"Not here. We'll talk in my bedroom, my equipment is there." Cyn walked away and she followed. They went down the hallway in the opposite direction of the guest bedroom. Emma had to move fast to keep up with his long strides. The man moved with an assured fluidity which could only come from years of having to remain undetected.

When they entered his bedroom she glanced over the space, taking it all in. The room was functional and clinical, a combination bedroom and office with muted gray walls devoid of a single adornment. A contemporary desk holding a flat-screen laptop occupied the alcove. Other than a small picture of Cyn and Blue next to the computer, nothing else was on the surfaces of the desk or the nightstands, not even a lamp or clock.

Plush gray bedding folded down to show stark white sheets made his king-sized bed an inviting sight.

While she studied the surroundings, he pushed several buttons in a control panel by the door. Emma eyed him warily as glass shields fell, fully closing off the area. She gulped at the reality that she was trapped in very close proximity with a Protector.

In his bedroom.

"Part of the house security system, soundproof and teen proof," was all he said as he walked to his bed, sat down and began to remove his boots. He yanked his socks off and threw them toward his closet.

Emma felt uncomfortable and remained standing just inside the door. The situation felt too personal. She fidgeted with the hem of her shirt to keep her hands busy.

He moved with a graceful ease of a man sure of himself, as he picked up his boots and put them beside the bed.

Did he think she would to sleep with him in exchange for his help? Would she do that? Was that the only way to get his help? What about Blue? Did he not care that his son was in the house?

She bit her bottom lip and surveyed the room purposely skipping over the huge bed.

When she forced herself to glance back to the bed, Cyn was preoccupied reading the display on his cell phone.

She swallowed at the blast of feral heat when he raised his eyes to her. His interest evident by the way his hungry eyes swept leisurely from her lips down her body.

She looked away from him and lunged for a chair just

a few feet away, deciding it would be easier to fend off his advances if she sat.

For now.

She jumped at the touch of a firm hand on her shoulder. He'd come up behind her without making a sound. The man moved fast. The feel of his breath on the back of her neck made her relive what had transpired between them in the alley. She almost leaned back into his warmth.

"Turn around." His smooth voice flowed over her like velvet.

Emma tried to swallow but her mouth went dry. She turned to find he stood very close.

God help her, she'd never seen a more handsome man than the one who stood before her now. Her body screamed for his touch. She wanted to be with him, her skin against his. But she wouldn't sleep with him as a form of payment.

What if during sex he sensed that she was part demon and killed her on the spot? But then again, maybe he would kill her just for saying no.

She forced herself to remain calm and placed her hand on his chest only to draw it back when the urge to caress him became too strong.

"Listen Cyn. I know most women throw themselves at you. I mean you're extremely good-lo... but, I, – I am not going to have sex with you right now. What happened before between us, out there in the alley? That was just because of the rush of adrenaline after your encounter with the demon...,"She stopped babbling, at a loss for words.

Cyn stood back with his arms crossed while he stared down at her. He raised an eyebrow and his lips curved into a crooked smile.

"I was going move the chair so you could sit by the

desk and I could get some more information from you. But I see your mind is on other things." He leaned in closer to her and his smile widened. "You said 'not right now', does that mean we'll have sex later?"

A scorching flush of embarrassment crept up her face. Not sure of how to respond, she huffed and pushed him out of her way as she stomped toward the desk.

A different, more methodical side of the man became evident as he asked her questions about locations and descriptions of everyone and everything she saw while at the compound. He questioned her about the types of buildings and any landmarks, how many demons, and where they were positioned when they transported her. The thoroughness of his questioning and the speed that he entered the data into his computer amazed her. His fingers literally flew over the keys.

Emma studied his profile as he typed. The man didn't seem real—no way could a human be so perfect. His plush lashes matched the perfectly arched eyebrows that framed his ice-blue eyes. Those eyes, they were a most disconcerting color. She'd never seen the like. When they locked with hers, it was as if he could peer into her soul. The slight indentation on his chin caught her attention. What would it feel like to press her lips there?

When her eyes rose to his, he was staring at her. She almost groaned, chagrined at being caught making a fool of herself yet again.

His eyes leveled on her lips and she gulped. Was he going to kiss her again?

She jumped when his intercom beeped.

Again, he cocked an eyebrow at her and his lips twitched.

Cyn relaxed back into his chair and pushed the talk button.

Emma leaned closer and peeked at the computer

screen. She couldn't make out any of the information on the screen. It was some type of code. She wondered if he used it because he didn't trust her or if it was out of habit.

Blue's voice came over the intercom. "Hey Dad, when are we leaving?"

"Give me ten minutes," Cyn told him and pushed the button again to disconnect.

He stood up and stretched, his movements reminded her of a sleek tiger as he walked toward what she assumed was the bathroom "I'm going to take a quick shower. Then we're going to a friend's for dinner."

He grabbed a small dirk off his dresser and walked away from her, did he plan to have to protect himself from her? She wondered if he'd forgotten she was locked in the room with him. She opened her mouth, but nothing came out when he pulled his shirt off over his head. His wide back was ripped — muscular and smooth. His broad shoulders tapered to a narrow waist.

She started to say something again, but then he dropped his pants and underwear at the same time. Even his butt was strong and good-looking, not flat at all, but well-shaped and muscular. His long lean legs had a light fuzz of blond hair that glowed on his golden skin. Mouth dry, at that point Emma had no choice but to remain silent and take full advantage of the scenery before her.

She knew the Protectors were stunning males, but this was her first time seeing one up close and fully nude at that. As Cyn continued into his bathroom, Emma's mouth watered. She dug her fingernails into her hands to keep from following behind him so she could keep watching.

The swish of the shower told her what he did now. She listened to the sound, and closed her eyes. Emma pictured his hands as they lathered that body under the spray of hot water. Were his foamy hands slow as they stroked over that strong chest and then down his flat stomach? Did his wet fingers trail to his muscular thighs? She would die happy if she could watch the man take a shower.

Emma shook her head at her repeated distraction and stood up.

She needed to concentrate on what was important right now. She should consider her options, not sit there drooling over the man in the shower. Rational thoughts evaded her when near him. She squeezed her eyes shut for a moment and began to formulate a plan of action.

First, she would convince Cyn to take her on her sister's rescue mission. Next, she'd talk Gerard out of his plan to capture Cyn. She had to come up with a plan to save Cyn, her sister and maybe even herself from certain death. To accomplish all of that, she needed to stay focused.

"Okay, that is a hell of a list," Emma muttered and paced around the room, while she waited for Cyn to finish in the bathroom.

If only she didn't have to involve anyone else in all of this. Emma had considered confronting the demons on her own, right after they took Briana. But she knew she didn't have a chance against so many. She'd even considered approaching higher-level demons serving in local government offices and asking for their assistance. But she was sure they wouldn't care about the demise of a half-demon girl. They were well aware rogue demons killed innocent humans yet did nothing about it. Scared of humans discovering their demon identity, they used the media and fed reporters and the police fake evidence to cover up the deaths.

The Master demon incited a large amount of the needless violence. How she hated that demon.

~ ☾ ~

One look into Gerard's soulless black eyes and it was obvious that he was pure evil.

~ ☾ ~

CHAPTER SEVEN

Deep in thought, Emma didn't hear Cyn cut off the water in the shower. She started, when she noticed him at the dresser. His back to her, he dug through a drawer wearing only a towel that was wrapped low on his hips. Her breath hitched at the sight of his still damp bare skin. Droplets of water clung to his muscles and glistened on his tawny skin as he hunted for clothing.

He turned. Cyn was definitely a perfect example of pure masculinity. Her eyes traveled slowly from his muscular broad chest down to his sculpted abdomen. When her gaze trekked further downward, Emma noted a slight movement under his towel. Mortified, she turned away.

Would she ever stop making a fool of herself?

Cyn cleared his throat and went to the control panel pushed a code in and the shields rose.

"Did you forget the security shields were still in place?" Emma asked.

"Nope," he replied without hesitation. "Couldn't leave you unescorted with my son here in the house."

He'd undressed in front of her on purpose. If he'd meant to entice her, it worked.

His towel slipped dangerously low and she caught a glimpse of the trail of hair descending from his navel to a place she had no business thinking about. "Are you taking me to my car on your way to your dinner?" Emma asked, trying hard not to stare. If only the damn towel would fall already.

When he looked at her, Emma pressed her lips together and feigned a sudden interest in the wall behind him.

"No. I am not letting you out of my sight until after I figure out what is going on," Cyn told her as he lifted his towel and secured it around his waist. Emma's annoyance at his words did not stop the pang of disappointment.

"If we aren't going to rescue my sister tonight then I want to go home. I have a life you know. A cat to feed, bills to pay," she snapped. "I can't just hang out with you until you decide what to do."

He came closer. A tantalizing hint of musky spice teased her nostrils.

The anger in his glare caused a shiver to run through her, not from fright, but from another emotion. Desperate for space between them she attempted to move back. Trapped by the chair behind her legs, she had no choice but to endure his proximity.

When he spoke, his voice held a dangerous edge. "You need me to save your sister right?" Emma bit her lip and nodded as he continued. "Then you play by my rules. I suggest you call and find someone to feed your damn cat."

With that frosty stare and the lethal tautness to his body, he was intimidating. Even naked, with only a towel wrapped around his waist, he was a frightening sight. Yet somehow, she knew he wouldn't hurt her.

"I don't have my cell phone here with me." She said, giving him her best glare.

At his fierce scowl, Emma understood what any demon confronted by him felt. She studied the pattern on the carpeting, not sure what to do next.

He went to his bed, picked up his cell phone and

handed it to her. "Call someone - we're leaving in about two minutes for dinner." His voice had softened.

She squared her shoulders and tried to give him a superior look. "Fine."

Cyn stood close by and peered over her shoulder as she pushed Wendy's number into the cell phone, probably to make sure she didn't dial 9-1-1 or something. Emma was disappointed when Wendy didn't answer. She left a message, making up some random excuse so that Wendy would stop by her place and feed her cat. When she turned around, Cyn walked out of the room fully dressed.

How did the man move so fast?

Emma walked into the living room where Cyn waited to blindfold her again. With a resigned sigh, she turned her back to him. She didn't want him to touch her. He affected her too much. So, she stood very still as he tied the suede wrap around her face.

Blue snickered then abruptly stopped. No doubt Cyn had given him the same lethal glare she'd received earlier. Strong hands guided her to the garage.

"We're taking my truck," Cyn told her as he helped her get into the vehicle. His hands on her waist, he helped her get into the vehicle.

Unsettled by his touch, she tried to relax into the lushness of the leather seat and waited.

On the way to dinner, Cyn told her about Roderick's family. They were to have dinner with Rachel, Roderick's wife and Brock, his teenage son. He instructed her not to say a word about Roderick's current situation.

Emma's curiosity peaked. She couldn't wait to see who the huge Protector's wife was.

"I didn't think Protectors were allowed to marry," Emma said.

Damn blindfold, she couldn't see his expression when

he remained quiet. She leaned back against the headrest, and figured he wouldn't answer.

"We are not banned from marrying. But if we want to marry, our superior must arrange it. Or, we can marry, if we meet our destined life-mate on our own. We risk expulsion from the Protector force if we choose to marry without our leader's permission." He spoke matter-of-factly, without any hint of emotion.

"Was Roderick and Rachel's marriage arranged?"

"No."

"Is Rachel is his life-mate?"

"I don't know."

She persisted. "So Roderick is no longer a Protector?"

"He is a doctor. But he still helps us out on occasion." Cyn cranked up the music —effectively letting her know the subject was closed. Questions still swirled in her head, but she tried to relax as hard rock filled the air.

A few minutes later, the truck came to a stop and Cyn removed Emma's blindfold. The bright moonlight showcased an impressive log cabin home. Tall evergreen trees surrounded the giant home, completely blocking any views of the surrounding area.

Cyn placed his hand on a small security screen and the front door unlocked, allowing them in.

The inside of Roderick's home shocked Emma. It was elegant yet welcoming. The family room showcased a pair of plush suede camel couches accented by pine tables and shelves brimming with books. A huge flat screen flanked one wall. On it, an animated battle game played.

A teenage boy sat on one of the couches absorbed with the action. He acknowledged their entrance with a slight bob of his head, while keeping his eyes glued to the screen. The boy appeared to be the about the same age as Blue— definitely Roderick's son. He had the same startling silver hair. The boy motioned Blue over immediately shoving a controller in his hand. Blue plopped down; his eyes widened at the screen even as he began to push buttons on the hand piece.

Emma turned just in time to watch Cyn walk through the archway and settle his large frame onto a high barstool.

"Hello Rachel," Cyn greeted the sleek brunette beauty as he rested his elbows on the counter.

Emma entered the kitchen and gaped at Roderick's wife. The statuesque woman was a good match for Roderick who was enormous, a good four inches taller than Cyn.

Rachel's glossy hair was tied back from her face in a loose ponytail. Even in a casual red blouse and tan slacks, she resembled a runway model.

Emma felt dowdy in her crumpled clothes and mussed hair, which was in desperate need of a trim. Rachel was human, but with a gift of some sort. Emma sensed a powerful energy from her.

Roderick's wife studied her intently, as if to take in as much as she could. Emma cleared her throat and smiled. Rachel seemed oblivious to Emma's discomfort as she crossed the room and held out her hand. "Hi, I'm Rachel Crogan. The teen gamer in there, staring at the big screen, is my son Brock."

Emma shook Rachel's hand and wished she could have done more about her appearance. "Hello, I'm Emma."

"Please sit down" Rachel gave her a bright smile and motioned for Emma to sit on the stool next to Cyn's.

Emma eyed the proximity of the stool to where Cyn sat and discreetly slid it away from him and sat. As soon as she did, the heat from Cyn's body blasted her side and she resisted the urge to get back up. Feeling as if she dragged away from a magnetic force, she slid as far from him as she could.

"So what have you two been up to?" Rachel asked them, as she poured wine into crystal glasses.

Did Rachel assume they were a couple? Emma shifted and their thighs touched. She jerked away and Cyn turned to her, his lips curled up in a sly smile.

"I am providing protection for Emma, for a few days," Cyn replied to Rachel's question. "She has a high-level demon after her."

"Well Emma, don't worry." Rachel gave her a reassuring smile. "You are in good hands. Cyn is a great Protector."

Emma nodded, preferring to keep quiet and the odds of saying something wrong as low as possible.

Cyn gave her one of his wide smiles. "I intend to keep you very safe."

Damn him.

Emma tore her eyes from his mouth. The urge to reach out and touch him became so strong that she balled her hands into fists.

What the hell was wrong with her? The awareness of him overwhelmed her and it was beginning to annoy her.

She slid off the barstool and walked around the counter toward Rachel.

"Can I help you with anything?" Emma asked, already reaching for the wine glasses in Rachel's hands.

"Not really. Everything is ready," Rachel replied as she reached for her own glass and took a sip of wine.

Emma went to place Cyn's glass on the counter in front of him, but he reached out to take it from her. When his fingers brushed her hand, a tingle raced up her arm. She snatched her hand away hoping that he didn't notice.

She backed away and spoke to Rachel. "The food

smells delicious." Which was true, it did. After only a grilled cheese sandwich to eat all day, Emma looked forward to a full meal.

Rachel placed the dish onto a tray and then carried it to the dining table.

"I'll call the boys. Why don't you two go ahead and sit," Rachel told them. As they sat, Rachel studied Cyn for a moment. Emotions flickered across her beautiful face. Her eyes shimmered as she glanced toward the living room before she spoke. "Any news?"

"No, sorry," Cyn replied.

Emma knew they referred to Roderick and her gut twisted.

Cyn did not meet Emma's eyes when Rachel went to get call the boys.

Why didn't Cyn want to tell Rachel Roderick was alive? Sure that he had his reasons Emma remained quiet.

Dinner was delicious. The wine along with Rachel's easy-going nature and the boy's chatter throughout the meal helped Emma relax some.

During the meal, Emma caught several glances between Cyn and Rachel. In all probability, they tried to figure out if she was a friend or foe.

She was neither – just desperate.

As the adults finished up dessert, the boys announced they were done and ran back to the living room to continue playing the video game.

Throughout the meal, Cyn was subdued. He would just answer a question and return to his food without elaboration. When his cell phone rang, he left the room to talk in private.

Rachel swirled the wine around in her glass, her face pensive. "Earlier when Cyn called me, he told me you could see demons and know about the Protectors. How

~ ☾ ~

do you know these things? How did you get in trouble with demons?" she took a sip of wine and leaned back in her chair, waiting for Emma to answer.

A strong surge of energy moved through her, Emma stilled and blocked Rachel's reading of her. The source of her power became clear to Emma. Rachel was an empath. She could read emotions and feelings.

Great.

Emma ensured her thoughts and emotions were blocked. Since she wasn't sure what all she was supposed to tell Rachel, she decided it was easier to stick as close the truth as possible. "I can see demons for what they are, I am not sure why, but I have always been able to see them. I learned about the Protectors overhearing demons talk at a bar, The Inferno, where my sister and I went a couple of times. I sought out Cyn because I need his help. The demons have my sister and I need him to help to rescue her."

"I'm sorry Emma." Rachel turned away but not before Emma saw her anguished expression.

She must be thinking of Roderick.

Emma wanted to tell her about her visit to the demon complex, but she'd given Cyn her word. "I don't know what to do," Emma told Rachel, "I can't just sit around. I know Cyn has a plan, but I wish we could go now."

Rachel's voice was flat. "They can't just go without a plan. Demons are strange creatures. They take humans as slaves by force. I don't understand why when they have so many that go to them of their own accord. I just hope they are not doing this to get to Cyn. I'm afraid they've decided to get proactive and are laying traps for the Protectors."

The comment hit too close to home, a wave of guilt almost made her confess everything to Rachel. Instead, she forced a calm façade. "I don't know what the demons are planning. I just know I have to get my sister. She's all the family I have."

Emma really didn't know if, other than Cyn, Gerard wanted more Protectors, or why. Even though demons hated Protectors, it didn't make sense. Of course, according to what her father told her, Roderick and Cyn were two of the most powerful Protectors alive and a huge threat to high-level demons. But there had to be more to it. Most likely, a vendetta or some kind of purpose was behind it. Other than making demon life easier, that is.

Rachel stood up. "If you will excuse me, I need to speak to Cyn for a minute. Please help yourself to more wine," she told Emma as she left the dining room.

Emma strained to hear their conversation, but gave up after a couple of minutes with a frustrated sigh. She couldn't hear a word over the teenagers' loud game.

# # #

Rachel walked out to the back deck where he waited. Cyn hoped she had some answers to what Emma was, perhaps even why she was really there. He'd left them alone on purpose to see if Rachel could pick up something using her ability to sense emotions.

He blocked his emotions and thoughts as she neared him. The less she knew about Roderick right now the better it was for her. Although it tore at him, he hated not telling Rachel what he knew about Roderick. As much as he wanted to assure her Roderick was alive, he knew it would cause her additional grief later if it turned out to be a trick.

He would rather let her cling on to the idea that Roderick would return soon. He'd wait to see if he could get any confirmation about Roderick first and then let

Rachel know.

After Roderick's disappearance, Julian sent a in a pair of spies disguised as demons to infiltrate the Atlanta area demons. He hoped they would find information about Roderick and the location of their coven.

Rachel leaned on the railing next to him, with a crinkled brow. "I don't know what she is. I know she is at least part human. Perhaps she is part Fae, but I don't sense she's just human." Her brow wrinkled. "Maybe demon, very recessive, but it's possible." She began to pace as she tried to figure out Emma's origin. "Have you tried to seduce her?"

Cyn didn't mind telling her. "We kissed and she was willing. I didn't use any mind control. She didn't deny me. Although I got the feeling she wasn't too happy about it after."

"Interesting" Rachel shrugged and held her hands up. "Well I'm stumped, a human is easy to seduce with mind control and demons are tricky and prefer to do the seducing. The only species that can block your prowess would be a shifter or another Protector." She smiled at Cyn's offended expression. "I know, I know. Protectors are only males and you don't swing that way, but it was worth saying just to see the look on your face."

Cyn huffed and turned away from her. "Rachel, I am going to go to the demon compound. I need to rescue that girl." He heard Rachel's intake of breath and she placed a hand over her heart. "You'll keep Blue for me, won't you?"

"It's not worth it Cyn," Rachel told him, her calm façade gone. "The girl is in all probability there willingly or dead by now. We both know it. The demons won't let a human remain there against their will and live this long." Cyn heard her voice crack. "First Roderick disappears and now you want to follow? I can't bear to lose you right now Cyn. Who's next? Is Kieran planning to go too? When is enough going to be enough?"

Something squeezed in his chest when he saw the angst on her face and unshed tears glistening in her eyes. But he had no idea how to comfort her.

"Of course you can leave Blue here, but don't tell him where you're going." She wiped a tear away with the back of her hand. Cyn's heart jerked.

Without another word, she went back into the house.

Cyn stood for a while, listening to the crickets' melody in the background. It was well worth it to risk his life if there was a chance Roderick was alive. He had no doubt the Spartan would do the same for him. He couldn't ignore the gut wrenching sensation that had eaten at him since they arrived at Roderick's home tonight at seeing his wife and son's struggle to act normal in his absence.

Cyn walked back into the house a few minutes later. Emma sat in a chair in the living room and watched the boys play. She concentrated on the screen as if she were really trying to figure out the game. Cyn went over and put his hand on Blue's slim shoulder.

The boy glanced up with a frown. "I'm not ready to leave yet Dad. Can I stay over?"

Cyn nodded. "Yes you can sleep here. I need to talk to you for a minute Blue."

Blue jumped up, obviously sensing Cyn's tension. "What's wrong Dad?" The boy's entire body appeared taut, apprehension evident in his stance.

Cyn took the boys shoulders and looked him in the eyes. "Nothing's wrong. I have to go on a job, so I need you to stay with Rachel and Brock."

"For how long?" Blue didn't relax.

Emma watched the exchange between them transfixed. Cyn didn't like that Blue's fear of being away from him for too long was so obvious. He'd not gotten over his fear that one day his birth father would demand his return.

He shook him playfully, grinning to assure Blue. “Just a day or two at the most.”

Blue relaxed. “Oh okay.” He glanced at the screen then back at him, clearly torn. “Just for a couple of days at the most. Right?”

He nodded, and smiled down at his son. “Yes Blue, I promise I’ll be back in two days. Don’t get into any trouble. Come here.” Cyn hugged his son and laughed when the boy tried to squirm out of his hold.

“Geez Dad, you don’t have to get all mushy and junk.”

Belying his words, the boy appeared to be reassured as he flopped back down on the couch and began to play again.

Cyn observed his son for a few moments before they headed out. He hated goodbyes, even short ones.

~ ☾ ~

CHAPTER EIGHT

The drive back to Cyn's house was quiet. Sure that her voice would not get past the huge lump in her throat, Emma decided it was best to remain silent. How she wished she could come clean. The exchange between Cyn and his son tore through her like a knife and ripped her heart to shreds. How could she play a part in causing Blue to deal with the loss of his father?

Cyn appeared to be lost in thought as well, or maybe he attempted to read her mind, she wasn't sure which. The silence allowed her time to think and plan for the days ahead.

When they arrived back at Cyn's home, he removed her blindfold. The security system scanned her again before they entered the house. With a pensive air about him, Cyn maintained a noticeable distance from her. Maybe time with Roderick's family had affected him after all.

It was too quiet in the dark room as he engaged the security system. Cyn turned to her. "We need to get some sleep. Tomorrow we'll see about your sister."

Emma closed her eyes and thanked heaven. Her sister — he was going to help her get Briana back! Another night of worrying about Briana would not be as bad knowing that it would all end soon.

He pointed toward the kitchen. "You remember where the spare bedroom is right?"

She nodded but followed him as he headed in the

opposite direction. “What is the plan? I think we are going to need weapons and more men.” He ignored her and went into his bedroom. She hesitated for a moment, at the doorway and then walked in after him.

“Who is going to help us?”

Cyn stopped and faced her. “I am not going to share the plan with you. For all I know you are on their side, a damn decoy, and your sister doesn’t even exist.”

“If you don’t trust me then why are you helping me?” Unjustified rage filled her, perhaps because his words were too close to the truth. Emma stepped closer to him. She hated that she had to bend her neck back to look up at him. “Maybe this is a mistake, maybe I should just figure this out by myself.”

He held her by the forearms and drew her to him. First his eyes were piercing, his stare hard, but they softened when he spoke. “I don’t know why, but I want to protect you.” His tone and expression carried both surprise and confusion in equal measure.

No one had ever spoken such words to her. Emma almost couldn’t breathe as soothing waves of emotion flowed through her. She continued to hold his gaze even though her knees almost buckled when his eyes darkened with hunger. The urge to kiss him slammed into her. Of their own accord, her hands moved up his arms and behind his head. She dragged her fingers through his silky hair and brought his face down to hers.

As if he’d held back, he let out a soft growl before his mouth crashed down on hers and she was lost to the taste of him.

The feel of his hard muscular body against hers drove her crazy with desire. The contradiction of the softness of his lips and his powerful build amazed her. Emma’s pulse quickened when his tongue dove into her mouth. She moaned and swirled hers around it and was rewarded by his sharp intake of breath. To have this effect on such a man made her feel powerful, feminine.

His hands trailed down her back. He cupped her bottom and held her in place against him. His hard-on pressed into her midsection sending a rush of heat between her legs.

Mouths joined, she splayed her fingers and ran her hands across his back to touch more of him. Cyn's mouth moved across hers, as if he couldn't get enough.

When his mouth slid from her lips to her ear, Emma's heart beat so fast she could not catch her breath.

"Talk to me," he whispered gruffly in her ear. "Tell me to stop."

Control was lost. Emma grabbed his butt and thrust her hips into him sending a clear message.

"I don't want you to stop. Don't you dare stop."

He cupped her face with both hands and kissed her hard, a promise of what was to come. Emma fisted the front of his shirt to keep him from moving away from her. She did not want to break the spell of his nearness. A hiss escaped when he began to trail kisses down her throat while his capable hands slipped her jacket off her shoulders.

Emma did not object when she felt his touch under her t-shirt and he began to caress her bare skin. His rough hands were gentle as he moved her bra aside and cupped her breasts. She tugged at his shirt with trembling fingers.

Cyn backed away from her and removed her shirt. Then without taking his eyes from hers, he unzipped her jeans with unhurried and precise movements. They slid down her legs, his fingers skimming her skin along the way. She stepped out of the pool of denim, mesmerized by the hunger in his face. All she wore now was a lacy bra and matching panties made of the sheerest pink fabric.

~ ☾ ~

Once again she crashed against him and held her face up to him in a silent plea for more of his kisses.

Both ran their hands over each other as he walked her backwards. The fabric of the plush comforter cooled her heated skin when Cyn picked her up and placed her on the bed.

Dazed, Emma reclined and watched through hooded eyes as Cyn began to remove his clothing.

Without hurry, he removed his polo shirt off over his head, seeming to enjoy her rapt attention.

She admired his broad shoulders, muscular arms and flat taut stomach. The trail of light hair that led from the ripples to disappear into the juncture below definitely begged for exploration.

When he took off his pants, she licked her lips as need coursed through her. He was more than ready, a bead of liquid glistened on the tip of his erection.

He was perfection.

More bewitching than any portrait on canvas, Emma lay on his bed, her hot gaze consuming him. Her enticing chest moved up and down with each inhalation. Her body stunned him. For a small woman, she was just right – her breasts, full and supple and her legs went on forever.

Cyn enjoyed the sight of Emma's aroused state and took his time moving closer. He stood beside the bed and held his hands out to her. When she took them, he drew her up to a kneeling position. He kissed her again, and began to caress her breasts, his thumbs circling the pink tips. He watched the changing expressions on her beautiful face.

He pinched each peak, not enough to hurt, and elicited a throaty moan. His breathing hitched at the affect of his touch. Emma made a stunning sight with her head thrown back, eyes closed and those pouty lips parted

Totally lost in the moment.

He wanted her with such intensity. Almost too much. Every fiber of his being cried out for release — a primal instinct to bury himself inside her and thrust until both were spent. He wanted just as badly to take it slow and enjoy her.

He lifted her face and took her mouth with ravenous desperation.

She began to caress him with uncertain and timid movements. Every inch of his skin reacted like each nerve was on fire. Her touches triggered a path of heat that shot through him.

Emma was a contradiction. Inexperienced, almost as if he was her first lover. At the same time, she proved bold in her desire to explore his body.

Even after hundreds of years and many sexual encounters, tonight with her felt extraordinary.

Cyn trailed his tongue down her throat while he slid his hands around to cup her butt. When he held her against him, an avalanche of desire made it hard to suppress a moan at the incredible feel of her body against his.

He closed his eyes to more fully enjoy the myriad of sensations that coursed through him. Her hands traveled from his shoulders down his back to his butt and thighs. She caressed and kneaded his skin and at the same time trailed hot kisses from his throat to his chest. Her tongue darted and circled his nipple and he damn near lost it.

At this point he wanted to throw her back on the bed and ram into her hard and fast, but he held back and enjoyed her discovery of his body.

It'd been too long since he'd had sex. He was about to

embarrass himself.

Her hands moved to his hips and she began to suckle the sensitive skin of his inner thigh. He inhaled sharply and constricted his muscles. He couldn't take much more.

Cyn lifted her flushed face up to him.

"You've got to stop," he told her, his voice gruff.

He continued at the same unhurried pace she'd set and unclipped her bra. His breath quickened at the sight of her firm breasts. He then pushed her panties off. She kicked them away.

She was soft curves and enticing skin that glowed with a light sheen of perspiration laid bare for his pleasure.

The woman was amazing.

His took a moment to admire the sight of her stretched before him.

She blushed and turned her face.

"You surprise me." He told her.

Her widened eyes flew to his. "Why"

"You are bold and shy at the same time. I find it fascinating."

"I find you enthralling too," she replied, staring boldly.

They sunk into the bed together.

Finally.

Emma wanted to moan when he rolled on top of her and his arms closed around her. When his lips crushed hers, she was astounded at how perfect the moment felt. Emma reveled in the taste of him and the feel of his skin against hers.

His hair was soft and thick as it flowed through her fingers. It fell forward and formed a silken tent around them as they continued to feast on each other's mouths.

~ ☾ ~

She wished time would stand still at that moment. If only she could freeze the fantastic sensations forever. When his mouth suckled at her throat, she arched back to allow him more access. He nipped at the sensitive skin for a few delicious moments after which his warm lips moved down to her breasts.

He took her nipple in his mouth while his hand moved between her legs.

A quiver raced over her and Emma bucked into his hand. She didn't understand what her body did but it felt so good. Her head thrashed from side-to-side as she tried to hold back. She lost the battle and cried out when everything spun out of control.

Floating downward, she forced her eyes open. He watched her, his lips curved in a satisfied smile. "You are ready for me, but I want to enjoy you a bit more." As if she could form a coherent reply at that moment? The only word that came to mind was 'more'. Emma raked her fingernails across his broad shoulders.

Cyn continued his sweet torture and slipped a finger inside her as his lips took hers captive again. She'd never experienced anything as glorious as this.

Hands on her hips, he held her in place and slid lower, between her legs. When his hot mouth covered her and his tongue began to explore, Emma was sure she'd pass out from the intensity of the torrent his lips caused. He continued the sweet torment, his tongue giving her more pleasure than she ever thought possible. He suckled and licked her until her body trembled in release.

"I need you," Emma gasped. "I want you..." She wasn't sure what she wanted, but she didn't want it to end.

Ever.

Cyn panted. "Take me then." He moved back up and his mouth took hers, as he pushed deep into her.

The rumble of his deep voice at her ear enhanced the

sensory experience. “You feel so damn good. Just feeling your heat surround me is amazing,” his hoarse tone oh so sexy, at her ear. He paused for a moment and lifted his head. Pleasure darkened eyes raked over her face. He captured her mouth in a fervent kiss.

At this point, all she could do was let go and enjoyed the moment.

Then Cyn began pumping in and out of her again, finding and setting a rhythm. Grunting and moaning in her ear, he moved faster and faster, taking them to the climax they both craved. He threw his head back and his incisors snapped down as he began to peak.

His fangs sunk into her throat.

Emma felt as if she floated into space as wave after wave of intense climaxes hit her. Her body convulsed and her fingers curled in his hair holding him in place at her throat. The connection was intense. It was as if a gateway had been opened and their emotions intermingled and flowed between them.

He tensed and his body began to shudder. Somehow, she knew he felt as much as she did. The sound of his loud moans ebbed and flowed with hers.

With a loud growl, he came inside her. His heated release filled her.

He thrust one last time and collapsed on top of her.

He retracted his fangs from her throat and licked it, sealing the wound.

Totally spent, Emma caressed his back, her fingers tracing the muscular lines while the steady beat of his heart thumped against her breast.

“I’m sorry, I know I’m heavy,” He mumbled a moment later and lifted off of her. He lay on his back and held her against his chest.

“You are so beautiful.” His voice washed over her as she lay within his arms, her body sated and limp.

~ ☾ ~

Making love with Cyn was incredible. Exhausted, she lay snuggled against him with her eyes closed. Her body unsteady and her mind empty of all negative emotions.

A few moments later, Emma raised her head and peered at him. He appeared relaxed, his eyes hooded, a soft smile on his lips.

"Did you bite me?" Her hand went to her throat, rubbed the spot and then glanced at her fingers to ensure that she was not bleeding. She wasn't. "Why?" Emma frowned at him in confusion.

Her father had once told her that Protectors had vampire-like fangs that were only used to defend themselves and for their mate's pleasure, as they did not need to feed on blood.

Cyn had definitely bitten her.

His eyes went from her face to her throat. Uncertainty flickered in them for a moment before he shrugged. "I'm sorry. I lost my head for a minute. Did I hurt you?" He looked into her eyes; not breaking contact.

Unnerved by his stare, she grabbed a corner of the comforter to cover herself.

"No it was pleasant, but I thought Protectors only bit their mates."

"I don't usually bite anyone." Cyn smirked and nipped at her lips playfully. "But, I could feast on you for days."

He'd changed the subject on purpose. She placed her hand on his jaw. It was hard not to urge him to, indeed devour her as long as he liked with his handsome face so close.

She decided not to push the subject; instead, she asked him a question. "I've never seen eyes like yours. What makes them so light?"

After an uncomfortable beat, he looked up at the ceiling, a slight coloring on his face. "A reflective shield. I know my eyes make some people uncomfortable. That's why I wear sunglasses during the day, most of the time."

Emma turned him to her. "I think they're beautiful. A bit disconcerting at first, but I really like them."

He kissed her in response. "It's one of the changes we go through as Protectors. Since we hunt for demons, which are nocturnal, we need to have excellent night vision. The reflective shield works great at night, but it gives our eyes a strange sheen during the day."

In the curve of his arm, she relaxed into him again, and laid her head on his shoulder.

"What's your full name? I know Cyn is just a nickname, right?" Emma asked him next.

"Cynden Alexander Fraser," he replied.

"You have an accent. Where are you from?"

"My brother Kieran and I are Scottish. We were born in the Highlands of Scotland, near Inverness."

"You are a long way from home, Scot."

"Aye" Cyn replied with a purposely-pronounced accent. "I have to admit Georgia has little resemblance to me home."

His voice took a faraway tone. "I haven't been to Scotland in a long time. Kieran returns every fifty years or so. His accent is still quite noticeable. Protectors are a mobile lot. When you're immortal, you can't stay in the same place for long. It's been almost a decade since I've been to the Fraser lands."

Emma remembered reading about the large clan. "The Fraser's were a powerful clan."

"They are still a powerful clan. We're not extinct, you know," he told her, pride evident in his voice.

Emma studied his handsome profile. She couldn't believe the difference between the savage killer/demon-fighter and the man who lay next to her now.

In bed.

After sex.

~ ☾ ~

Incredible sex.

"Is your brother here in Atlanta?"

"Yes, Kieran and I came here about twelve years ago. We're both assigned here for at least another five years. Roderick too." She saw a shadow of worry cross his face.

"Roderick and Briana will be all right. I just know it." She told him.

Without warning, the intimacy of the moment rattled her. She couldn't resist and hugged him to assure that it was real. Although not a virgin, she had never experienced a moment like this.

Their lips met in a sweet kiss.

They were both quiet for a few moments.

Cyn broke the silence first. "Who are you, really?"

"A lost girl." *Trying to find her way home.*

"You're not like any woman I have ever been with."

Emma tensed. Though she enjoyed making love with him, he probably wasn't as satisfied. He was more experienced than she. Cyn was only the second man she'd ever slept with.

Unsure, she started to move away from him. "I wouldn't know." Emma snapped, to hide the hurt.

As fast as she could, she slid out of the bed.

Beside her at once, he took her arm and turned her to him. "I didn't mean it in a bad way. It was good. Incredible, actually. It's just that it felt so different. It was...intense. There's something different about you..."

Emma stilled at the earnest look on his face.

In this moment, she wished she could risk telling him the truth about herself. She wanted to trust someone, especially the person that could save Briana. But she couldn't risk her sister's life by confessing her demon heritage. Not only would he be repulsed at having been intimate with her, he'd probably kill her instantly for lying.

~ ☾ ~

"I don't know what to tell you Cyn."

Cyn's brow narrowed, he didn't release her arm. "Where are your parents?"

She was honest with her answer. "My father was killed by demons. My mother lost it after that. She abandoned my sister and me. We ended up in the foster care program until the Blake's adopted us. I haven't seen my mother in over twenty years. I don't even know where she is." She shrugged her arm out of his hand and began to put her clothes back on.

"Why didn't one of your parents' families take you and your sister into their care?" He asked her puzzled.

Oh God, she had to get away before she told him everything. She yanked her pants and t-shirt back on. She zipped up her jeans and bent to pick up her bra and panties off the floor. "You said we needed to get some rest..." She walked to the door and then turned to him. "Unless you want to tell me what the plan is for tomorrow."

"I'm not going to go over any plans with you, Emma No offense." Cyn stood with his arms relaxed at his sides, fully nude.

The man was spectacular. She'd never forget the sight of him.

Brows furrowed, he pushed his hair back away from his face with one hand and stared at her for a moment.

Disappointment or resolution, one or the other, or both crossed his face.

"You're right. We better get some sleep. Good night Emma."

She just nodded and walked out. Once out of his view, she let her shoulders slump forward with her own regret as she went down the hall and into her room. He hadn't asked her to spend the night with him.

In the spare bedroom, she hunted through a chest of

drawers and found a white t-shirt. After she brushed her teeth and changed, she fell into the bed and waited for sleep to claim her.

It couldn't come soon enough.

She began to worry about Briana. Her sister was the only family she had left. There was no way she'd lose her too. She had to get Briana back and convince her to move, maybe to a small town far from Atlanta. She tried to imagine a place where no one knew them and with no demons. Or at least no demons that would physically threaten them. Inner demons — that was something else completely.

As soon as she pushed the thoughts of her sister away, Cyn took her place.

Her first lover was a bitter memory. She'd given herself to her Alex Brody, a boy in high school. When his country club obsessed mother found out he was seeing 'the foster kid' she demanded he never see her again. He hurt her deeply by never speaking to her again. After Alex, she'd done her best to stay away from men, both human and not.

She didn't fit in either world.

Although sweet, making love with Alex had been nothing like the passionate encounter with the man down the hall. Her body craved Cyn's touch again. She squirmed as frustration filled her. It was just as well that he did not ask her to stay with him, she thought glumly. If Cyn had asked her to spend the night in his bed, she would have had to say no. She could not allow herself to get close to anyone.

Not now. Not ever.

She'd lost everyone she ever loved and didn't want to feel that ache yet again. Not that she loved him...not really. She was just feeling the echoes of their intimacy.

Emma flipped onto her back and sighed. She'd never

spent an entire night with a man. What would it have been like to wake up next to Cyn? She stared up at the ceiling and relived the amazing moments she'd just experienced. Would it always be like that with him?

She turned to lie on her side and punched the pillow. "Don't be stupid Emma. Your future is death."

Cyn sat back from his computer. He'd watched Emma toss and turn until she'd fallen asleep. It had taken great restraint to keep from asking her to stay the night with him. He had to be careful; something about Emma gave him pause.

He leaned back and glanced toward his bed. Although he was tired, the empty bed just wasn't enticing — not without her.

He'd heard her say those words before she fell asleep. *"Don't be stupid Emma. Your future is death."* What exactly had she meant by that? Was she being a martyr of some kind?

He checked his computer. There was an email from Kieran. Julian received a report back from the droid spies. There was nothing new regarding Roderick. The only promising bit of information was that they'd discovered the exact location of the coven's current position and that they were not due to change for another three days.

They had three days to find Roderick, and rescue Briana Blake.

If she even existed.

For reasons he couldn't understand, he wanted to believe Emma. He considered going to her. Instead, he walked over to his bed and stretched out. He needed to rest for a few hours before they left.

Tomorrow, it would start.

~ ☾ ~

CHAPTER NINE

Gerard looked up from his desk and fell back with an exasperated sigh. His demon guards dragged the spy into his office.

The guards had beaten and tortured the man for hours and he didn't seem inclined to answer any of their questions. Gerard's eyes narrowed as he studied the man. Not one bruise was visible on his face.

He stalked toward them, dagger in hand. Without pause, Gerard stabbed one of the guards through the heart killing him. The demon fell and evaporated.

"You idiots! This is not a human. It's a droid! I can't believe you wasted all this time beating a damned droid and didn't even realize it. Did the lack of blood not offer any of you assholes a clue? Dumbshits."

The remaining guards froze. They looked at each other in terrified confusion and held their collective breath — obviously, dreading of whatever punishment he would give.

Heat of rage coursed through him. It felt good. A sword appeared in his hand. Gerard's fiery stare landed on each of the guards and he was rewarded by expressions of absolute terror on their faces. Then with one fell swoop he severed the droid's head. The guards moved out of the sword's path dropping the droid. The body landed with a solid thump on the floor. The head rolled under a chair.

Carlo, his second in command walked into the room.

"I apologize, Sire. I was not there during the interrogation of the droid." The stocky demon peered at the remains with a look of distaste. "With all respect Sire, I think you should have left it in working order. I would have better luck at downloading its memory bank."

Carlo stepped over the droid and went to stand by his desk. He spoke to the guards ignoring Gerard's glare. "Guards, take the remains to my shop. I'll see what I can salvage."

The guards were more than happy to follow his orders. They picked up the droid's parts and exited the room faster than Gerard had ever seen them move, leaving only Carlo and his personal guards.

Gerard stalked to his desk and slammed his fist on the solid black marble top. Carlo merely sat down and waited.

Through the tinted windows of the room, the moonlight beam gave the space an eerie glow. Carlo's ever present black attire blended in the murky light.

"You already know who sent the droid. It's doubtful that you will get any useful information from it." Gerard told Carlo. "That damn Protector, Kieran Fraser, is too smart for that. Especially after the idiot guards destroyed anything useful," he finished, not one to admit he'd participated in the destruction of the droid.

"We need more experienced help. Most of our guards are new or lower demons and can hardly complete any task we set before them." Carlo voice was dull.

Gerard grunted. He hoped that little idiot Emma succeeded in convincing Cynden Fraser to try to save her sister. He needed to leave this place and replenish his coven with better followers.

Emma. He sat, a slow smile spread across his face.

Emma Blake would die.

It couldn't be helped. He'd implanted an explosive

device along with a spell star into the side of her neck. The spell star made it impossible for anyone to sense her demon blood.

A shame really, she was the prettier of the two sisters and he'd been looking forward to having her. She would have made a good sex slave. But, she was the more loyal of the two. Emma would die for her sister. He wasn't sure Briana would be as accommodating.

Just as well though. He had to admit, last night with Briana had been pretty adventurous. She was voracious and eager to please him, which made it easy for him to exploit her demon nature. Soon she'd forfeit her humanity and it would be his to do with as he wished. He enjoyed sex with the young half-demon. So far, this idea of his to use the sisters as bait had been well worth it, in many ways.

Carlo cleared his throat and brought Gerard back to the present.

"When we capture Cynden Fraser, we will bargain with the Protector's leader, Julian, for Thames. The Supreme demon must be released." Gerard told his first. "The plan is coming along. The droid won't pose any problem."

Carlo shook his head. "I don't understand why we wait Sire. We already have one Protector. Roderick Cronan is one of the strongest Protectors I've ever seen. Even chained to a wall, he's managed to kill one of our guards. Perhaps their leader will barter for him alone."

His men had expected him to kill the Protector for murdering the demon. But he had bigger plans for Roderick.

"I don't care that a guard is dead, the pissant disserved to die if a chained man could overcome him," Gerard snarled at Carlo. "I might turn both Protectors into powerful demons."

~ ☾ ~

"The Roman will bargain for the Spartan. He needs his strongest warriors," Carlo insisted.

"Yes, Julian might bargain for one, but having two is better leverage. We must be patient and hope that Julian remains unaware that the freeing of Thames means utter destruction to the human race and total power for the demonic realm."

"You forget one thing Sire," Carlo said. "The Protectors are now aware of our location. The droid must have at least reported that much."

"They don't know we have Roderick. If they suspected, they would have attacked already. No, they believe him dead — slaughtered on the street by rogue demons. They won't come without cause. We must remain until Cynden Fraser is lured here."

Gerard was secure in the knowledge that Julian would not risk the loss of the two Protectors; especially once his new weapon arrived in Atlanta. Warrior demons were coming to join with his group of higher-level demons. They were expensive to hire, but stronger than most high-levels and would be quite a challenge for the outnumbered Protectors.

As far as bargaining for the release of Thames, he knew who would be the arbitrator. Kieran Fraser.

Kieran would not allow his brother to die. The Protector would broker the deal and force their leader to bend to Gerard's demands.

More relaxed, Gerard sat in a plush chair that faced the window which afforded him a view of the sizeable courtyard. Several of their human followers were outside tending to the gardens in the moonlight. *How disgusting*. He could care less about the damn flowering bushes. Much more picturesque was his power over the humans. The humans installed an entire wall of windows at the old warehouse. They'd spent their own money and resources to plant a garden and tend it in an effort to please him. His lip curled. They were such weak creatures.

Most of them would have to be disposed of soon. Once Julian freed Thames, he and his guards would relocate to an abandoned castle he'd just acquired in Belgium. The owner was more than happy to deed his castle and lands to him in order to save his wife from dying. Gerard turned her into a demon, giving her immortality. The exquisite woman would be his. In time, he'd return for her. The man would not live much longer.

The plan was in place, Roderick and Cynden would be turned into demons. He would stay in Atlanta long enough to see the Protectors turned. Ironically, their comrades would be forced to kill them. Or if all went better than planned, he'd be fortunate enough to witness his two new-turns slay them all.

"Sire, you are putting a lot of stock in the girl, Emma. I hope she will follow through," Carlo gave him a concerned look. "The half-demon may decide to save herself and run."

"The girl is too loyal to her sister. She'll follow through," Gerard replied and waved the man away.

Emma was a walking time bomb. She was naïve enough to believe him when he told her the explosive unit was an untraceable homing device and he would remove it upon her return. She also believed he'd release her and her sister upon delivery of the Protector.

Gerard felt no guilt at the thought of killing either of them. They were walking abominations. How he'd like to punish their full blood father for daring to procreate with a human woman?

In time he would have to replace Briana. Take a new lover or two, but not until after he used her body a few more times. He rather enjoyed the way the girl gave herself to him. She enjoyed their rough sex. Aroused at the thought, he motioned for a demon guard to approach.

"Go fetch Briana, have her prepared for me and leave her in my chamber." Gerard sat back and smiled, he wondered if he should go watch in case Roderick killed another of his useless guardsmen when they went for Briana.

~ ☾ ~

Chapter Ten

Cyn woke with a start when his computer beeped. Groggy, he rolled over and saw Kieran's face on his computer screen. By the shadows of trees behind him, it looked like his brother was still outdoors.

"Hey, I got some information."

He sat up and shoved his hair out of his face, annoyed. He forgot to get it cut, again. Cyn motioned at the computer monitor for Kieran to continue. "The security shields are in place."

"The demons discovered the droid and disabled him. But the other spy is still active." Kieran paused. "Roderick is alive."

Cyn jumped out of the bed and stared at Kieran's image. "No shit! We have to get in there and get him out before they kill him."

Kieran nodded. "I agree brother. I'm coming back home from Louisiana. Meet me at my house. I'm headed there now. See you in about an hour."

Cyn glanced at the time on the computer screen. "See you soon."

After a fast shower, Cyn got dressed and went to wake up Emma. He walked in to find her bed empty.

Hearing her, he turned to see her come out of the bathroom. Preoccupied with wrapping a towel around her, she wasn't aware of his presence. He waited for her to notice him, but she never looked up and ran right into his chest.

She jumped back startled.

"I-I was about to get dressed and come find you," she stuttered.

She'd combed her hair back away from her face.

Nothing hindered his view.

She was so beautiful.

His body reacted.

He saw the same heat reflected when their eyes met. "We leave in thirty minutes. Would you like something to eat?"

Emma nodded, her eyes never leaving his face.

"Ah hell," he moved toward her, unable to stop himself from reaching for her.

When his lips covered hers, she sighed and wrapped her arms around his waist. He wished they had more time.

These would be their last few minutes alone.

She felt so damn perfect in his arms.

Just a few minutes. If he could just spend a few more minutes with her, maybe he could calm the searing need that nearly had him trembling.

No, they didn't have time.

She was dangerous. He couldn't form coherent thoughts around her. It shouldn't be this hard to walk away. The urge to be with her was too strong, like a tangible thing. It was new for him to not be in complete control and he didn't like it.

Emma's hand touched the side of his face and she looked into his eyes. She spoke his thoughts. "Can't we be together one more time, Cyn?"

He couldn't deny her.

He groaned, and gave in to desire.

~ ☾ ~

Impatiently, he yanked his pants off, and his erection sprung free. He tugged away her towel, baring every inch of her in one fell swoop. He lifted her up and she wrapped her legs around his waist. He carried her to the bed and sat with her on his lap, so she straddled him.

"Ride me Emma," he told her. "Hurry love, we don't have much time." He lifted her by the hips and pushed up into her. Emma drew a sharp intake of breath as he filled her heated moist center.

She leaned forward and placed her hands on his shoulders and looked at him, her pretty face puzzled. Had she never done this before?

Emma frowned and bit her lip as she peered down to where they were joined. She raised her hips and when he began to slide out of her, she pushed back down. Hissing in pleasure, he was mesmerized at the sight of her above him. The feel of her snug heat made him buck under her.

Cyn shuddered as she pushed him back onto the bed and began to rock her hips up and down in a steady rhythm. He kept his hands on her hips — in heaven, but allowed her to set the pace. At first, her movements were slow but as she neared climax, her tempo increased. The sound of flesh hitting flesh and their moans filled the room.

Cyn teetered near the edge. Through half-closed eyes, he watched Emma. She was enticing, her eyes closed, lips curved into a sensual smile.

When she shuddered and fell against him, Cyn held her in place and continued to drive in and out of her. Not able to hold back long, he held her against his chest and rode the wave of completion.

She lay on his chest for a few moments. When their eyes met, he glimpsed a flicker of unguarded emotion.

He kissed her. She didn't kiss him back.

The moment was over. He could literally feel her pull

away from him and reassemble her walls. When he slipped out of her, Emma got off the bed without a word. She donned her bra and top before shimming into her jeans. The entire time she kept her eyes averted.

He wondered why she acted so uneasy after making love. Something about intimacy bothered her. He decided not to ask, as it didn't matter. After they rescued Roderick, he would never see her again. He threw his clothes back on.

"I'll be in the kitchen," Cyn called as she turned toward the bathroom. "We leave in ten minutes."

# # #

Cyn sat at the kitchen table drinking coffee. Why did Emma distance herself from him after making love? His bite may have frightened her. He definitely shouldn't have bitten her. Not once had he ever bitten a woman during lovemaking. He wasn't sure what came over him that drew him to do that. Perhaps she feared him still.

No, she had most definitely enjoyed sex with him. And he hadn't bitten her this morning. Emma was an enthusiastic lover. When she walked into the kitchen a few minutes later, she looked away when their eyes met. She dropped her bag onto a chair before going to the counter to pour a cup of coffee. Inexplicably, it troubled him to see her so subdued.

Cyn held out a bagel to her that he'd already buttered.

"Thank you," she muttered as she took the bagel and bit into it.

"Are you alright?" he asked before downing the last of his coffee.

"Great, why do you ask?" She raised her eyes to his as if daring him to say something.

What the hell do I say now?

~ ☾ ~

They stared at each other not moving, it seemed that neither of them were sure what to say or do next.

Finally, he decided it was best to just avoid the conversation. “We better go,” He walked past her out of the kitchen.

Emma’s changing moods intrigued him. Everything about her called to him.

Watch your back. Kieran’s words came back into his head. Could this all be a ploy?

Her stance was rigid when he picked up the strap to blindfold her. Cyn almost changed his mind, but he could not risk her knowing the location of the house. He had to consider Blue’s safety. He tied the blindfold and took her by the arm leading her to the garage. “Sorry, I have to take precautions.”

“Of course,” Emma replied, her voice flat.

# # #

They rode the motorcycle to the outskirts of Atlanta before Cyn stopped to remove her blindfold. Once she donned the helmet again, they rode on.

When they finally stopped outside an old white farmhouse, Emma looked around puzzled.

The old two-story, though in dire need of new paint, stood proud against the darkening background of tall pines. Several of its shutters clung in desperation to the weathered boards flanking the sides of the windows. One fallen victim leaned haphazardly against the house on the wide front porch.

Cyn drove around to a square dirt patch in the back of the house and helped her dismount. She took the helmet off and stepped back, careful not to brush against the bulky silver Harley Cruiser already parked there.

The arc of Cyn’s long leg sweeping over and off of the

bike was a graceful thing to watch but her appreciation came to an abrupt end when he motioned to the ground next to her feet. “Can you grab that piece of wood for me?”

She handed him the square block of wood that he slid under the kickstand to keep the bike upright on the ground.

“This is my brother’s place,” Cyn told her looking up at the farmhouse.

The back of the house wasn’t in much better shape than the front. The door to a screened-in porch hung at such an awkward angle it couldn’t even close. The obvious cause behind the constant creaking of the rusty hinges as it opened and closed in the breeze.

Cyn noticed her raised eyebrows. “Kieran’s not much into home improvements.”

That was a huge understatement.

Emma followed closely behind him and scanned the area, feeling ill at ease. She sensed the other Protector as soon as they got to the rickety back door and stepped onto the porch.

Emma’s hand shook as she risked steadying herself on the doorframe. What if his brother could sense her demon nature? She held onto the fact that the spell star to camouflage her true identity had worked so far.

Without knocking, they stepped into a stunning modern and enormous kitchen that looked to double as a meeting room of sorts. An oversized oak table in the center of the room surrounded by six leather executive style chairs filled the room.

A stainless steel side-by-side refrigerator and stove lined one wall, along with a microwave and dishwasher. On the adjoining wall, there was a large farm style sink which was surrounded by a tan and rust speckled granite counter. A computer and coffee maker rested side by side. She made special note of the steaming cup of coffee, cell phone, gun, and sword that lay near the computer.

The dense tree line surrounding the house could be viewed from the large picture window on the wall opposite the sink.

Emma moved behind Cyn when two men walked into the kitchen.

The first man to enter had to be Kieran, Cyn's brother. He was as tall as Cyn and had the same golden hair. But unlike Cyn, Kieran's hair just reached his shoulders. The Protector was leaner than Cyn with the clearest green eyes Emma had ever seen. They were almost transparent. His demeanor was harsh. He spared her one brief glance before lifting his chin at his brother in greeting. Like Cyn, Kieran was handsome, but more intense and aloof.

The other man, also a Protector, had just arrived. He wore a heavy coat and his sword hung prominently across his back. This male was exotic with caramel skin and luminescent gray eyes. A bit shorter than the brothers, the Protector had a strong jaw and a broad muscular chest. Under his unbuttoned leather coat, his gray t-shirt stretched across his well-formed pecks. The man sported the same feral look about him that was second nature to Protectors. He wore his midnight black tresses braided down his back. More hostile than Kieran, this Protector took his time to eye her with distaste, his lip curled all the while. Cyn approached the intimidating Protector and put his hand on his shoulder.

"Rowe. It's been awhile."

Rowe returned the gesture and gave Cyn a pointed look, his expression solemn. "If Roderick's alive, we'll get him." His deep voice coated in middle-eastern accent.

Cyn turned and motioned toward Emma, who tried to stay behind him as much as possible. "This is Emma."

"Emma this is Rowe and my brother Kit." He told her as he motioned toward each in turn.

Kit? Cyn's nickname for his brother didn't fit the somber man. When Kieran glared at Cyn, his nostrils flaring, she understood why he disclosed it.

Kieran's eyes snapped to her and Emma swallowed hard. She was surprised when he relaxed and gave her a subtle nod. Rowe ignored her.

"We won't eat you lass. Sit down, have some coffee." Kieran had managed to maintain more of his Scottish accent while still sounding remarkably like his brother. The familiarity halfway assured that she was safe from Kieran. However, she wasn't so sure about Rowe.

Kieran went to the coffee pot and topped off his cup. Cyn shook his head, flashing a crooked smile at his brother. "Kit is addicted to coffee. If he goes any length of time without it, he loses his mind."

The Scot disregarded his brother's comment and gestured at a map spread out on the table. The mood in the room changed when men stood around the table and studied the map. Kieran circled areas with his finger and briefed them about the newest information on the location of the demon compound.

Emma moved to stand by Cyn. Without taking his eyes away from the map, he motioned for her to take a seat. Too uneasy to sit, she remained standing.

"We know the demons are in this area, our droid sent general coordinates, but it was discovered before we could confirm an exact location. This area does make the most sense. Demons have to stay close enough to the city so they can get there, have their fun and be back under ground by daylight." Kieran indicated a large circle around the city center. "They also have to be far enough out of the city so they can hide and keep their human followers."

~ ☾ ~

Cyn addressed her. “As you saw when you were there, they keep humans to feed from. Most of the humans are there voluntarily. They serve as food for the older demons which may be too old or weak to hunt. Humans are also used to train the young ones how to feed.”

Repulsed, Emma shuddered. She’d never felt the urge to feed from a human or demon for that matter. Being a half-demon meant that she didn’t need blood to live. Even most of the full-blooded demons she’d run across sought to blend in with humans and got their blood from demon-owned blood banks. Before her encounter with Gerard, that is.

The men continued to analyze and study the map. After a while, Emma began to tire. She poured herself a cup of coffee and sat in a chair on the end of the table to watch them. The men were well trained. Some of their conversation flew over her head as they tossed around coordinates and strategies. Although frustrated at her lack of understanding, she drank down the strong brew and absorbed as much information as she could.

An hour later, Cyn and Rowe decided to go scout the areas Kieran indicated on the map.

Emma jumped up and went to walk out with Cyn. She didn’t want to be left behind with Kieran. Even though he was Cyn’s brother, he was still her natural enemy.

“I won’t be long,” Cyn wrapped his arm protectively around her shoulder and held her to him, not seeming to care they had an audience. Cyn brushed his lips across her brow. When he tipped her face up to him, a stab of emotion that she couldn’t quite identify took her by surprise. If they had more time, if things were different, she could fall in love with this man.

“You have to stay here. We’ll be gone for a short while. Kieran will stay with you.” She glanced uncertainly at Kieran, who at the moment, spoke with Rowe.

~ ☾ ~

"It will be okay, Kieran won't harm you. He'll keep you safe." Cyn assured her.

"It's not just that. I don't want to sit around waiting. I can be of help. I was there, remember?" The tensing of his shoulders indicated he would not change his mind. She gave him her best pleading look.

Cyn proved unbending, "I won't take you with me now. You'll have to wait."

She glared at him, but remained silent knowing she could not force him to take her.

After Cyn and Rowe left, Emma sat on the edge of one of the leather chairs in the kitchen and watched Kieran pour himself yet another cup of coffee. Some of her apprehension lifted when he topped off her cup.

Soon Emma tired of sitting in the quiet room. Other than studying every detail of the kitchen, there wasn't anything else to do. Kieran didn't seem to feel uncomfortable by the silence in the room.

Finally, after almost an hour of Kieran not speaking a word, Emma became restless.

"Can I ask what you are reading?"

Kieran looked away from the paperwork in front of him and glanced at her, almost as if he'd forgotten she was there. "The information Cyn got from you."

"Do you mind if I explore the house?" she asked.

"Go at it," he replied, his attention already away from her.

Upon leaving the kitchen, she was impressed. Though the exterior of the house was in shambles, the entire interior was well maintained. Most of the furniture was of the highest quality. Like Cyn's home, Kieran's place was sparse but expensively furnished.

In the spacious living area, a buttery suede sofa and a pair of chocolate leather chairs faced a sizeable stone fireplace. But that was extent of the room's furnishings.

~ ☾ ~

She ambled down a hallway to find a small guest bathroom and two good-sized bedrooms. The bedrooms were almost identical, each with a large bed and single dresser. Across the hall, she peeked into what was obviously Kieran's master bedroom. The dimly-lit room housed a beautiful rustic unmade bed fashioned from tree branches. The askew black bedding suited the somber man. Not wanting to invade his privacy, she went back to the living room and out the front door.

Emma strolled out to the front porch bathed by rays that filtered through the tall pines. She closed her eyes and took a deep breath lifting her face up to the warmth of the sun. Would her life ever be simple again? Would she be able to enjoy the simple things like the sun on her face after tomorrow?

The enjoyment didn't last long. Kieran's sharp voice startled her.

"Come inside." He scowled at her from the doorway. When she entered the house, he waited for her in the living room.

"Remain in the house. Cyn will be cross with me if you're not here when he returns."

Kieran walked away without another word and went back into the kitchen.

The day was not progressing as she'd hoped. Other than Cyn and Rowe scouting, not much headway had been made toward rescuing Brianna. Emma sat in the living room for a long while and leafed through a book on folklore. Literally appalled at how many discrepancies it contained. Kieran kept a lot of books on the paranormal. Emma wouldn't have expected such a collection from someone who lived it every day.

She let out a breath and put the book down. Surely, there was something useful she could be doing. Too anxious to sit any longer, she went to find Kieran. Maybe she could get him to have a conversation with her?

Kieran sat at his computer and typed in what looked like the same type of code language Cyn used.

The room was quiet except for the tapping of keys. Emma cleared her throat. “Er, Kieran, I was wondering. If the Protector’s mission is to destroy demons, why is Cyn raising Blue?”

Kieran didn’t answer her right away. Then he faced her, his expression pensive. “Our mission is to kill those that are a threat to humans or others who cannot defend themselves. We don’t bother any demon unless it threatens someone unable to defend himself. As far as any other type of relationship for us, it can get complicated,” Kieran frowned in thought. “Blue was a baby when Cyn rescued him from harm. He considers the boy his own now.”

Emma liked the burr of his Scottish accent. Cyn’s was barely perceptible. “What about when Blue matures? His demon nature may become dominant and it may be hard for him to overcome it, even living with a Protector.”

“Cyn is hoping Blue will be able to. He is only half-demon and is well cared for and taught the Protector way. We’ll have to wait and see. Then cross that bridge when we reach it.”

Emma’s heart skipped. Kieran didn’t seem to think badly of half-demons. She wondered if he would be as accepting of her. What was she thinking? Maybe under different circumstances, she could’ve found out. But there was no sense in even considering any kind of relationship with Cyn. Not after what she was about to do.

“What time are we going to the demons’ compound? Are more Protectors coming to help?”

She saw Kieran’s jaw tense and knew she’d pushed him too far. But he surprised her.

~ ☾ ~

"At dawn. A few more are coming. We are stronger than the demons, but we can be at a disadvantage depending on their numbers. From what you told Cyn, it sounds like they have twenty to thirty demon guards at all times. There are some higher-levels there as well."

His clear eyes locked with hers. The air was suddenly scarce in the room and she couldn't move. "Don't think that because you're sleeping with my brother, any of us will hesitate to kill you if this is a trap."

Emma tore her eyes away from his. Her stomach in knots, she believed him. Already she'd begun to wonder herself if she could betray Cyn.

"I wouldn't blame you," was all she said and then jumped at the ding of the doorbell. "Who is it? More Protectors?"

Kieran shook his head. "No, they wouldn't ring the doorbell. It's dinner." She remained at the kitchen table while Kieran spoke to the delivery person. With a silent prayer, Emma hoped Cyn would come back before the other Protectors arrived. What if one of them was able to figure out what she was despite the spell star? She shuddered at what could happen in his absence.

Kieran came back into the kitchen area with a stack of pizza boxes. He opened one and took out a slice, and bit into it as he tilted his head to talk to someone on his earpiece. He motioned for Emma to eat, but she shook her head. She was too nervous to eat. If only Cyn would hurry up and return. She wouldn't feel at ease he did.

The realization shook her.

A few minutes later, just as the sun was setting, Cyn and Rowe arrived. Both men went straight to the pizza boxes.

Cyn grabbed two slices and handed one to her.

Rowe sat down to eat without a word or glance toward her. It was an improvement from his hostile glare, but she'd still feel more comfortable if he left the room.

It was tempting to head to the living room, but she wanted to hear as much as she could about what happened on their scouting mission and any plans they'd formed to rescue her sister.

She ate her pizza in silence. The men didn't speak either, each eating a second piece while she finished her first.

Kieran and Cyn exchanged a glance.

Cyn held out his hand to her. "Come Emma." When she hesitated, he took her by the arm and tugged her out of the room and up some stairs and into a guest bedroom.

"We have some things to discuss in private. I need you to stay in this room. We'll sleep here tonight."

Emma narrowed her eyes at him. "First of all, I expect to be part of my sister's rescue, so I should know the plan. Second, what do you mean by *we* are sleeping in here?" She emphasized the word 'we'.

He took a breath as if trying to gain patience. It reminded her of when he spoke to Blue. "Emma, we are not going to discuss our plans with you. And you're welcome to sleep anywhere you want in this house. Just remember there will be several other Protectors here, under the same roof. Perhaps you would prefer to bunk with Rowe?" He waited for her reply with his arms crossed and one eyebrow cocked.

Emma bit back the desire to groan in frustration. She walked to the bed and sat on it. "So what do I do for now?"

Cyn sighed. "Get some rest. We will be leaving at dawn. Do you want me to bring you some more pizza?"

Not hungry, she shook her head.

As he went to leave, the voices of more Protectors arriving drifted up the stairs and Emma saw the tension in his body.

"What's wrong?" She asked, sensing he was wary.

"It's not safe for so many of us to be in the same place at the same time. Higher-level demons can sense our presence."

Cyn studied Emma for a lingering moment. Did she know how exquisite she was? Even with her hair disheveled from the long day and scowling at her displeasure of having to stay in the bedroom, he found her sexy. She plopped down on the bed and her boots landed with a thud on the floor as she kicked them off. Her socks were next and she threw them aside with impatience. Pink toenails peeked out from her pants leg when she raised her knees and wrapped her arms around them. She glared at him then leaned her cheek on top of her knees and sighed.

The urge to forget about the rest of the Protectors in the house pressed him to get in bed and hold her.

Reassure her.

Instead, he went to her and stroked her cheek. "Look, we can't go in without a plan. I'm as impatient to go in there as you are."

What the hell was wrong with him? His main focus should be Roderick's rescue, not to comfort the bewitching woman.

~ ☾ ~

CHAPTER ELEVEN

"Ah my brother returns from tucking in his charge." Kieran said as Cyn returned downstairs to greet the newly arrived pair of Protectors.

He went to the two new arrivals, Thor and Fallon and each pair exchanged the standard greeting.

Cyn was glad to see Thor. The oldest warrior present, at over a thousand years old, was also the most experienced against high-level demons. Thor, who looked to be in his late twenties, was a fiery tempered Viking. The red-haired male couldn't seem to get used to modern life. He preferred to live in the colder climates, though Cyn suspected that the fact that the giant Norseman killed almost half the demon population in Pittsburg was more the reason for his current gig in Iceland.

Fallon greeted Cyn next with his usual cool reserve. The Brit was the youngest of the Protectors there. He was born into English aristocracy during the eighteenth century. Like most Protectors, Fallon transformed in his early twenties, but when Julian approached him to become a demon slayer, Fallon refused the call. He chose to remain in England living the plush life of a Lord.

When his parents died of old age and Fallon still looked like he was in his twenties, people began to fear him. Even his friends turned on him when they noticed he was not aging. Some even speculated that he was a vampire. Shunned from society, Fallon finally realized that he couldn't deny his fate any longer. He searched for a Protector to help him. He found a friend and guide in Roderick, who trained him to become what he was born to be.

Fallon would battle to the death for his mentor.

The Brit's translucent violet eyes took Cyn in and then he looked up toward the ceiling. "Think that's a good idea? She's part demon."

Air rushed out of Cyn's lungs. It felt as if he'd been punched in the stomach. The gut reaction he'd had when he first met her was right. He should have known she wasn't just human.

Demon? He didn't want to believe it. But there was no questioning of Fallon's keen senses, the Brit was always right.

Yet he asked. "Are you sure?"

The English Protector shrugged elegantly, his mannerisms still very much those of an elegant lord. "Yes, although I don't sense any hostility. She may not even be aware of her own heritage. I do however sense strong emotions toward you," his lips twitched with a hint of amusement. "It seems she may be falling in love with you my friend." He grinned at Cyn's shocked look.

"Let's concentrate on the mission," Cyn answered through gritted teeth, and ignored the other Protector's throat clearing.

He turned to the table, but not before he noticed that Thor and Fallon watched him with intent and considering looks.

In all the years of his long life Cyn had been successful in keeping his distance from women. He took great pains to not see anyone more than a couple times so that they did not develop any feelings for him. A relationship clouded a man's thoughts, which could be deadly in battle. He wasn't sure how he felt about Emma caring for

~ ☾ ~

him. God, it couldn't be good.

A low growl from Rowe alerted them and Cyn followed the Protector's line of sight to the doorway where Emma stood, her eyes darted back and forth between the men only to widen when meeting his.

"Just wanted to make sure you hadn't left without me," she told him and turned on her heel.

Thor's laughter boomed at Cyn's scowl. "You've got your hands full with that one."

# # #

Several hours later, after they discussed plans for Roderick's rescue, Kieran and Rowe took the first watch while others went to sleep.

Cyn walked into the guest bedroom. A weariness settled deep within.

Although his body did not tire easily, he wanted to lie down and not think for a couple of hours.

Waiting for the perfect time was always the hardest. More than anything, he wanted to leave and go get Roderick now. But he knew they should strike at daylight, when most of the demons would not be as strong.

He took his shirt off and kicked aside his boots, and then he headed into the bathroom to shower.

As the hot water pounded on him, his thoughts turned to Roderick. *What was Roderick enduring?* The demons hated Protectors and, no doubt, they enjoyed torturing his friend. Cyn wondered if the Spartan would be the same after all this time in their hands.

Almost two weeks of captivity by demons could change a man for life, even Roderick, one of the strongest warriors he knew.

If the demons hoped to get the best of them to come

after Roderick, they'd succeeded.

What kind of trap were they walking into? A well-planned trap meant to capture the strongest demon slayers. Maybe this was bigger than just Roderick and him. He stuck his head under the stream of water concentrating on what lay ahead. The demons only expected him and maybe Kieran. They'd provided enough clues and information through Emma so that she would lure them there.

Was she fully aware of this whole scheme of theirs?

He pictured her straddling him just that morning and grunted.

Shit—definitely not the path his thoughts needed to go down right now. Not burdened by common sense, his body demanded her. Cyn hadn't planned to be with her again. But the prospect of it made his pulse quicken.

Demon. She was part demon. Yet he hungered for her. She could be one of them, a killer. The reason the Protectors existed. He should be wary of her, feel guarded about her, but he didn't.

He wanted her. Not just for tonight, but to claim her as his.

Naked, Cyn slipped into the bed and under the blankets. Emma appeared so fragile. She had curled up with her back to him, taking as little space as possible.

He closed his eyes and thought about Fallon's words. That she had strong feelings for him.

Perhaps she did, but hate was as strong as love, if not stronger. He didn't give a shit which one it was. Right now he just wanted her. The realization of how much shook him.

He slid closer to her and inhaled her familiar scent. Aroused he hugged her around the waist and drew her to him.

"Cyn," Emma moaned, throwing her head back. It was

unbelievable how much he craved the feel of her softness against him. He trailed kisses down her neck and cupped her breasts teasing her pebbled nipples.

"I want you," he whispered in her ear.

Emma's defenses melted from Cyn's caresses and the three words eroded any willpower against him. Her judgment completely clouded by his intoxicating touch. The need to be with him became too strong for clear thought.

I can't do this. How could she spend an entire night with him? A tear of frustration glided down her cheek. What would happen tomorrow? Of course, she would never see him again, of that she was sure.

"Turn around Emma. Face me." Cyn's husky voice teased her ear.

Emma did as he asked. When she faced him, his eager mouth immediately took hers. They kissed and Emma was grateful for another chance to be together.

She wanted to treasure this moment. Her fingers traveled over the smooth skin of his back and traced every wonderful inch of him.

His hardness pushed into her center and she shifted closer to him. It felt as if she could not be close enough. She needed to become totally surrounded by the feel of him.

As much as Emma ached for Cyn to be inside her, she fought to refrain from grabbing for him. He rolled her onto her back and held her arms up over her head. He feathered kisses on her breasts and took the time to lave each one as she begged him to enter her.

Cyn's chuckle was low. "Not yet, I want to make this last Emma. I want to enjoy being with you."

He suckled her breasts and tortured her with his

hands. His finger slid in and out of her, Emma responded by riding his hand. His thumb began to play havoc on her body when he circled it around her swollen bud.

In a frantic effort to give him pleasure as well, she found his hardness and wrapped her hand around it. Matching the rhythm of his movements, she slid her hand up and down the silky flesh. Cyn pushed into her hand, a hoarse moan erupted from him. When his movements quickened, Emma whimpered as tremors shook her body.

Emma bit her lip to keep from crying out when she came. He waited for her body to settle. Then he climbed on top of her.

The orgasm did not sate her hunger for him. Emma almost wept when he finally pushed into her with deliberate slowness. The sensation of their union took her higher.

"You're incredible," he told her, eyes locked with hers.

Emma urged him on by wrapping her legs around his hips. She wanted every inch of him deep inside.

Cyn moaned at the feel of Emma's heat as it surrounded his length. His incisors snapped down when she tightened around him. He pumped in and out of her hard and fast, not able to hold back. When she turned her head giving him ample access to her creamy throat, he couldn't resist.

His fangs broke through her velvety skin and her blood rushed into his body fueling the ardor of the moment to a combustible intensity. His entire body shuddered in response as their senses became intertwined.

Emma flailed wildly when she climaxed. Her soft

mewls vibrated in his ear at the same time her muscles constricted around his length, milking him. Not able to withstand the wonderful kneading, he growled as wave after wave of release spilled out of him.

All his strength momentarily sapped, Cyn floated back to the stark reality. He closed his eyes when she began to massage his back, her fingers like magic against his heated skin.

They lay like that a long time, the room silent, except for their labored breathing.

"It ends tomorrow doesn't it?" Emma whispered into his ear while she ran her fingers through his hair. She asked the question, but they both already knew the answer. He wasn't sure if she asked him or herself.

"Yes." He lifted his head and was struck speechless when her heavy lashes lifted and her eyes met his. Never had he sensed emotion as deep as that reflected in her beautiful honeyed gaze.

Without warning, all the emotions of the last days appeared to hit her at once and Emma began to weep.

Cyn lifted off of her to hold her, and stroked her back. He didn't ask her why she cried. Instead patted her shoulder feeling awkward, not quite sure what to do. Even though he was an immortal, he had little experience with women's emotions. One thing he knew beyond a shadow of a doubt — he hated to see Emma cry.

"Shhh, tomorrow you'll be with your sister and all will be fine," he whispered to her.

When she calmed down, he wiped her tears away with a corner of the sheet.

She looked up at him, her pretty tear streaked face sad. "I am not sure why I'm crying." She put her hand up to Cyn's face. "I just wish things were different."

Cyn kissed her and held her. He didn't answer her. While she cried, she'd forgotten to keep her guard up and he'd been able to read her thoughts.

Now, he was certain she would betray him.

He was also sure he felt something for her. He cared for Emma.

Damn.

Not until much later when she fell asleep, her breathing even and soft, did he reply.

"So do I."

# # #

The weak rays of the dawn's light peeked through the window coverings providing dim lighting. Kieran didn't look surprised when Cyn walked into the kitchen and poured himself some coffee. Kieran must have noticed the tension in his brother's face as Cyn took a seat and drank the coffee in silence.

"It is possible for us to find a mate Cyn. But it's highly improbable," Kieran told his silent brother. "We have to accept that most women are with us for one of two reasons. They either want to fuck us or fuck us over."

Cyn nodded, his face grim. "I know." Then he let out a breath. "That's why we have to save Roderick. He's one of the lucky ones. What he and Rachel have is rare."

Kieran glared in response and his body visibly tensed. "Our reason for existing, and this includes Roderick, is solely to destroy demons. Women have no place in our lives." Kieran shoved from the table and turned away, his shoulders rigid. Cyn could only imagine what old memories assailed his brother.

He started to ask, but just then Fallon, Thor, and Rowe walked in. The Protectors were all armed and ready to go.

Cyn grabbed his leather jacket from a hook behind the door and shrugged on the heavy garment. It was completely loaded, with sterling silver daggers hidden in special side pockets, the weight of it a solid assurance.

Besides his daggers, he carried a short broadsword at his hip. His bigger, longer sword, he secured across his back.

Four Protectors walked out and mounted separate motorcycles modified to go over two hundred miles an hour.

One Protector remained behind.

~ ☾ ~

CHAPTER TWELVE

The rumble of motorcycles woke Emma with a start.

Cyn was gone.

She listened for a moment longer. The house was too quiet.

Damn it, they left me behind.

She jumped out of bed and flew around the room throwing on her clothes. Her bag in hand, she raced down the stairs into the kitchen.

Emma stopped dead in her tracks when she spotted a Protector at the kitchen table. With his hands rested on the tabletop, he seemed deep in thought, but looked up expectantly at her entrance.

She held her breath. One look at his narrowed eyes and she knew they had figured out she was demon.

The Protector must have remained behind to kill her.

The male tilted his head to one side and studied her, his eyes roaming over her with boldness.

His violet eyes traveled down her body before rising again to meet her own. She didn't care if he was a Protector, he wouldn't look at her that way if Cyn were there.

Who was she fooling? Would Cyn even care?

"I'm Fallon, Lord Fallon Trent. I can see why you enthrall him. And you are correct– Cynden would slam me against a wall right now for looking at you 'that way'." His velvety English accent did little to settle her nerves or overcome the fact that when he stood, he was a tower of walking death. “It seems I lost the coin toss, so I am to be your escort to demon-town.”

A mixture of relief followed by disappointment flowed through her. “Why didn’t Cyn wait for me?”

Fallon shrugged. “Cynden didn’t mention wanting to take you. Like I said we tossed a coin.”

His words cut into her. She pushed the hurt away and lifted her face to him. “Let’s go then.”

Fallon continued looking at her for a few moments as if deciding whether or not he wanted to say something else. Instead, he shrugged and began to check his coat and arranged each one of his daggers. The Lord picked up his sword and motioned for her to walk out before him.

She hesitated and glanced up at him and narrowed her eyes. “You go first.”

He gave her a mocking half smile. “I am not going to hurt you. But...I know what you are and if you try anything stupid, have no doubt, I will enjoy killing you.”

Emma felt as if her legs were going to give out from under her. She ensured her expression was blank and mutely nodded at him. “I need a weapon.” She held her hand out.

Without hesitation, he handed her a dagger. It surprised her, but she jammed it into her purse before he changed his mind.

He motioned toward the back door. “Let’s go dance with the devil. Shall we?”

# # #

Fallon drove a silver jaguar. It was beautiful and fast. Emma sat frozen as they flew down the road. What was it with these men and speed? She studied his profile. Despite the fact that he concentrated on the road and appeared oblivious to her presence, she knew he tracked her every move.

Emma clenched the armrest as Fallon took a sharp corner. “Why don’t you just kill me and get it over with?”

“I wouldn’t mind doing just that. But for one, I think Cynden would probably be cross with me if I slay you without reason. And secondly, Gerard sent you, so you must be the key to accessing the demon’s compound.” Fallon glanced at her and then back at the road. “Besides, since you are going to double-cross us, I will get to kill you anyway.”

Emma swallowed. Fallon’s powers were exceptionally strong if he could get past Gerard’s spell star.

Each Protector was so different, Emma thought, as she continued to study the male, out of the corner of her eye.

This one was even more unique than the group she’d already met. Although he possessed the extraordinarily handsome features, the common denominator with Protectors, he was more refined than the others. An aristocratic air resonated from Fallon that made her wonder about his background. His chestnut hair had been styled with care, not a strand out of place. Graceful and sleek, he reminded her of a male model. His long lashes would definitely be cause for envy. His patrician nose was so perfectly chiseled, any prominent plastic surgeon would fight to take credit for nature’s handiwork. His biceps bulged under the supple leather of his coat as he handled the steering wheel. The masculine yet elegant hands recently manicured.

How could someone, so obviously meticulous about his appearance be a demon slayer? Pretty boy or not, he definitely had that lethal air about him. Maybe he was gay. *Hmm...now that would be a shame.*

“I prefer women. I assure you, I’m not gay.” His

smooth voice caused her to snap her head toward to him. His lips were curved in an amused smile.

Oh God! He heard all my thoughts!

Warmth crept over her cheeks; she wanted to slap the grin off his face. Instead, she concentrated on blocking her thoughts.

A few minutes later, Emma reached into her bag. The back of her hand brushed against the hard plastic of a pen shaped remote tracer Gerard had given her. A stark reminder of what she had to do. Once activated, the remote would send a signal to Gerard. The problem was how to trigger the device without Fallon sensing it and killing her on the spot.

To distract Fallon, she took out a stick of gum and put it in her mouth. She almost offered him some, but one look at his stern face and she decided against it. As she replaced the pack of gum back into her bag, her fingers grazed the remote. She knew she needed to push the button.

But she couldn't do it.

Her heart raced. Surely Gerard would sense their presence without the tracer. She looked out the side window and did her best to breathe normal.

Thankfully, Fallon didn't give any indication that he sensed her discomfort.

They caught up with the four motorcycles and followed the riders down the winding country road until arriving at what looked like an abandoned industrial facility.

Fallon touched a button and the car's engine became silent. The motorcycles also switched to a stealth mode and glided without sound at a slower pace. They parked behind what looked like a deserted warehouse. The area felt somewhat familiar to her, but Emma didn't remember the place clearly. She'd been terrified when here last and barely able to see anything in the dark.

She waited for Fallon's instructions, not daring to move.

In silence, she watched the Protector's movements. Hurt and concern pierced her chest when Cyn and the others dismounted from their bikes and ran around to the side of the warehouse. He didn't even bother to glance her way.

It's better this way. She blinked rapidly at the sting of tears.

After the Protectors disappeared from sight, they climbed out of the car. Fallon motioned for Emma to follow him, as he ran around the back of the same building.

When they rounded the corner, she didn't see the other Protectors. They'd already gone inside.

Fallon opened a rusty door with measured slowness. Emma gasped when the creak startled some birds that flew out noisily. The Protector gave her an aggravated glare.

In a swift motion, he drew his sword and held it in one hand. Fallon's warm fingers wrapped around hers and he pulled Emma behind him into the warehouse.

Inside the building, the stale air barely stirred as they made their way into the dim and silent space. Able to see in the dark, Fallon moved with soundless swiftness through the obscurity.

A low, electrical hum filled the air. Then total silence fell again. Emma strained to hear or catch a glimpse of the other Protectors to no avail.

Fallon hesitated and leaned back against the wall. "Let's wait for the party to start, shall we?" his voice just the faintest whisper in her ear.

Emma nodded as she continued to listen intently, but the only sounds she heard were water droplets from the pipes that hung from the rafters and the wind outside.

Fallon must have heard something because he moved onward keeping a slow pace, not stopping until they entered an open area of the building. The badly lit room was gigantic; the only relief from darkness came from a line of minuscule grimy windows across the top of one of the high walls.

Without warning, demons materialized and attacked. Fallon dropped her hand to strike back at them.

Emma fell against a wall and stifled a scream.

His skill astonished her. Fallon fought with blinding speed and elegance. Immediately, two demons were felled, the smoke of their disintegration drifted over the area like thick mist.

Emma took advantage of Fallon's distraction and sprinted away from him. She ran down the side of the building. Disoriented, she concentrated trying to see through the haze and weak lighting.

Where was Cyn? Gerard had been clear. He would only release Briana in exchange for him.

The sound of more swords clashing guided her to where the other Protectors fought. Emma followed the loud clinks until she spotted him. A silent scream lodged in her throat at the sight before her.

Cyn and Kieran were back-to-back warring against so many demons, she couldn't count them all. The brothers were magnificent to watch as they battled. They seemed to read each other's minds and fought in unison —their movements like a well-choreographed dance. Demons charged and fell back just as fast from the Protectors' swords cutting them down.

Strong hands grabbed her from behind. This time Emma shrieked as a demon threw her over his shoulder and took off at a run down a long hallway.

Cyn would follow her. Emma knew he would.

~ ☾ ~

Now faced with the reality of the situation, regret clawed at her conscious and she couldn't follow through. Cyn didn't deserve to be betrayed, he fought for good. He dedicated his life to fighting against those out to harm innocents.

She would warn him not to follow alone. With the help of the Protectors, there was a chance she could still save Briana.

Thor, Fallon, and Rowe joined them and began to battle the demons. Cyn heard Emma's scream. After killing two demons that attacked him, their efforts clumsy at best, he checked to ensure the Protectors had things well in hand.

"Go." His brother mouthed at him.

It was the second phase of their plan. Follow Emma's trail that hopefully would lead to Roderick. Cyn ran after the demon that carried her over his shoulder. It was obvious from the slow pace that it was making sure he could follow them. Cyn forced himself to stay a short distance behind.

Emma bounced on the high-level's shoulder. Her hair fell forward blocking his view of her face. She pounded on the demons back with her fists and demanded for him to put her down.

She brushed her hair aside. Spotting him, she motioned with both hands for him to stop.

Had she changed her mind? *Too late.*

"Don't..." her words were muted by the creaking sounds of the wind ramming the sides of the building's metal walls.

The demon turned a corner and Cyn lost sight of them. He slowed and held his sword out in front of him ready for battle.

~ ☾ ~

The unmistakable evil emanating in the air ensured that Cyn sensed the demons before he saw them. He turned the corner, and beheaded one with swiftness. Then he flung out daggers and killed two more. As fast as the demons evaporated, others took their place.

They were all low-levels and some hesitated after they realized he was a Protector. Apparently, they were not fully informed. Their wariness gave him a chance to kill a couple more.

Communicating with the Protectors through his earpiece, he was aware they continued to fight, and followed the plan and stayed away from where he was.

Just as Cyn felled the last low-level, six warrior-demons surrounded him. It astonished him to see so many in one place.

High-levels, like the Protectors did not usually congregate.

What could be so important that they would risk themselves like this?

He turned in a circle slashing his sword through the air to keep them at bay. When they rushed him, he fought with all his might. Relief in killing one became frustration at being attacked by another.

Cyn hissed in pain when a demon managed to cut into his right upper arm. He swung around and killed the one responsible. But with so many high-levels, he was not strong enough or fast enough to take them all. A hard blow dropped him to his knees.

Cyn dropped to his side after another solid hit, yet managed to throw a dagger at his closest foe.

He missed.

The vulnerable position made it hard to defend himself from the onslaught of blows. When his sword was kicked out of his hand, several demons overcame him and wrenched his arms behind his back. Heat seared the nape of his neck and darkness fell.

When the fog inside his skull began to clear, Cyn knew he was in deep shit. He swallowed in an attempt to moisten his parched throat. He didn't have to attempt to move to know he was strapped into a chair, his wrists bound behind the backrest. Based on the throbbing in his shoulders, he'd been there at least a couple of hours. He scanned the space without lifting his head.

Heavy blood-red drapery covered the windows and tapestries with renaissance scenes hung from the walls. A gold-gilded carved desk and ornate chairs completed the obvious attempt at medieval decor. The computer that rested on the desktop looked totally out of place.

A sense of desire weaved around him. A female, most definitely a succubus, stood by a window leering at him with open lust. The sex demon guarded him, an interesting choice given that succubi were notoriously untrustworthy. He blocked her onslaught of pheromones.

Cyn began to assess his injuries. A couple of broken ribs and a deep cut to his sword arm were already healing. He flinched as he rotated his dislocated left shoulder back into place.

The succubus neared. Cyn ignored her and prepared himself to face Gerard, sensing the demon's presence before he entered the room.

With his back ramrod straight, Gerard swept in with long strides. He stood behind his garish desk like a king at his throne. Several high-level demons filed in behind him.

Cyn rolled his eyes and waited for the demon to speak. Gerard's jet black hair fell past his shoulders. The strands that framed his pale face, made it look even more so. The demon wore black from head to toe. His clothes were well made and fashionable. The modern choice of clothing was a stark contrast with his taste in decor.

Gerard's eyes were so dark that it was impossible to see his irises. When he glared at him, cold chills crawled down Cyn's spine. Pure evil emanated from the demon.

The Master-demon gave him a bored look. "Well I have to admit that I'm disappointed by you Protector. I expected more of a challenge from someone with your reputation. Trapping you was too easy." His lips curved into a smile. "Maybe your brother will put up more of a challenge." Cyn didn't respond. He hoped Kieran would get away.

Gerard waved his hand around the room and motioned to the demons. "You see Protectors are not the only ones who work together."

Cyn sneered. "Your kind only comes together when it benefits each of you." Cyn looked around the room with disgust. "Then again, trying to kill us would benefit your demented asses." He growled when a demon came from behind him and bit into his neck. As the anger pulsed through him, Cyn's fangs snapped down. He twisted out of the demon's grip and bit down on to his neck, tearing out the demon's artery. The foul creature stumbled back and collapsed.

Gerard sneered and motioned to a couple of low-levels. "Take that idiot out of my sight. Do what you want with him." The others dragged the dying demon out of the room. Cyn noted they were only too happy to comply.

The high-levels walked out of the room behind them. Cyn had no doubt additional demons were on the hunt for Kieran.

Now just four bulky ones, who were obviously Gerard's personal guards, remained in the room.

When Emma walked into the room, Cyn's stomach pitched. She glanced at him, her face devoid of any emotion, and went straight to Gerard. The Master stared at Cyn and yanked her closer by her hair. Her face pinched in a pained grimace but she didn't cry out.

Gerard studied Emma with amusement when she tried to tug her hair out of his hand.

Cyn could only stare, transfixed, when Gerard drew Emma to him and took her mouth with his.

When Emma wrapped her arms around Gerard's neck, bile rose. Cyn wanted to turn away, but refused to do so.

It was a good lesson. This was the way of women that faked interest in someone like him, treacherous every one of them.

Gerard turned Emma around so she could face Cyn. Although a bit pale, she smiled at him with empty eyes.

"I hope you enjoyed her while you could. She's a good fuck, isn't she? Of course, you understand that I don't plan to share her with you after today."

Cyn's eyes met her emotionless ones. Without looking away from her, he answered Gerard. "I've had better." He saw her flinch, the movement barely perceptible.

His words affected her. *Good.*

"Unless you plan to fuck her in front of me, can we move on to why I'm here?"

Gerard's lips curved and he raised an eyebrow. "You're not a good liar Protector. You feel something for her. Emma, show our hero your little toy."

Emma took a pen out of her pocket and held it up. "It's a tracking device — it was deactivated so you wouldn't find it."

Cyn refused to react. Instead, he just stared at her until she looked away. He addressed Gerard. "So we have established the bitch lied to get me here. Please, enough with the damn drama. What the hell do you want demon?"

~ ☾ ~

"I planned to kill you. I still might, but first I am going to force Julian to agree to exchange you and the Spartan, Roderick, for our Supreme Ruler. Of course, now I will have another Protector as well. Bringing your brother with you is an added bonus, more bargaining chips against the Roman." Gerard sat behind his desk as a demon came and took Emma out of the room. Neither Cyn nor she looked at each other. He wondered why she hadn't told Gerard about the other Protectors, but then figured she didn't think it necessary.

Cyn looked up at the ceiling with a bored expression. "Thames will never be freed. And you know the Protector's code does not allow for bargaining of any kind."

Gerard growled. "Oh he'll deal for your release. The Roman knows that without you three, crimes against humans in the area will escalate out of control."

"You can try. Go ahead waste your time."

The succubus, who had up until now, remained quiet, stepped closer and leered at Cyn, "Thames will be freed. Have no doubt, we will succeed."

Her voice was a siren's call. Cyn steeled against it.

Cyn recoiled from the sex demon when she approached. Gerard watched and laughed when she took Cyn's face in her hands. He turned his head away when she tried to kiss him. The succubus kissed his jaw slowly and licked him. Her tongue laved his skin from the corner of his mouth to his ear. She turned his face to her and smiled, the tips of her fangs rested on her bottom lip. "I could make you forget her and any other woman you've ever had Protector." She slid her hand to his crotch and squeezed. "Not quite awake and already a good size. Too bad, I would love to play with it." Cyn grimaced but was proud at his lack of response to her ministrations.

~ ☾ ~

Gerard shoved her aside. “Perhaps later Gia. Right now I have a plan for our guest that doesn’t include pleasure of any kind. Well actually, I’m lying. I will receive much pleasure while watching him tortured.”

Gia didn’t seem thrilled. She glared at Gerard, but said nothing.

~ ☾ ~

CHAPTER THIRTEEN

After they dragged her into a room, the demons shoved Emma in and left with a slam of the door behind them. Quickly, she explored the area and searched for an exit.

The onyx walls, bedding, and draperies gave her the creeps. An oversized wrought iron bed and two overstuff chairs upholstered to match the wall completed the morose look of the room. A deep red throw over the back of one of the chairs provided the only color in the depressing space.

She yanked back the thick drapes to find a bricked–in window.

"Damn it."Emma stumbled to a chair and collapsed into it.

Cyn hated her now. She would never forget the look on his face.

It was quick, but she'd seen hurt flicker in his eyes before he masked it. Emma also witnessed the change in him, from shock to sheer hatred. The knowledge that he despised her now was the hardest thing she'd ever endured.

When she'd entered Gerard's office, her escort motioned to a demon guard who stood behind Cyn and held a sword pointed at his back. She got the message loud and clear. One wrong move or word on her part and he would pierce Cyn's heart.

What now?

~ ☾ ~

Had it been worth it? Would Gerard let Briana go? A tear slid down her face and she swiped it away with the back of her hand. This was no time to feel sorry for herself. She had to find Briana.

Besides, she was tired of sitting around and waiting. It was time to go and look for her sister.

Emma cracked the door and peeked out into an empty hallway. Excited at her good fortune, she darted from the room and ran down the hall to hunt for the area where her sister was kept.

She only made it a few feet when a demon grabbed her arm.

"Master Gerard doesn't want you out and about by yourself."

Emma yanked her arm away. "I want to see my sister." She kneed him in the groin.

"Fuck!" The demon yelled cupping the affected area. She took off running as fast as she could, the stumbling demon not too far behind.

Finally, she turned down a corridor that seemed to go on forever until she came to an intersection. As she rounded a corner, it became clear that she was on the right track. The area looked familiar from the last time she'd seen her sister. That part of the building had very little lighting, which limited her visibility and forced her to slow. She came to a metal door that was cracked open and slipped inside.

The empty room was the same one Briana occupied the last time. There was no sign of her sister or any of her belongings. She froze when footsteps approached. With a snarl on his lips, her angry pursuer burst into the room.

"Where is she? Where is my sister?" Emma backed into a corner and yelled at him.

The demon shrugged, "Damned if I know. But you need to come back with me. Now."

~ ☾ ~

Emma dodged his first attempt to grab her. “I don’t think so.” She tried to run around him to the door.

But he was fast. The demon snatched her by the back of her neck. She tried to knee him again, but this time he avoided it and backhanded her across the face. Emma’s ears rang from the slap. It took all her strength not to pass out but she couldn’t stop her legs from betraying her. After she crumpled to the floor, he picked her up and carried her back to the same room.

Once inside, he tossed her onto the bed.

Then the demon left and this time the clicking of the lock ensured she would remain.

# # #

Piercing agony scorched through Cyn’s entire body. He’d been trained to numb himself and not feel so much of it, but it crept through his defenses. The demons had crushed his left knee and broken several of his fingers demanding to know where Thames was.

Fangs elongated past his bottom lip, he growled from the pain when they picked him up and half dragged him back to Gerard’s office. Unable to fight them as he was bound too tight, he decided to wait for a more opportune time.

Back at the office, Cyn managed to bite a demon as they strapped him back into the same chair he’d sat in earlier. The sting of broken ribs dug into his lungs when the demon punched him in the stomach. He spat the blood onto Gerard’s gaudy rug.

The room began to spin and Cyn closed his eyes slumping forward. After a few beats he shook his head and tried without success to regain his equilibrium.

A commotion broke out. Roderick was dragged in and strapped into a chair next to his. Still bleeding from

Cyn's bite, the demon shoved Roderick as he helped strap him down. With an angry roar, Roderick head-butted him. The demon howled and jabbed Roderick in the jaw.

Roderick shifted his jaw back and forth and raised an eyebrow, taking in Cyn's appearance. "What the hell are you doing here?"

At the sight of Roderick's wan and bruised face, his fury blazed. But he managed a droll look. "I happened to be in the neighborhood. You?"

"Heard the ambiance was pleasant." Roderick looked around the room with disgust. "Apparently I heard wrong."

Despite their situation, both Protectors grinned at each other. Cyn was relieved that Roderick was not only alive, but also appeared to have his wits about him. It gave him renewed energy. He bent down, lifted the chair off the ground and swung it around hitting a demon and knocking it to the floor with a grunt.

Roderick chucked. "I'm impressed, neat trick. I haven't tried that one, yet."

"Laugh all you want assholes, Gerard will be here soon," one of the demons told them as they began to leave, "You won't enjoy what he has in store for you." The room emptied, except for two burly guards, which remained by the door.

# # #

Emma leapt to her feet when the door opened. A succubus sauntered into the room. The blonde demon looked around the room as if measuring it. She swung a key ring from a long red fingernail. The succubus was about her size, but with bigger boobs. She sized Emma up and raised her eyebrows, as if in disbelief. "I don't get the big deal about you. You have that Protector crazy for you and now it seems Gerard wants you prepared to be with him tonight." She smiled, revealing the tips of her fangs.

"I am Gia." The succubus walked up to her and looked her up and down with disdain, then grinned. "I get to play with your Protector tonight. He is quite a looker and well hung too." Gia pushed her golden hair back from her face.

Emma stiffened. The female was trying to get a rise out of her.

She succeeded. "What the hell is going on? I am not going to prepare for shit! I want to see my sister now." She stomped closer to where Gia stood and shoved her, "and stay away from Cyn bitch."

Gia laughed. "You are a fool. Do you really think Gerard will keep his promises to you? You're not even a full-blooded demon." She slapped Emma across the face. "And bitch I will not only touch the Protector, but I will fuck him so good he will forget all about you by the time I'm done with him."

Emma went to grab her by the hair, but the succubus proved to be fast. She dashed out of the room, a trail of laughter behind her.

Emma kicked the locked door. The metallic taste of her own blood filled her with rage. She held her hand to her mouth and drew back blood stained fingers. The damned succubus busted her lip. She barely felt it as she replayed Gia's comment. "*Do you really think Gerard will keep his promise to you?*"

Oh God. What have I done? What are they doing to Cyn?

Several demons entered the room. Emma tensed. *What now?* They held her down while some human females tore her clothes off.

~ ☾ ~

Emma fought and screamed until she was hoarse while they massaged perfumed oil all over her. Then she was dressed in a black, sheer gown and gold chains were placed on her ankles and wrists.

Emma raised her wrist and inspected the jewelry. "Seriously?" The male demons carried her to the bed.

She remained there, dumbfounded, not sure what else to do. Her life had spun out of control.

Why hadn't she seen Briana?

Briana was dead.

The consciousness of it hit and Emma's stomach lurched. She ran to the bathroom and threw up. She continued retching long after anything came up.

Determination alone gave her the strength to stand up. After rinsing her mouth, Emma walked out and paced the room in wait for Gerard. When he came, she would try her best to kill him — with her bare hands.

# # #

Kieran's sword arm throbbed. He'd never fought so many demons at once. Although most of them were low-level and lacked battle skills, they made up for their shortcomings with sheer numbers. While he fought, he'd become separated from the others. He gasped for breath as he ran down a corridor. Julian's call sounded in his earpiece.

The Roman's strong voice boomed though his earpiece. "Fallon, Thor and Rowe, get out now. West end exit is clear. Kieran go on ahead about two hundred feet, there will be a door on the left. Go in and wait for direction."

Kieran wanted to argue, but he was so tired he could barely keep ahead of the demons. In a burst of adrenaline, he dashed down a winding corridor and found the door, opened it, and stepped in. His breathing was labored as he waited in a cramped closet-sized room. His pursuer's footsteps rushed past.

A few moments later, he heard Fallon's voice over the distinct rumble of the Protector's motorcycles. "We're off the premises." *Good.*

He began the task of accessing any injuries while he waited in the pitch black for further instructions from Julian. Suddenly the door opened and a high-level sex demon, an Incubus, stepped inside and closed the door.

Kieran raised his sword, but he was so drained that the demon easily disarmed him and held him against the wall. The Incubus was his same height, but was stronger at the moment. Kieran went for the dagger in his boot and kicked his foot out to retrieve it.

The male huffed at him. "Kieran if you stab me in the ass, I'm going to knock you out." Then the demon stepped away from him and held his hands up. "I'm Sebastian, Julian sent me to help out."

Kieran had heard of him. Sebastian was a powerful Incubus, but no one knew exactly what side he was on from day to day. It was rumored that he sold his services out to the highest bidder. It didn't seem to matter whether the person that hired him was a demon, a Protector, or a human. So Sebastian must have been the other spy, not a second droid like he'd assumed.

Kieran kept a close eye on the Incubus, who picked up his sword and handed it back to him hilt first.

"We don't have much time. Gerard is planning to implant explosive devices in your friends. We have to beat him to them." Sebastian opened the door and stepped outside. He scanned the hallway and motioned for Kieran to follow.

They walked in silence until the Incubus stopped by a door and held up two fingers, to let Kieran know there were two demons inside. Sebastian opened the door and two bulky demons blocked his entrance.

One eyed them with suspicion, obviously too dumb to realize who Kieran was. "Master Gerard wants no one to enter here until after the implants are..."

Sebastian cut his head off before the demon finished the sentence. He turned when he heard the body of the other demon hit the floor as Kieran did the same.

Both bodies evaporated as they hurried inside to release Roderick and Cyn.

The escape was relatively easy. They encountered and dispatched a couple more demons. The Protectors left the building through a side entrance Sebastian led them to and jogged to the waiting vehicles. Kieran and Roderick got into Fallon's Jaguar since Fallon had taken Kieran's motorcycle as planned.

Cyn climbed on his motorcycle and sped off into the night.

Almost two hours later, Cyn walked into his house. It seemed like a long time ago that he'd left the house with Emma.

Emma.

He refused to think about her.

Her betrayal hurt worse than any of the injuries and cuts the demons inflicted on him.

Now he understood Kieran more. No wonder his brother refused to even consider any kind of interaction with a human woman. From now on he would rely solely on the females Julian provided for sex.

His brother had offered, but he'd refused to spend the night at Kieran's house. He wanted— no he needed to be alone.

Thankfully his brother took Blue and Brock to his house after he dropped Roderick off.

~ ☾ ~

Once home, Cyn walked through the empty space to his bedroom. He reeked of demon. He peeled off all his clothing and tossed it on the floor. Tomorrow he would burn them.

He still smelled. “Gah!”

With tense fingers, he pushed the code to lower the security shields and made a beeline for the bathroom.

He allowed the hot streams of water to wash over his bruised body until the water was no longer warm.

With just a towel wrapped around his waist, he fell back on his bed and huffed out a deep breath.

Emma. The woman had lied to him from the very beginning, and he’d actually fallen for her.

What an idiot.

~ ☾ ~

CHAPTER FOURTEEN

"The Supreme Ruler must be freed. That should be our ever-present goal. Nothing else matters." Gerard slammed his fist down on the table, sending several glasses of blood tumbling to the floor. He hit the table again while he studied the face of each high-level demon that surrounded his conference table in the dimly lit meeting room.

"We understand how important it is for us to secure Thames' release," Lionel, a British born Master demon replied with a bored expression. "Unfortunately, the Protectors have him in a well hidden location. You had two of them here and they didn't reveal any useful information before they so easily escaped. Either they don't know or your guards need lessons in torture." Lionel purposely pointed out his failures.

"The Protectors didn't know anything. If they knew even one blasted useful thing, believe me they would have talked." He spat out each word while he jabbed his index finger towards Lionel.

Lionel pushed Gerard further. "The only Protector that knows Thames' exact location is the Roman. You're wasting our time. I don't appreciate you having all of us gathered here, putting our lives at risk just so that you can parade around feeling important."

The demon enjoyed the game but his eyes did widen when Gerard's fangs dropped and he leaped across the table to grab him around the neck. They grappled on the floor snarling. Gerard shoved Lionel's face into the carpeting gratified at the demon's groans. Lionel struggled without avail to loosen his hold.

Sebastian stood up, stretched and yawned. "I for one agree with Lionel. We might as well paint targets on each other's asses while we're at it."

Several demons laughed as the damn Incubus continued. "With or without Thames, it's apparent that our kind is quite successful at multiplying and getting everything we require to thrive amongst the humans."

Gerard shoved Lionel away and jumped to his feet, his rage now focused on Sebastian. Each step that he took toward the Incubus was measured and controlled, on the verge of losing control yet again.

"Well, well, so the Incubus thinks he can just stand here and point out the obvious. I don't give a fuck about the success of our kind as you put it. Those low level demons out there are not what are going to assure us total power. The only one who can assure us total control of the world is Thames. Only when he is free will we have ultimate power over all."

When Gerard was within a few inches of Sebastian, he snarled at the younger demon. "I am not even sure you are actually on our side. You are a whore that sells out to the highest bidder."

Gerard didn't pursue his challenge any further when Sebastian's fangs sprung and a deep growl emanated from low in the younger demon's throat.

It had proved impossible to gauge Sebastian's power level the times he'd tried. Gerard didn't trust the Incubus, but he didn't want to alienate him either.

The Master demon turned away flinging his hair into Sebastian's face. He went to stand at the head of the table and glared at the room.

When Sebastian retracted his fangs, he was

disappointed, he hoped for the opportunity to order his guard to attack the pompous male.

Gerard threaded his fingers together in front of him, and spoke slowly. “Thames was spawned for the sole purpose of ending light and casting the world into beautiful darkness. The Supreme Master’s powers are far beyond those of any other demon on earth. Somehow almost a thousand years ago, the Protectors became aware of his existence and captured him. But I have no doubt whatsoever that I will be instrumental in his liberation. The freeing of the Supreme means great powers to those who assist him.”

Gerard glared at Sebastian, who rolled his eyes, but Gerard was undeterred. “We will persist in our campaign to free him, even if we have to kill each and every Protector to reach our goal. Many Protectors died during Thames’ capture and hundreds of demons have died over the years trying to free him. I for one am willing to die trying.”

Gerard spoke on for some time and finally quieted when he realized only a few of the low-levels who were too afraid of him to leave, remained in the room.

Sebastian stood outside the door as Gerard stormed out, shoving demons out of his way, “What the hell do you want Incubus?”

“I’m leaving. Have to head back to my club. The sun is setting.”

“Fine, I don’t need you here any longer,” Gerard replied and stalked down the hallway toward his bedroom.

“I wasn’t asking for permission,” Sebastian called after him.

One day he’d kill the fucker.

Gerard spoke to the demon guards that stood outside

the bedroom door. "Don't let anyone disturb me under any circumstance."

He trembled in anticipation of releasing his frustrations on the half-demon inside.

If he had feelings, he'd feel sorry for Emma right now.

# # #

One of the demons told Emma that Briana willingly stayed with Gerard. She refused to believe it. Was her sister alive, but one of Gerard's minions now?

Is Briana capable of doing something like this?

Her sister was impulsive and rebellious, but not mean. On the other hand, a half-blood was susceptible to influence when in the constant presence of high-level demons. It wouldn't be hard for Gerard to turn Briana against everyone and everything she knew.

Had she done all this for nothing?

What about Cyn? Not sure if it was wishful thinking, but she didn't sense his death. Ache pierced her chest, at the thought. If they'd killed him, it was her fault. She shouldn't have trusted Gerard.

Even if she'd done it all to try to save her sister, she'd betrayed Cyn and brought him here to die. After he'd been willing to help her. Tears threatened and she blinked them away. She would save him, even if she had to die to do it.

After all, what did she have to lose now?

She needed to get a hold of her emotions for now and face Gerard. She would not let him see how much she hurt. He would enjoy it too much.

Gerard spoke to someone outside the door and she steadied her breathing. She collapsed into a chair. It proved impossible to quiet her thoughts. They were a complete mess. Her hands curled into fists with the urge to attack the demon as soon as he entered. He needed to die and she would gladly do the honors.

Gerard entered the room and stared at Emma. She remained immobile in the chair, her hands folded on her lap. When she looked up at him she could only hope he didn't sense her feelings.

His eyes raked over her, black and cold. She couldn't suppress a tremble of repulsion. By the curve of his lips, he enjoyed her distress. The Master demon walked to her and stopped just short of the chair and reached down to stroke her cheek. She turned from his hand.

"I am going to do so many things to you tonight. You will be begging for more of my touch, beautiful Emma."

Emma bolted up from the chair and glared at him. "The hell I will. I am not going to have sex with you, Gerard — ever. Where is my sister? Is she even alive? I want to see her now."

Gerard grunted and let out a deep breath. "Drama tires me," he told her impatiently waving his hand, as though to dismiss her remarks. "I don't need your consent to take you."

Anger spiked her words. "Let Cyn go, I want to see him leave."

"No."

"We made a bargain and you're not keeping your end of the deal. I demand you release him now."

His eyes roamed over her body leisurely. The sheer gown didn't hide much of her nudity. But at the moment she was too angry to care. Let him look all he wanted, he would not touch her.

"I can have you regardless, why should I bargain? Come to me." Gerard ordered.

An invisible force pulled Emma toward him. She fought against it, but he was too powerful.

In seconds, she was only inches away from him. He

grabbed her head and brought her face to his. His mouth took hers in a hard kiss that wasn't meant to arouse but to punish. In sheer panic, she bit his lip and kneed him in the groin at the same time. With a grunt, Gerard stiffened and released her. Emma turned to run toward the door. But before she could take two steps, he grabbed her by the hair and dragged her back. He held her against him with one hand; with the other he turned her head to expose her neck. When his lips touched her throat, Emma lost control of her emotions. She punched his face with all her might.

"Fine let's play rough. I enjoy a feisty woman." Gerard pressed his fingers onto the back of her neck. She instantly went limp. The only thing she could do was glare at him with defiance.

Emma gagged when his mouth covered hers once again and he forced his tongue past her lips. Gerard drew her head back and stared into her eyes while he dragged a long fingernail down her throat and pierced her skin. He licked at the trickle of blood that spilled. Pain slammed into her when his fangs plunged in to her vein. She could do little more than whimper when he fed from her.

Aroused he rubbed his hardness into her while he suckled. His breathing became ragged. There was nothing she could do to stop him. She was alone with no one to help her.

A tear slid down her cheek and splashed on the side of Gerard's face. He retracted his fangs from her neck. His face contorted with fury. "You cry? Little bitch, do you know how many women beg to be in my bed? After I am finished with you, I will toss you to the guards. They can take turns with what's left of you."

"I see my sister returned." Briana's voice took the Master demon's attention away from her.

~ ☾ ~

Gerard let go of her and Emma fell to the floor like a rag doll. Her eyes widened in shock when her sister crossed the threshold. Briana was alive and well, dressed in her usual low cut blouse and short skirt.

Emma still couldn't move although a tingling began to travel down her body. Gerard's numbing touch was fading.

Ignoring her, Briana sauntered up to Gerard and caressed his face. Her sister kept her attention on the Master demon, reverence evident when she looked up at him and rubbed her thumb over his bottom lip. "I missed you, Sire." She then ran her hands through his neck and brought him down to kiss her.

Horrified, Emma watched Briana and Gerard's passionate embrace her mind a whirl. Had her sister turned? Was she a full demon now? Did Briana really plan this with Gerard all along? No! Surely her sister was just under his control.

Finally she found her voice, and whispered hoarsely, "Briana, go away, leave this place. You have to save yourself."

Briana directed another look of total adoration at Gerard before she went to where Emma lay. She kneeled down next to her and peered down at her.

What used to be the same honey brown eyes as hers — were red-rimmed now.

"Emma you were always such a damned good girl. I don't want to save myself. I'm where I want to be. I belong here, with Gerard," Briana sneered. She looked over her shoulder at Gerard. "Can we send her away? I need to be with you now, I'm on fire for you Sire and I am running out of patience."

Gerard didn't answer Briana. His eyes roamed over Emma, a hungry expression on his face. "I like the taste of her blood, I will have you both."

~ ☾ ~

Briana glared at her, obviously not inclined to share. "Fine, but I'm first." She rose and went to the Master demon.

As her sister began to undress Gerard, Emma stared at her sister in disbelief. However, she still tried to catch Briana's attention hoping that together they could figure out a way to escape. But Briana didn't spare her a glance, seeming to forget she was even in the room. Her concentration was solely on Gerard. Not able to move, Emma had no choice but to remain on the floor.

Could Briana hate her so much now, that she'd allow Gerard to hurt her?

Perhaps her sister thought herself to be in love with the Master-demon. She tried to see Gerard from a woman's perspective. He was sleek and extremely attractive. The strength of his powers could be very appealing to a half-demon who needed to be accepted. Briana basked in his full attention — confident his black eyes following her every move.

Gerard remained motionless as Briana licked a trail down his chest. Her hand slid down his flat stomach. A loud moan escaped from him when she unzipped his pants and freed him.

Briana slid his pants down past his hips, while her lips covered the skin from where the material slid. Emma's eyes widened when her sister kneeled and took him fully in her mouth.

Lost in the gratification he received, his fingers curled in Briana's hair and closed his eyes.

Stunned, Emma dragged her eyes away from the sight of a world she could never be part of. She wiggled her fingers and realized she could move now. Her eyes caught a flicking motion of Briana's hand, as if her sister was signaling for her to leave.

Emma was not sure at the moment if Briana helped

her out of concern, or jealousy, but she wasn't going to hang around and find out.

She kept an eye on the couple to ensure they didn't see her and dragged herself slowly toward the door.

Just as she reached for the doorknob, the door flew open and strong arms grabbed her, one hand covered her mouth to keep her quiet. Emma was lifted and carried into the hallway.

The demon guards outside the door were gone.

"Don't fight me. I'm getting you out of here." A masculine voice whispered, as he placed her to her feet. She met the male's eyes and desire slammed into her, sending trails of heat to pool at her center, ecstasy overwhelmed her senses.

Her rescuer was an Incubus. A sex demon.

Perfect.

The Incubus met her eyes for a moment then took her hand. "Come."

Emma allowed him to tug her along the hallways as they ran out of the warehouse. It became clear he knew exactly where to go and had taken care to remove any obstacles.

~ ☾ ~

CHAPTER FIFTEEN

A few days later Emma ignored the steady rhythm of the rain that pelted the bedroom window. It was the middle of the night and as usual she couldn't sleep. She looked at the clock on the nightstand. It was two o'clock in the morning. Weary, but not sleepy, she sat up and reached for a tissue to blow her nose.

Staying at her apartment wasn't safe at the moment and with nowhere to go; she'd gone to Wendy's.

What have I done? Emma asked for the hundredth time. Tears began to fall from her swollen eyes. *Oh my God, I betrayed you and may as well have killed you myself.*

Renewed grief filled her and she fell back into her bed. Her sobbing shook her entire being. Emma cried bitterly, until she was so exhausted and empty she just moaned.

Images of Cyn and their time together tumbled nonstop through her mind. A constant reminder of what she'd done to the only man she ever loved. The physical pain of heartache became almost unbearable. She curled into a ball and tried to fall asleep.

Sleep must have claimed her because a nudge woke her and she dragged her eyelids open to Wendy's concerned face.

"Oh Honey," Wendy exclaimed. "Let me get a cool compress for those eyes."

Wendy disappeared into the bathroom and came back with a wet washcloth.

~ ☾ ~

"Here put this over your eyes while I make us some tea."

Later in the kitchen, Emma sipped her tea and took a small bite of one of the Danishes Wendy had gone out and bought that morning. Emma had to admit, after a shower and some sustenance, she felt a bit better.

Eventually, she would have to go back to her apartment and move on with her life. For now, Emma was grateful for her friend's presence and that Wendy hadn't pushed her to talk. Instead, she'd just fretted and fussed over her.

"I'm not sure what I need to do now," Emma sighed, "I'm so drained."

Wendy picked at her own pastry. "Obviously things didn't go well. What can you do?"

"I don't know. Frankly I just want to go back to bed and stay there for a month or two." Or, *however long it will take for the hurt to go away.*

"What happened to Cyn?" Wendy finally asked.

"He's dead." Emma's voice shook, the tears already falling. "I got him killed for nothing. Briana is still there, under Gerard's control."

"Oh my God." Wendy's covered her mouth with her hand, her rounded eyes locked on her. "Are you sure they killed Cyn?"

"I'm pretty sure. I hope not. I love him Wendy. I didn't even tell him." Emma closed her eyes at the constriction in her chest. "It hurts so much. I can't believe I killed him."

"Oh Emma stop it. You didn't kill him, those idiot demons did. I told you that Briana wouldn't leave. I know you want to think better of your sister, but she isn't like you."

Wendy didn't say anything else. She must have realized Emma already hurt enough and didn't need to

~ ☾ ~

hear anymore.

# # #

A month later, wearing distressed jeans and a light jacket, Emma walked into Inferno, and tried without success to block the blaring techno music and flashing strobe that blinded her. She'd never been a clubber because the combination of loud beats, smoke, and lighting gave her a headache.

Several males, both human and demon turned when she walked by them. A male demon stepped in her path in an attempt to get her attention. She pushed past him and went to the glass bar that flanked the entire length of the club's wall. Emma sat on a barstool and ordered a club soda. She spotted Sebastian on the dance floor.

Although a fast beat song played, the Incubus and his companion danced to their own slow song. The woman writhed into him and threw her head back as if in the throes of passion as Sebastian fed from her sexual energy.

Yep, the woman was having a major orgasm. Emma's eyebrows rose.

Sebastian held the woman who now convulsed against him. He moved off the dance floor and half dragged her to a nearby chair. Emma watched Sebastian lean over and peer into the woman's eyes, no doubt to erase her memory of what just occurred between them.

He turned when another woman came up behind him and wrapped her arms around his waist while she swayed to the music. It was evident he didn't suffer from low energy. The Incubus removed the woman's arms and urged her toward the crowd on the dance floor and away from him.

He must have sensed Emma watching him and looked

toward the bar, scanning it until he saw her. With a sensuous curve on his lips, he strolled toward her.

Emma studied the attractive demon. Dressed in black jeans and a silky teal shirt, he looked more like a movie star than a club owner. His shirt was unbuttoned and pulled out of his waistband. Probably the work of the woman he'd been dancing with. He wore a black undershirt that molded to him perfectly. He was tall and in good shape, with an angular face that gave him a rugged appeal. Sebastian wore his black hair trimmed and tussled. Then again, that too could be the woman's handiwork.

"I see you ensure your customers have a good time," Emma told him when he leaned on the bar next to her. "I wonder how she'll explain it to herself when she gets her bearings and realizes she's just been well pleasured."

Sebastian looked back toward the woman, his eyes flat. "She's woken up next to some slob many a time not remembering his name or even if they had sex. At least this time, she kept her clothes on."

"You know how to pick em," Emma teased him.

He motioned for the bartender to make him a drink then he turned his attention back to Emma. He regarded her and smiled. "True, I tend to shy away from good girls like you."

"You didn't the first time we met," She replied, grateful he'd not used his sexual powers on her since.

"That day I didn't know if you were a good girl or not." His eyes twinkled with mischief.

Sebastian's smile faded. "I know you didn't come to dance. Not that I don't enjoy your company, but why do you insist on returning time and again? I've told you, I am not going back to the Gerard's warehouse. I'm surprised he hasn't torched this place after what I did. The only thing I can figure is that he must not know it was me who helped you escape."

Emma placed her hand on his arm. He didn't move away, but held her with his gaze. "Understand me Sebastian, I have to know if my sister is all right. I must get her out of there." *And I want to kill Gerard to avenge Cyn.* "I need your help, I can't do it alone."

Sebastian picked up his drink, then took her arm and guided her around the bar toward his office.

Once they stepped inside his stylish workspace, he closed the door. He emptied his glass. "I told you—your sister was the one that went to Gerard with the idea of trapping the Protectors."

"But she's young and susceptible. I'm sure if I could talk to her alone, she will realize she's making a serious mistake. Sebastian, I know Briana fancies herself in love with Gerard and she's always been impulsive. I assure you she didn't expect that anyone would actually get hurt."

Sebastian went to his polished metal desk and opened a drawer. He took out a gadget and threw it at her. She caught it and studied the item. Emma recognized it as the remote for the tracer Gerard implanted in her neck. "I don't understand. What you are trying to tell me with this."

"When we removed the implant from your neck, we had to dispose of it immediately. We took it to an open field so that we could safely detonate it." Sebastian explained speaking slowly to ensure she understood. "Emma, the device was an explosive, you were supposed to die."

With a shaky hand, Emma rubbed the jagged scar on the side of her neck. "I didn't know."

"I know. Look, both you and your sister are half demon. Your father was a high-level so your demon heritage is strong and it can consume you, especially if you open yourself to it. Your sister is no longer human."

Sadness threatened to envelope her, but she steeled herself against it. He spoke the truth. She just didn't want to accept it. Resigned, she started toward the door. "You're right, but I find it hard to give up on her. I love her and I know that she must still care for me, we are all we've got."

She stopped and managed a smile toward him. "I owe you my life Sebastian. I'm not sure why you helped me, but if I can ever do anything for you, call me and let me know."

The longing in Sebastian's expression told Emma what he wanted from her. The desire in his eyes spoke volumes. He was attracted to her.

Although she found him appealing, Emma wouldn't be ready for a relationship anytime soon. The grief of losing Cyn was still ever present and raw.

"Give me time Sebastian, okay?"

He nodded, accepting her reluctance. "Take all the time you need."

Emma hesitated, but she had to ask, her heart constricted as she spoke. "Do you know if the Protectors were able to escape?"

"I can't tell you anything about them," Sebastian replied, his eyes didn't meet hers. "You shouldn't ask about them, it's dangerous, they are our enemy."

His answer disappointed her, but she didn't persist. "Good night."

# # #

It was a bright night. Cyn leaned against a building's wall and looked up at the full moon.

He was assigned to the midtown sector of Atlanta and currently stood across the street from the Fox Theatre.

The blinking lights of the marquee cast a glow over the patrons who rushed in late for the play.

He walked down the street and scanned behind the large hotel buildings. Movement caught his attention and he stepped back into the shadows.

The muffled sound of laughter traveled over the sound of a car alarm. He relaxed when two couples came into view. The foursome chatted and walked past without noticing him. They parted ways, one heading to an all-night coffee shop and the other to their car.

The man held the door for his date, who gave him a grateful peck on the cheek. The familiar scene had unfolded before him thousands of times in all the years and he'd never paid much attention. However, this night he watched the car drive away until it disappeared. It bothered him, for the first time in a long time that he would never have a normal life. He'd been human once, but it was so long ago that he remembered very little of those short years before becoming a Protector.

Love, marriage, and family were things most Protectors gave up. Being immortal, they would see those they loved age and die.

Roderick himself confessed his sadness once to Cyn at the thought that he might have to watch his son Brock die of old age, while he remained young. Julian believed that Brock might be destined to be a Protector, but they wouldn't know for a few more years. Cyn and Roderick didn't know of any other Protectors to have offspring and Julian wouldn't tell them if there were.

Cyn shook his head. The Roman kept too many secrets in his opinion.

He pushed the thoughts away and became vigilant again. He was on the lookout for a gang of young demons that attacked college students in the area. So far, it was a quiet night. Not many demons around. He wondered if

Kieran had better luck spotting demons, so he called his brother's unit. Kieran answered on the first ring.

"Anything over there? Nothing here. " Cyn told him as he walked down a side street.

"I've seen quite a few demons headed into Inferno. But they're more interested in getting laid, than killing," Kieran replied. "By the way, I just saw a woman who looked just like Emma going in. It was strange. I followed her inside out of curiosity, but I lost her in there. It's packed."

"I'm sure the management loved you walking in there." Cyn replied. "Call if anything comes up; we need to find the rogue demons." He ended the call.

Damn it, the last person he wanted to think about tonight was Emma. Footsteps neared and he tensed as a woman stepped out of the shadows and faced him. "Emma?"

The woman laughed, it was throaty and sensual. "I almost wish I was." She stood under a street light with her feet planted apart. She swept her long hair away from her face. It was the succubus, the same one he'd seen back at the Gerard's. Gia.

Succubae took power and life energy from sex. Although not dangerous, they were exceptionally strong. She was about the same build as Emma and stunning.

Her red-rimmed eyes roamed over his body and she licked her lips. "I've been looking for you."

Cyn didn't relax his stance. "I'm not in the mood to fuck a demon. Go look someplace else." He told her, his voice flat.

Gia took another step toward him. "I bet I can help you forget the woman who betrayed you. After a night with me, you won't remember any other woman you have ever been with. Wouldn't that be nice?"

Cyn had to admit the idea did have merit. He hated

that Emma filled his thoughts daily. He wanted to forget her and be glad she was gone, but he couldn't. When they escaped from the demon's warehouse, Sebastian told them an explosive transmitter had been placed in her neck. Ever since, he'd wondered if she was dead.

Cyn sneered at the succubus. "I bet I will forget all kinds of shit if I kill you too."

"She's with him you know. Emma is with Gerard. From what I can tell, she doesn't care about you." The succubus smiled. "Even when he told her you were dead, she didn't act like she cared. Their only regret is that we were not able to free Thames."

She's not dead.

The female's words affected Cyn, but he fortified himself not to ask more about Emma.

"Now come with me Protector. It will just be sex between a man and a female. I want that thick cock of yours inside me." Her pheromones encircled him its tendrils of temptation wrapping around him.

He forgot to block her affect.

Arousal assaulted him and his pulse quickened. His jeans grew very snug.

When his breathing became labored, Gia moved closer, her eyes gleaming with satisfaction.

He drew strength and took a step back to avoid the draw.

With a loud growl, Cyn swung his sword barely missing her throat. Her eyes flashed with fear.

"I won't miss next time Succubus. Leave me be."

"Fine, suit yourself." She maintained eye contact for a few more moments then finally gave up and turned on her heel.

Cyn spotted a businessman exiting a building across the street. Gia made a beeline toward the man.

Cyn watched Gia's retreating figure as the effects of

~ ☾ ~

her seduction attempt dimished. He shook his head to clear it. He felt bad for the man who had already put in a long day. He was going to be much later getting home now.

Had Gia lied to him? Was Emma really alive? It was too much of a coincidence, Kieran thought he saw her and now the succubus told him she hadn't died.

And with Gerard.

Did it matter?

An hour later, still on patrol, the hair on the back of Cyn's neck lifted.

Demons.

He took off at a slow jog, turned a corner, and saw them.

There were three of them behind a restaurant. The demons fed from the neck and wrists of a man who lay on the ground. From his lack of reaction, Cyn figured him to be passed out from blood loss.

He pushed Kieran's number into his earpiece and ran toward them.

The demons were slow to react. Apparently they didn't expect to be confronted by a Protector. As soon as one sprung up, Cyn swung his sword. The demon's head flew across the pavement and landed next to a dumpster. One of the other demons pulled out a gun and aimed it at him. The first shot narrowly missed his head. The second bullet hit him in the shoulder.

If it were possible, his glare would have bored an actual hole into the demon's face. Before he could pull the trigger again, Cyn flew toward the demon that turned to run. He didn't get far before Cyn cut him down.

The third low-level drew out a sword although he appeared hesitant use it. "Hey, we weren't going to kill the guy." The demon whined. "We were just hungry."

The buzzing of his fury barely allowed Cyn to hear the

words clearly, he wanted to kill him now. But he paused and looked over at the passed out man. His chest moved, he was breathing. The fresh bites on his neck and wrists no longer bled. Cyn turned back to the demon that continued to hold up his sword, but looked less afraid.

"Next time, order a pizza idiot. Go ahead. Get the fuck out of here." The demon took a step back. "Next time I will not hesitate to kill you," Cyn snarled.

The demon dropped his sword. The cheap metal clanged noisily on the pavement. As fast as his legs could carry him, he disappeared around a corner.

Cyn bent and drew the unconscious man's cell phone out of his pants' pocket. He dialed 9-1-1 and dropped the phone back on the man's lap. With the demon's discarded sword in hand, and the other's gun shoved into his waistband, he waited a few yards away, for an ambulance to arrive.

"I guess you didn't wait for me." Kieran walked toward him.

"They were low level demons, I handled it."

"Why did you kill them? We are just supposed to warn them." Kieran's eyes widened. "Oh Shit." Kieran mouthed 'Julian' and motioned to his earpiece, when he realized their leader overheard them.

Cyn's earpiece beeped.

It was Julian.

A very pissed off Julian.

~ ☾ ~

CHAPTER SIXTEEN

The next evening, Cyn lay on the couch and watched a Rugby game. He'd been unable to sleep and hadn't gone to bed. A hard punch to his shoulder startled him from sleep. Instinctively his fist flew out and hit the person so hard it knocked them down.

Fully awake now, Cyn jerked up in time to catch the look of shock on Blue's face. The boy scrambled to his feet and ran to his bedroom slamming the door behind him.

There was a crumpled piece of paper on the floor next to the couch. He picked it up and scanned it. It was Blue's report card.

Straight A's.

His gut clenched. He'd forgot all about Blue's parent-teacher conference that evening, and to make matters worse, he'd just broken a promise he made to Blue. That he would never strike him.

God knew the boy pushed him on that pledge, testing him over and over. But Cyn never hit him.

Until now.

It was a great week so far — enduring Julian's wrath for killing the low-level demons, and now this.

He got up and went to find his son.

Cyn opened the door to Blue's bedroom to find the boy in front of his blank computer screen. When Blue noticed Cyn entering the room, he squared his shoulders and glanced at him. Without a word, he looked back at the monitor.

The glistening in the Blue's eyes shot a sharp ache square into the center of his chest.

He was a Protector. He never planned to be a parent. But now that he had Blue, he couldn't imagine his life without the boy in it.

For three centuries, it had just been him. He didn't have to worry about anyone else. But things were different since Blue, and he loved it. He stepped closer to him and reached for the boy's shoulder, Blue shifted away from his touch.

"I'm sorry son. I didn't mean to hit you. You caught me off guard."

Blue shrugged and tried to act nonchalant, but his voice shook. "It was my fault."

"No Blue. It was not." Cyn took him by the shoulders and lifted him out of the chair. Blue looked up at him. "It wasn't your fault. I should have been with you at the parent-teacher thing. I forgot. I'm so sorry."

"It's okay Dad." A sigh of relief escaped Cyn as the boy threw his arms around his waist and hugged him. Blue moved away his face flushed. "Uncle Roderick and Aunt Rachel were there. Afterwards, they took Brock and me out for pizza."

"Let me see your face." Cyn inspected Blue's face closely while he squirmed. Thankfully, there was no bruising or swelling.

"How about I make it up to you? We can go dirt biking Saturday."

Blue's eyes widened, a wide grin spread across his face. "I don't have a dirt bike."

Cyn smiled at him. "After that report card, you will." Blue hugged him again, this time not letting go right away.

Blue ran to his bed, plopped down and picked up his

cell phone. "Wait till Brock hears about this!"

The security alarm chirped to let him know someone had arrived. Since whoever it was knew the code, it was either Roderick or Kieran.

When he walked into the kitchen, the site of Roderick's backside greeted him. The Spartan was bent over digging in his refrigerator.

Cyn let out a breath. "I know I fucked up. I forgot all about the school thing tonight."

Roderick straightened with a beer in each hand. He handed Cyn one, then opened the other and drank from it.

Cyn put the bottle aside and leaned on the counter in wait, sure Roderick was about to give him a stern lecture. Instead, his friend gave him an amused grin and shrugged. "You know, I never thought we would be discussing parent-teacher conferences. I was more comfortable killing Nazi demons during World War II than I am sitting down, listening to a teacher telling me that Brock can add well." Roderick looked toward Blue's room. "You should have been there."

"I know — what can I say? I just apologized to Blue. Thank you for being there for him." The Spartan nodded, his discomfort was palpable.

"What else is up Roderick? I know you didn't just come over to bust my balls about the school conference." Cyn asked.

Roderick took another swig from his beer but his eyes did not quite meet Cyn's. The large man rubbed his chin as if in thought. "Okay...it's like this. I'm worried about you, so is Kieran. We think that woman, Emma, got under your skin." Concerned eyes met his. "Cynden, if your head is not where it's supposed to be, you can die."

Before Cyn could answer Roderick held up his hand. "I'm not done." He pulled out a chair turned it around and straddled it. “Let’s talk this through. He counted off on his fingers. For one thing, Protectors don’t develop feelings for a female unless it’s our mate. Secondly, there has to be a reason why you feel tied to her, if she isn’t your mate. We need to figure this out because we can’t afford for you not to have it all together, up here,” Roderick jabbed at his temple with his forefinger.

Cyn held a finger up to stop his friend’s lecture. “Roderick, I appreciate the Dr. Phil talk, but I’m okay. I am fine, up here.” He pointed to his head.

Cyn looked over his shoulder to make sure Blue wasn’t nearby. “Maybe it’s just that I haven’t gotten laid in a while and well you know.” He ran his hand through his hair. “Shit I don’t know.”

Roderick chuckled, then sobered. “Nope that’s not it and you know it.”

Cyn huffed and gave in. Then he grabbed a chair and sat opposite his friend. “Okay, she’s been on my mind. A lot. I don’t know how I feel about her, to be honest. Kieran said he saw Emma, or someone that looked just like her, walking into Inferno the other night. That same night a succubus mentioned her. I think she’s still alive. In all probability, she’s fully embraced her demonic side now.”

Cyn reached back for his beer, popped it open and took a long swig. “Maybe I need to visit Inferno and find out for myself.”

Roderick’s eyebrows shot up and he laughed. “That will go over well. Sebastian will have a fit if a Protector goes in there and scares the shit out of his demon patrons.” A grin split across Roderick’s face. “Actually, that sounds like fun, mind if I come along?”

Roderick looked as though he was relaxed and at ease. Cyn hoped he was getting back to normal.

“How are things with you and Rachel?” He asked.

~ ☾ ~

"Great. With her, it's great," Roderick's eyes clouded, his lips pressed together.

Cyn nodded. "What about with you?"

"It's like a slow lifting fog. The first couple of days we hardly left the bedroom, I can lose myself in Rachel and not think. I'm back at work and moving toward a normal life. It gets better day-by-day. I'm working on it. And I got my old friend now. Roderick motioned to his broad sword, attached to his belt. You should see the looks I get at the hospital." He downed the rest of the beer and stood up.

"You wear your sword in the hospital?" Surprised his friend could get away with it.

Roderick shrugged. "No one has had the balls to tell me it's against policy yet. Rachel thinks it's hilarious." His loud laugh filled the room. "Well, speaking of Rachel, she was drinking a glass of wine when I left. I better get back and take advantage of that."

The Spartan looked down at his boots for a beat then back at him. "I had to talk to you. I know that you can handle yourself, Cyn. Just make sure you think about what I said. I'm not sure what course of action needs to be taken, maybe you need some time off or something."

Cyn remained in the kitchen after Roderick left. Emma's expressions, when they made love came to mind. The picture of the curve of her neck when she turned to give him access to her throat made him bite back a groan and close his eyes.

Roderick was right. The woman was playing havoc with his mind.

Could a half-demon actually be his mate?

~ ☾ ~

CHAPTER SEVENTEEN

"Here kitty cat...." Emma held a bowl of cat food and tried to coax her cat out from under the bed. The orange tabby moved further back and hissed, its yellow eyes tracking her every move.

"Fine suit yourself, but you can't stay under there forever." Emma put the bowl down and got up. "I don't know why I even try."

Months earlier, she'd brought the cat home after she found him on the side of the road. He'd been hit by a car. He wasn't hurt bad, and recovered fast.

When she got home from work the day after, she found him stretched out on her couch. As soon as the cat spotted her, he hissed and darted under her bed. Like most animals, he sensed the demon in her which made him skittish. Maybe she'd find him another home.

"It's strange that the kitty doesn't like you. He hung out with me while you were gone." Wendy called out to her.

Emma went into Wendy's bohemian inspired living room. "Why don't you keep him? He hates me. He's been around me for weeks and is still scared of me." Emma sat on the floor next to Wendy's denim upholstered couch and picked up her glass of wine.

"Yeah I might just do that," Wendy told her with a laugh. "I think the cat may not like you because you haven't taken the time to even name him."

Emma nodded. "Yes I did, his name is Kitty Cat. Right

now I have a new name for him, but it's not nice."

Things were almost back to normal. Emma was glad for Wendy's easygoing company. More times than not, she would find a way to cheer her up.

"I think it's safe for me to go back to my apartment now."

Wendy's eye widened. "I don't know, maybe you should ask Sebastian what he thinks. He wasn't too thrilled about you refusing to stay at his place and moving in with me."

"I couldn't stay there. Sebastian saved my life and I owe him. But he wants more from me than I'm ready to give," Emma replied. "You know Wendy, as attractive as Sebastian is, I can't even think about being with him. It will take me a long time to get over Cyn." Her throat constricted. "Shit, I can't even say his name without losing it."

Sebastian deserves more than that.

As if on cue, Emma's phone rang. It was Sebastian.

"Your sister is here."

# # #

Emma strode into Inferno with a purpose. When she spotted Briana dancing, she pushed through the swaying crowd. Her sister danced with a human male who was already entranced by her. Emma hurried onto the dance floor and shoved the guy aside. She stood in front of her sister, hands on her hips.

Caught by surprise, Briana didn't react at first; she just stared at her blankly, as if she didn't remember who she was. Recognition sparked and she stalked off the dance floor.

Emma grabbed her arm.

Briana glared at her. "Wow! You're willingly hanging

out at Inferno? I can honestly say I'm surprised. You've changed sister." She made her way toward the bar at a leisurely pace. Once there, she signaled the bartender for a drink. "I hope you have a good reason for interrupting what would have been a great meal for me." She looked back toward the dance floor as if trying to locate the guy she'd been dancing with.

"Come back to Sebastian's office, I need to talk to you. It's important." Emma tugged on Briana's arm and her sister reluctantly followed her.

When they entered the office, Sebastian stood up and motioned for them to sit. With a reassuring look at Emma, he left them alone.

Emma took her sister's hands in hers. "Leave with me Briana. We can move away and start all over. Gerard is pure evil. He will kill you."

Briana jerked her hands out of Emma's hold. She went to stand by Sebastian's desk and gawked at her. Her skin had a darker blue undertone than before and her eyes were red-rimmed. She was a full demon now. Her hands shook with the need to feed when she fidgeted with an errant strand of hair.

"I am not going anywhere with you." Briana let out an exasperated breath, "Emma, we have to accept who we are or should I say what we are. I don't want to go through life pretending to be human. I won't do it anymore. Gerard has shown me so many things. Things I never thought I could experience. I can't imagine life without him. I need him. I love him."

Her sister would lose more and more of her humanity the longer she remained with the Master demon. In desperation she grabbed Briana by the shoulders and shook her. "He doesn't love you Briana. He is not capable of it. He gets off on torturing people and suffering. Don't you see his wickedness every moment you are around him?"

Briana shrugged her hands off. "Perhaps, but it's still worth it."

"A good man I love died trying to save you." Emma's voice shook.

Briana's expression remained bland and aloof. "Gerard assured me no one would get hurt." She stepped away from her. "Look Emma, I didn't ask you to save me. If you want to go back to that pathetic little life, work nine to five at that bullshit job at the bank, then go ahead. Forget about me. I don't want that, I want what I have now."

"I'm begging you Briana, just come to my place. We can hang out like we used to and talk," Emma pleaded.

Sebastian entered again. He spoke through an earpiece.

Briana's red-rimmed eyes stared back at her. She shivered at the emptiness in them. Her sister huffed with irritation and headed toward the open door. "Don't try to come after me again. If Gerard tries to kill you, I won't step in next time. I've chosen my path. Now leave me alone." She left without a backward glance.

Dejected Emma sank into a chair and covered her face with her hands. When she looked up, Sebastian was at his desk. He read information on a piece of paper in his hand to someone through his earpiece and disconnected.

"She's right you know." Sebastian told her, as he inched his hip onto the corner of his desk and regarded her. "She has turned. Briana will not leave him now."

"What about you Sebastian? Have you turned as well? Have you given yourself over to your demonic side too?" Emma shouted at him, taking her anger out on him.

"I'm a full-blood demon Emma. I don't pretend to be anything else. Unlike you and Briana, I didn't get a choice." His voice held a hint of envy when he continued.

~ ☾ ~

"Not all of us have that luxury."

"I'm sorry. I'm upset. I had no right to yell at you." Emma stood. "I'll go home to my *pathetic* life now." She held her hand out to him and he took it in both of his. He was a good man, regardless of his bloodline.

"Thank you Sebastian, for everything." She kissed his jaw.

Her steps heavy, Emma trudged through the throng of people and kaleidoscope lighting without noticing any of it. The weight of sorrow threatened to consume her and she prayed she'd make it home before losing it. The hum of traffic lulled her somewhat when she exited Inferno and headed around the back of the building to her car.

Without any warning, she was slammed against the building and held firmly in place. A muscular demon pressed his body against hers and pinned her arms to her sides.

Red-rimmed eyes zeroed in on her throat.

He was hungry for blood.

Emma attempted to scream, but his strong hold on her throat impaired her ability to breathe. Her vision began to fade as she gulped for air.

"Gerard sends his regards." The demon told her nuzzling her neck. "Since I have to kill you anyway, I might as well get a taste before I do." His fangs snapped down and she tried to scream, but it came out like a hoarse cough.

Emma struggled to shove him off of her, but he was too strong and didn't budge an inch. He bit into her and began to feed. The metallic smell of her own blood filled her with panic.

His hold on her lessoned and she was finally able to shriek.

"Step away from her." The Protector's voice vibrated with rage.

~ ☾ ~

Emma collapsed to the ground when the demon turned away to fight.

"Cyn" her whisper went unheard when the swords clashed. She held her hand to her neck. Blood seeped through her fingers so she applied pressure on the wound her eyes trained on the combatants. Was he really there?

He was alive.

She couldn't see his face for they fought in the shadows. But she knew it was him. As soon as the demon fell to the ground and disintegrated, she got up and ran toward him. She stopped short a distance from him.

"Cyn! You're alive!"

She went to take a step toward him but stopped when he backed away.

His expression was stoic and he regarded her without even the slightest flicker of emotion. Obviously, he was not happy to see her. She wasn't surprised.

He cocked an eyebrow at her. "Sorry to disappoint you."

Emma's shaky legs threatened to give out from under her, but she forced herself to remain upright. She understood why Cyn would despise her. "Regardless of what you think, I'm glad you are all right."

Cyn's face remained vacant. "Let me check your wound." His warm fingers pressed into her neck. Tears sprung to her eyes at his touch, the touch she thought she'd never feel again. But unlike before, there was no intimacy in this contact. He was just doing his job.

When he bent to check her neck, she inhaled his familiar musky scent. She ached to reach out and touch him, for his arms to be around her.

"The bleeding is slowing. You'll heal." He told her, his eyes flat. If he noticed her shakiness, the only indication he gave was when he wrapped his arm around her waist to support her as he led her to the car.

At her car, he opened the door for her. Emma didn't get in, not ready to say goodbye to him just yet.

"I see that you have picked a lifestyle." Cyn told her and motioned over toward Inferno with his head. He propped her up against her car and then moved away from her. When they locked gazes, she drank in the sight of his beautiful ice blue eyes.

She couldn't let him leave. She wanted to tell him how wrong she had been. Needed him to know that she loved him, but instinctively she knew he wouldn't believe her.

"I'm sorry Cyn. I thought I was saving my sister. I want--"

Cyn moved so fast she was shocked when he yanked her against him. "Stop lying to me demon." Both froze at the effect of their proximity, her eyes locking on his lips.

His mouth came down on hers. Immediately his familiar taste overflowed her senses. She went to put her arms around his neck but he jerked away from her.

"Good bye Emma."

Emma watched him walk away.

The elation at knowing he was alive was overshadowed by the hurt that he would never trust her again.

She remained in the same spot, not moving until long after he left.

~ ☾ ~

CHAPTER EIGHTEEN

The cloudy day enhanced the lushness of the Highland's green foliage surrounding the cemetery near Inverness, Scotland where Kieran and Cyn stood side-by-side.

The latest Fraser Laird had been laid to rest and they'd come to pay their respects.

Cyn stepped forward and touched the tombstone. "God speed Calum."

He took a deep breath. "Nothing smells like home".

Kieran nodded. "Yes and it's as beautiful as I remember. Unfortunately we should leave soon, before we're spotted."

Cyn noticed a man approaching, a short distance away. "Too late."

"You two are definitely Frasers. You're spitting image of my forefathers in the portraits that hang in my home." The man walked up to them and held out his hand. "Welcome, I am Ian Fraser, the new Laird. I take it you're the American Frasers my father spoke of so often. I'm sorry you didn't get to see him one more time." Ian's eyes misted as he looked at his father's tombstone. It was obvious he'd cared deeply for his father. "I'm sure Da would also be disappointed that he missed you." He studied Cyn closer. "The resemblance is uncanny. You seem so familiar, have we not met before?"

Kieran interrupted. "We are indeed the American Frasers, I'm Kieran and this is my brother Cynden. I met your father once. He was a good man."

"Aye he was." Ian motioned toward Fraser castle. The great castle still stood proud. It had been well taken care of over the years. "Please come, family is always welcome to stay. I will have your luggage collected at the inn if you have already checked in."

Kieran started to decline, but Cyn stopped him. "I think that's a good idea. We need to talk. We leave tomorrow, so it will just be overnight."

They walked into the large estate. Both brothers hesitated when the memories of their past life there assailed them.

In the entryway, a portrait of Malcolm, Kieran and himself startled Cyn. He glanced at Kieran who peered at the picture and then back at him. The sight of Malcolm's familiar face shook Cyn so much, he had to look away. Next, his attention went to the portrait of his parents and he smiled remembering them. Ian Fraser waited patiently as they looked at the portraits.

Ian frowned and his eyes narrowed as he glanced from the portraits, to them, but he didn't say anything. "Come meet my family," Ian told them and led them toward the great room.

They followed the new laird to the space where their family had gathered for generations. The brothers were introduced to Ian's wife, Maggie, and two of their four children.

That night in a guestroom, Cyn paced not able to sleep. It had been over a hundred years since he last stepped foot inside the castle and yet he instantly felt at home. He looked out the bedroom window and thought back to the last time he lived there, slept in that very room. Nearly three hundred and eighty years ago.

~ ☾ ~

# # #

Northern Highlands, Scotland 1634

The Laird, Malcolm Fraser, reined in his horse and slowed it down to trot alongside his younger brother. Cyn ignored him.

As of late, along with the change in his personality, Cyn also changed physically. Through a painful process, he'd grown to a towering height and filled out his already muscular physique. Goliath, the immense charger horse, Cyn rode upon, trembled as if he wanted to continue to ride hard.

Blood thirsty, like him.

The only time Cyn felt like himself of late, was on the battlefield. Once they headed back to their homestead, he became sullen and withdrawn again. Dread of what awaited enveloped him.

Malcolm gave him a worried look. "I'm not sure what has caused this change in you brother, but I can sense your unhappiness at heading home." His brother knew him too well.

"Cynden you have always been the easy-going one of us. You have our mother's patience and care about the clan's folk."

Until recently, I've become a different person.

Out of the corner of his eyes, Cyn could see Malcolm studying him. "Good turn back there. I do not think the MacLean's will want to trespass our lands anytime soon."

"Aye," Cyn answered without emotion.

"Mayhap we can celebrate our return with a betrothal brother," Malcolm tried again. "Tis time you take a wife and give the servant girls a reprieve. The housekeeping and cooking have declined since you've been using our serving wenches almost nightly. And quite thoroughly at that, it seems by their lack of energy during the day."

Cyn didn't answer as he already contemplated bedding the chambermaid upon arrival. Three weeks without a woman was far too long for him.

"The Campbell's lass, Marlene is of marrying age," Malcolm continued, determined to have the conversation with him. "She's a bonnie lass. Don't ye think?"

A grunt was Cyn's response. The thought of marriage did not sit well with him. He knew it was his duty to the clan, to marry and have children. But he'd never met a woman that didn't bore him after bedding them a couple of times. He didn't even try to get to know them anymore.

Besides, he wasn't sure he could stand to have anyone around him every day and night. Nearly every night in the last months, it was either nightmares that haunted him or excruciating pains that awakened him. He woke panting and sweating from either hurt or fright. It felt if his muscles separated from his bones, the aches so extreme he wondered if he might go mad.

When he'd asked his brother questions about hurting and nightmares, Malcolm just gave him puzzled looks, not sure what he talked about. His brother Kieran at just ten and four was too young to ask.

Now he kept what happened to him a secret.

The isolation of his situation was the worst part. His days were a trial. Tired and in a foul mood after the restless and painful nights, he trudged through his duties ignoring the curious looks of his clans folk.

He withdrew more and more from his family. Lately, he spent more time with Goliath than with his clan. The only time he had a respite from the nightmares was on the battlefield or after bed sport with a wench or two.

At his brother's questioning look, he realized Malcolm

wanted an answer, but not the one he was to give. He granted Goliath his wish and they thundered away from his brother.

That night the entire clan celebrated the return of the men sharing their evening meal in the great room. Everyone was in good spirits. Even Cyn relaxed, already eyeing a new serving wench. He sat next to Malcolm at the main table and studied the revelry around him, not quite a part of it.

"I worry about him." Cyn overheard Malcolm's wife, Lizzie, as she spoke to his brother. She repeatedly glanced at him, which made it obvious they were speaking about him. "Have you talked to him about taking a wife?"

"Aye, but he wasn't too keen on the idea." Malcolm answered her, kissing her brow. Lizzie sighed and dropped the subject.

Cyn drank deeply from his tankard and watched a messenger enter the room and stand before Malcolm.

The laird acknowledged the boy. "Speak lad and then have your fill from the trenchers before departing."

The young man's eyes bulged, as he took in all the food on the tables. "Thank you my Laird, I bring a message from Sir Julian D'Arco, He wishes to speak to you on the morrow."

The next day, Cyn woke with a heavy head and the new serving wench in an exhausted slumber, next to him. He rose noiselessly, as not to wake the girl and walked to the window. It was a warm morning and he didn't bother covering himself.

He would have to avoid Lizzie this morning. She'd be cross at him for keeping the serving girl away from her duties. He decided to get dressed at once and leave out the back way through the kitchens. He would grab some bread and cheese to break his fast and go to the stables.

~ ☾ ~

Once he got Goliath, they'd go to the nearby loch to bathe. Afterwards, he'd head into town and visit a certain tavern where he always received special favors.

Movement beneath his window got his attention. A regal beast of a horse, the likes of which he'd never seen before, pranced continuously.

A man with the physique of a warrior stood next to the horse. The stranger looked up at him. His penetrating stare observed him without expression.

The visitor the messenger announced the night before. *This must be Julian D'Arco.*

He abandoned his plan to avoid his brother's wife and dressed with swiftness. Cyn rushed out of his room to learn what news the visitor brought.

As he reached the library, its doors had already closed, which gave him no choice but to wait in the hallway and pace. Malcolm met with the stranger in private. A rare occurrence as Malcolm usually included Cyn in all matters. This didn't bode well.

Lizzie approached and hit his shoulder. "You are an ogre Cyn. Where is Maureen? If you don't take a wife soon, then find a mistress to use so that the household is not affected." Although her tone was terse, her eyes twinkled playfully at him. Lizzie was a beauty, with long red hair and sparkling green eyes.

He shrugged at her noncommittally. "I'll consider it."

She huffed and stalked away. He watched his sister-in-law's retreat. He liked Lizzie. She was the perfect wife for his stern brother, fiery and not afraid to stand up to the Fraser men. Perhaps one day he would find a wife such as her.

Finally the door opened and his brother called him inside. Tense, he walked in to find a taut faced Malcolm sitting opposite the visitor.

The burn in his gut told him his life was about to

change.

A month later, Cyn rode away from Fraser lands for good. Goliath whinnied barely holding back, anxious for the open road ahead.

For the next five years, Cyn trained to be a Protector and demon slayer with the best warriors known to mankind, Gladiators and Spartans.

Then he stopped aging.

# # #

Present Day

"So it's true." Ian Fraser leaned back in his chair and studied his ancestors with renewed clarity. "Da told me about our secret ties to the Protectors when he became obvious he wouldn't live long. I didn't believe him, not at first. But he was adamant and I began to imagine it was true."

Kieran and Cyn sat across from him and waited for what they'd told the Laird to soak in.

They'd taken turns explaining the Fraser Clan's ties to the Protector army. They told him of their experiences since they'd left Scotland.

"We try to inform each new Laird just to be sure they haven't inherited the gifts of the Protectors. Since you have a wife and have sired children, I take it you haven't received the call," Cyn told him. Ian already looked to be in his early forties.

Ian shook his head. "I can't say I have."

"Have any of your sons?" Kieran asked him.

"No... maybe. My first born, Tristan, has changed drastically since he turned twenty. I just figured he was just trying to find himself. You know prove his manhood. But he has become increasingly distant and brooding of late. He's got his mother and I worried." Ian confided.

"Then, we will talk to him. Can you tell us where we can find him?" Cyn asked. "After we speak to him, we will let you know if it's the call."

Ian nodded. By the dazed look he sported, it was obvious he was still overwhelmed by all the information. "He's probably in the stables. He's home from the University for his grandfather's funeral."

The laird rubbed the bridge of his nose. "It must be something to be immortal. I am not sure I envy your calling. But I know it's an honor to be chosen. Yes, go to my son and help him."

# # #

Tristan would be a Protector. He showed all the distinct signs. The Fraser brothers knew what it was like for the young man, not knowing what was happening to him. After they'd explained his destiny, a relieved Tristan had jumped into the air excited to know that all the dreams and strange pains were for a purpose.

For now, Tristan would remain in Scotland and wait for Julian to contact him. Since he just turned twenty, it could be only another year or two. Already at well over six feet the strapping young man, with golden hair and bright green eyes, would be an excellent Protector.

They drove away from Fraser lands in silence until the village came into view.

Cyn tore his eyes from the abundant green lands they passed.

"Time to go home, aye Kieran?"

"Aye, back to face our demons."

Cyn snorted at his double-éntendré.

~ ☾ ~

CHAPTER NINETEEN

The demon's had moved. The warehouse buildings were gutted and abandoned. The few humans they'd found did not remember anything.

Cyn kept vigil from a short distance away and watched several police units and ambulances drive away. The Protectors had called them in case any of the humans needed medical assistance.

"The bastard got away," he mumbled under his breath.

Maybe he should do the same. Once they found the demons' new location, he'd ask Julian for a transfer. Blue was old enough to adjust to a new place. He was sure the boy would welcome the adventure of a new city or even country.

Fallon's silver jaguar pulled up and the British Protector climbed out of the car. He ambled over to where Cyn stood.

"Julian is worried," Fallon told him, after they greeted each other. "Quite a few high-level demons remain in Atlanta. He wants us to find them before more people die."

"More humans went missing last week," Cyn told him, "I'm sure a lot of them are being kept as a food source. Once we find their new location, we will increase our patrol of the surrounding areas."

Fallon didn't reply, instead he looked around with disdain at the neglected area overgrown with weeds. Old decaying barrels and wooden spools lay strewn haphazardly over the old parking lot. Several smaller buildings looked about to fall over from neglect and the air was putrid from the chemicals that had been dumped haphazardly.

The Brit frowned at him. “This place is horrid.”

Cyn followed Fallon’s line of vision. “Yep, this area is pretty ugly. But Atlanta as a whole isn’t that bad. You might as well get used to it, your highness. You’ll be living here for a while.” Cyn liked to banter with Fallon, who was easy to irritate.

“You can address me as My Lord,” Fallon replied haughtily.

Cyn punched him in the gut, knocking Fallon back a few steps.

“Or Lord, Lord Fallon is fine,” Fallon wheezed, and threw a punch back, across the Cyn’s jaw.

Cyn flung himself at the Lord, satisfied at hearing Fallon’s “umphf” as they tussled to the grown.

“I can’t leave you two alone for long, can I?” Kieran walked up. “Why don’t we just shoot up a flare and let the cops know we’re here?”

Cyn removed his hand from Fallon’s throat and the Brit lowered his fist. He jumped up and held his hand out to help Fallon up. But Fallon slapped it away, got up, and then proceeded to brush debris off his pants. Cyn stared at him for a moment and then shook his head. “Sissy.”

Kieran glared at them but didn’t comment seeming to understand this was their way of getting to know each other. His brother had been on the other side of the area keeping an eye on the activities. If any demons were left behind, he would have followed them.

“Did you see any blood-breaths?” Cyn asked already knowing the answer.

~ ☾ ~

Kieran kicked at the dirt. “No I didn’t see anything. When did they leave? Roderick and I have been patrolling around here for weeks. We never saw any movement.”

Cyn shrugged “Who knows, but they got past us. It’s alright, we’ll find them.”

“Where are you staying?” Kieran asked Fallon, changing the subject.

“I bought a house in the area called Druid Hills. It will do for now.” The British man gave them a bland look that told he found his new home sub-par. Fallon was quite wealthy. The Protectors were well compensated by Julian. However, Fallon’s wealth exceeded that of most of the Protectors.

It was obvious the Brit did not like the idea of being forced away from his beloved England. But he’d been in the country almost twenty years and it was past time for him to relocate.

The first rays of sunlight rose on the horizon. It had been a long night. Cyn regarded the other two. “I’ll talk to Roderick, he knows Sebastian better than the rest of us. Maybe he can talk the Incubus into getting some information for us.”

# # #

Sebastian leaned back in his chair in the office at Inferno, and pressed his fingertips against the bridge of his nose. Although the last twelve hours had been tense, he was still surprised to find he had a headache.

An Incubus with a headache.

If not for the stiffness in his shoulders and the throbbing at his temples, he would laugh.

Detectives had just left, after they questioned him and all the staff for hours. Inferno was closed down until the local authorities finished their investigation of a murder on the premises the night prior.

A demon had slaughtered a woman in the middle of his packed club. Several panicked humans started a hysteria, which ended in the police arriving before he and the staff could contain the situation.

He knew the media would have a grand old time once the coroner released the report of bite marks on the victim's throat and death from blood loss at Inferno. The press would call the young demon a vampire wanna-be or some sort of fantastic name that would bring unwanted attention to Inferno.

"Oh great," he mumbled at his security monitor. He watched the two Protectors as they made their way toward his office. Cyn and Roderick walked past his already nervous staff. "The day just gets better and better."

The Protectors strolled into Sebastian's office and remained on their feet. Roderick approached him. "Hello Sebastian, you look like shit."

Sebastian stood after looking at each of them for a moment. "Fuck you, Roderick. What do you want?" He didn't bother to hide his irritation and glared at them. "I am not in the mood for visitors today."

"What can you tell us about Gerard's current dive?" Cyn returned the glare cutting straight to the reason they were there. "As one of his high-level minions we're sure you know where they moved."

"I am not exactly in Gerard's inner circle." Sebastian replied staring at the ceiling while he clenched his jaw. It proved hard not to lose his temper. "After you two got away, he was beyond pissed and suspected that I might have helped in your escape. I took a big chance and returned for Emma after I found out he planned to kill her too."

~ ☾ ~

Sebastian noticed Cyn tense at the mention of her name, a slight frown formed and his eyes snapped to meet his. *Interesting*

"I don't think he saw me, but someone might have. So as you can imagine, they are not sharing any information with me at the moment."

Roderick glanced at Cyn who narrowed his eyes at Sebastian. "Why was Gerard going to kill Emma? She brought him Cyn."

"He never planned to let her live. I am told the sister was the one that planned the whole thing. Briana is full demon now and remains with Gerard voluntarily."

Sebastian turned his full attention to Cyn. "Emma believed her sister's life was in danger. She was stupid to believe Gerard, of course, but her sister is her only family."

"Only a fool believes the word of a demon." Cyn's voice was flat as he turned the conversation back to the original subject. "Have you heard talk about Gerard's preferred hangouts? Perhaps from some of your customers?"

"As you just said, only a fool believes the word of a demon, so why waste your time and mine?" Sebastian brushed past them out of the office.

# # #

Roderick stared after Sebastian. "Well that went well." The Spartan motioned to the monitors showing the bar and dance floors.

In the monitor, Emma walked up to Sebastian and hugged the incubus. The Protectors walked out of the office.

"I heard what happened and came as soon as I could. I'm so sorry. Want to go have a cup of cof..." she stopped talking when she saw Cyn and Roderick. Her eyes widened. Sebastian placed a protective hand on her arm and held her in place.

Cyn's eyes honed to where Sebastian touched Emma and he fought the urge to ram his fist into the male's face.

"Coffee would be nice Emma." Sebastian told her. He wrapped a possessive arm around her shoulders.

Although his stomach pitched, Cyn set his jaw and ensured his expression remained blank as he neared them. Emma looked down and shuffled her feet. She seemed uncomfortable, but didn't move away from Sebastian. The thought of her with the Incubus filled him with rage.

He didn't realize he'd stopped moving forward until Roderick elbowed him.

Thankfully, Emma stepped away from the Incubus to go sit at a barstool nearby.

"Hello," Roderick acknowledged Emma before he turned his attention to Sebastian. "I never got a chance to thank you for helping us escape Sebastian. Thank you."

"It was a job Roderick. No thanks are necessary. But, I am glad to see you are well."

Roderick didn't respond, just held out his hand. Sebastian took it and they shook hands. The Protectors started toward the door.

"One minute." Sebastian stopped them from leaving. "I think perhaps there is something we can do to help one another."

Sebastian looked to Emma whose gaze flickered to Cyn and back to him. Her brow crinkled.

His torn expression grabbed Cyn's attention. "The girl that was killed here last night had an uncanny resemblance to you, Emma. I am almost certain that the demon thought he was killing you. This was not a random or accidental death. You need protection." Then Sebastian turned to the Protectors. He was quiet for a moment, his lips pressed together in thought. "Perhaps, we can work together on this. You can provide protection for Emma and I can find the demon's location through my sources."

Automatically, Cyn stepped toward Emma. She eyed him warily as she slid off the barstool and then glared at each of them. "I have a say on this decision." She moved to stand at Sebastian's side. "I don't want to be under anyone's protection. I can take care of myself. I can stay here," she pointed to the ceiling to Sebastian's apartments above.

The men remained silent and listened as she continued, "Maybe if I find Briana, she will help us find the Master demon's location and...." She stopped talking when Cyn glowered at her and Sebastian gave her a stunned look.

"Briana cannot be trusted Emma." Sebastian's aggravation was evident as he spoke. "You will have to stay with a Protector. I cannot keep you safe here. Too many demons come here nightly. And I have to leave in order to find their new location."

Roderick held his hand up. "I have to make a call, wait a sec." He walked a short distance away, speaking into his earpiece. "Julian?"

Cyn and Emma looked at each other and then immediately looked away. He didn't trust anyone else to watch over her, but at the same time wasn't sure he trusted himself to be near her.

Roderick returned, and interrupted the awkward silence.

"Julian is ok with Sebastian's idea. He thinks that Emma should stay with you Cyn, but we can ask Kieran or Fallon to guard her."

Cyn was grateful to his friend for giving him an out. But the thought of Emma alone with any other man, even his brother, didn't sit well with him. What the hell was wrong with him? He didn't even trust the woman. "That's alright, I can handle it."

"*It* is standing right here and *it* can hear you." Emma told him through gritted teeth. "Why can't I stay with you and Rachel?" She asked Roderick while ignoring Cyn's stare.

"Rachel's gone skiing with the boys. I doubt she would look kindly on me inviting a beautiful single woman to stay at the house while she's gone." Roderick answered her, his face soft.

"Oh. Well then I will to return to my apartment and take my chances." She turned and walked toward the front door, all three men followed the soft sway of her hips. Sebastian and Roderick promptly looked away when Cyn cleared his throat.

# # #

"This can't be happening," Emma whispered under her breath for the third time as she grabbed clothes and threw them in a small overnight bag. She took a quick inventory, not sure how many days she would be gone. She collected t-shirts, several pairs of jeans, a sweater, and an extra pair of flats. She opened her underwear drawer, grabbed a bunch of panties and bras, and tossed them in the bag.

Cyn's presence was overwhelming. Not yet ready to face him, she sunk into the bed.

He waited in her small living room. She'd known that once the three males made up their mind that she needed protection—she had no chance. Although, she still argued with them for almost an additional hour. Once becoming aware that woman was in danger, they all turned into knights in shining armor and insisted on saving the damsel in distress.

It was dreadful to be near Cyn. He'd barely spoken to her on the drive to her apartment. He'd hardly even looked at her. Just the fact that he was in her apartment, made her stomach churn with anxiety. She patted her midsection to keep the butterflies at bay.

Perhaps this was a second chance with Cyn. There had to be a way for him to understand how much she loved him, and maybe she'd find a way to gain his trust again. Emma grabbed the bag's strap and swung it over her shoulder. She gave her bedroom one last glance and came to a decision.

He is going to know how I feel about him and I am going to gain his trust again, even if it kills me.

Easier said than done.

On the drive to his place, he stayed on his cell phone the entire time. He didn't disconnect once they arrived, but merely threw her bag on the bed in the spare bedroom and then headed straight for his own. She heard the distinct whirl of his security shields as they lowered.

Later she sipped a cup of tea in the kitchen, and waited to talk to him. Cyn walked right past her, set the security alarm, and left without a word.

She groaned out loud.

She was not going to let him get away without hearing what she had to say. He would not continue to ignore her. Emma understood his keeping a distance. Her colossal mistake could have cost him his life. So it was unlikely that he would ever be her friend or even fully trust her. But more than anything, she wanted to give him her side of the story, get him to understand her desperation to save Briana.

Even though she didn't expect it, she still needed his forgiveness.

Emma walked around the empty house and touched the surfaces as she went. Cyn and Blue's home was definitely all male. No pictures, knick-knacks, or décor of any kind on his walls.

She practiced what she was going to tell Cyn when he returned. He hadn't given her a chance to talk since he took her under his protection. She would be ready when he came home and would somehow get him to listen.

If she failed, she would ask the bank manager for a transfer. Hopefully, either Wendy or even her sister would want to go with her. She'd try one last time to convince Briana to leave Gerard.

It was late in the evening when the sound of someone entering the house awakened Emma. Cyn walked in and didn't hesitate when he saw her lying on the couch. With barely a glance in her direction he continued toward his bedroom. Emma got up and followed him out of the living room. She caught up to him in the hallway.

"Cyn, I need to talk to you."

He stopped with his back still to her. "I am tired. Can't this wait?" His tone was clipped.

Emma reached out to touch him, but knowing he'd not appreciate it, she drew her hand back. "Five minutes, just give me five minutes."

"Fine," he turned and walked back into the living room and sat on the couch. His wary eyes followed her as she went to the other end and eased down. She pressed her lips together and tried to remember the speech she had prepared. But now with his intense gaze on her, she was at a total loss for words. He cocked an eyebrow waiting for her to speak.

"I," she cleared her throat. "First of all, I want to tell

you that I am sorry for not telling you the truth about Gerard's plans. I really believed he was going to kill my sister and I had no other choice. I was completely unaware that she was part of the entire scheme." She hesitated when she noticed that his expression did not change. He was so different from the man she'd shared time with the last time they'd been in the house. Although she sensed tension under the calm façade, that was all she got from him, nothing else. Disconcerted at his lack of emotion, she swallowed and continued through the dryness in her throat.

"Cyn, I know that you could have died. I know that you have no reason to trust me and I am sure things will never be right between us again. But please, believe me when I tell you that I am truly sorry. That day... I tried to tell you not to follow when demon grabbed me. During that whole scene in Gerard's office I couldn't warn you. The guard behind you held a sword pointed at your heart." Although he remained silent, his frosty stare unsettling, she trudged on.

"My father was a demon. A high-level, but he was a good father, who took care of us until his disappearance. After he died, my mother abandoned us because we reminded her of him too much. All I have is Briana."

Cyn went to stand and Emma held her hand up. "You agreed to five minutes, there is one last thing I want to tell you." She swallowed hard and steeled herself. She had to tell him everything since he would probably not give her a second chance. Her hands trembled, so she clamped them together on her lap and continued.

"I am in awe of your courage, your strength and your nobleness. And I am very grateful that you are alive. I couldn't bear the thought of Blue without his father. And lastly, I want you to know that you are the best thing that has ever happened to me. You made me feel things that I have never felt before... in my life."

He looked at her, but his face did not soften, his eyes moved somewhere past her.

She swallowed blinking back tears, her words barely a whisper now. "I know it doesn't mean anything, coming from me, but I love you Cyn. I fell in love with you and it tore me to pieces to do what I did to you." She looked at him and his eyes finally met hers, she hoped he read her mind and knew she told him the truth. "I do love you."

He gave no reaction whatsoever. Tears threatened, so she looked down at her lap. "That's it, that's everything I have to say."

Cyn didn't move for a few moments. Without a word, he stood.

Something inside her snapped. She was so mad at him for not acknowledging her apology. She jumped from the couch and blocked his path. "I know I fucked up beyond repair and I am very sorry. I wish there was a way I could make amends, but there isn't."

"What do you want Emma?" His stance remained tense, as if he held his anger in check.

"Just for you to understand."

"Good night Emma," Cyn replied and went around her toward his bedroom.

Emma trudged into the spare room in complete misery. Embarrassed and exhausted, she undressed and donned Cyn's oversized T-shirt. She'd kept it from her last stay.

She fell into bed and started to cry, unable to stop. When she ran out of tissues, she got up and went to the bathroom and grabbed an entire roll of toilet paper and took it to bed with her. Emptiness and loneliness swelled within her. Stabs of grief sliced at her heart. She gave into it and allowed sorrow to take over.

Emma vowed that once she got over this heartbreak,

she'd never love again. She pushed her face deep into the pillow so that Cyn wouldn't hear her sobs.

~ ☾ ~

CHAPTER TWENTY

Cyn shoulders sagged.

For what felt like an eternity, he'd stood outside Emma's bedroom door and listened to her cry. The entire time, he fought not to run in and soothe her. He feared he'd lose the battle, so he went to his bedroom and continued listening through the security system until she quieted and fell asleep.

A beep on his computer grabbed his attention.

It was Kieran.

"Sebastian has a lead. We're going out to see what comes of it, after sunrise," Kieran spoke to Cyn through the computer speakers.

"Where are we meeting?" Cyn asked Kieran, only half listening.

"I'm going with Roderick. You are on guard duty. Remember? Get some sleep." Kieran eyes narrowed and he studied Cyn's face. "Look Cyn, if Emma's presence bothers you this much, maybe you need to bring her here."

After he assured his brother he was fine, Cyn disconnected and walked out of his room. He went down the hall. He paused outside Emma's room.

Sighing in defeat, he opened the door and went in.

Cyn stood by the bed for a long while and looked down on the sleeping woman. She lay on her back, her hair spread over the pillow. Emma's right hand, fisted at the side of her face, still held a tissue. Her reddened nose did not distract from her beauty. She slept in his white t-shirt.

She kept it.

He caressed her cheek. He wanted nothing more than to climb in bed and hold her.

Instead he cursed under his breath and stormed back out.

Cyn stalked to the living room and lay down on the sofa where he spent a long time tossing about as he tried to get comfortable.

# # #

Trudging through the thick haze, Emma's bare feet sank into the muddy earth. Some part of her knew it was a dream, but it felt so real. She continued onward through the wooded lot, able to see the narrow path by the illumination of the full moon.

When a thorny bush ripped at the hem of the white t-shirt she wore, it scratched her thigh through the fabric. The sting of the thorns caused her to falter before she continued onward.

The cracks of a whip resounded, followed by howls of pain and she attempted to run toward it. Her legs felt like lead, as if weights were bound to her ankles. Finally, she arrived at a clearing.

The scene she walked upon shocked her to the core. She let out a horrified shriek and stumbled backward.

Cyn was chained to a tree by his wrists. His arms stretched up over his head. His torso striped with lash marks. The ground drank the blood that dripped from his wounds. A demon whipped him. She tried to run toward Cyn, but before she could reach him, Gerard yanked her back by the hair.

He held her in place, not flinching when Emma dug

her fingernails into his hand. He swung her around and slapped her across the face so hard, she saw stars.

"It's time to pay dear Emma." He whispered into her ear while he stroked her throbbing cheek in a rough caress. His long fingernails cut into her skin as they trailed down the sides of her face. Emma continued to struggle, but his hold was too strong.

The Master demon's cruel eyes met hers and she shivered at the evil in them. "You have a decision to make."

"No!" Emma screamed when Briana appeared, also chained to a tree. Her sister's sobs echoed through the trees.

"Stop! Let them go!" Emma kicked him and held a dagger that appeared in her fist, at Gerard's neck. "Let them go or I swear I will cut your damn head off!"

Before she could utter another word, the dagger disappeared out of her hand and into his. Gerard swung and hit her with the back of his hand. This time she fell to the muddy ground. She struggled against the overpowering urge to just shut her eyes.

He motioned for two demons to hold her. They took her arms and jerked her to her feet. Gerard moved to stand between Cyn and Briana. He held up the dagger.

"Look, not only is your judge and jury here, but she also brought the weapon that will end one of your miserable lives." Gerard stepped toward Cyn and yanked his head back by his hair. "So dear *Emma,* will I kill your lover or will I kill your sister?"

Cyn glared at Gerard with defiance.

Gerard made a great show with his arms open wide as he walked to Briana and held the dagger against her heart. Briana shrieked and tried to move away from it. Gerard looked back at Emma, his blood red eyes taunting her.

~ ☾ ~

"The choice is yours. If you don't make it, I kill them both."

"Why are you doing this? I can't make this choice." Emma looked from Briana to Cyn, who watched her with resignation in his eyes. He expected her to pick Briana.

"I can't choose, please..."

"I don't have all night!" Gerard snapped and stalked back to Cyn and began to push the tip of the dagger into his throat. A trail of blood trickled down Cyn's neck.

"Stop!" Emma gasped. She began to shake all over. "I made my decision."

Briana's eyes widened. "You bitch! You would pick him over me? Your own sister!"

"No, I am not picking either one."

The demons let go of her arms. Her legs gave out and she fell limp to the ground. "Gerard let them go. Take me. Kill me in their place."

"No Emma!" Cyn strained against the chains. "Don't do this, he will kill us all anyway." Emma looked at him and mouthed, I love you.

Everyone's eyes followed the dagger's flight through the air until it impaled Emma's chest.

A scream echoed in her ears, she wasn't sure if it was Cyn's, Briana's, or her own. The blackness of the fog wrapped around her as she fell to the muddy ground.

Emma's horror-filled cry woke Cyn.

Is someone in the house?

He jumped up and ran into her room. He scanned the darkness to ensure nothing was amiss. It was empty except for her.

"I can't! I can't do it! No, no." Emma jerked violently in her sleep. Her hair was plastered to her tear-streaked face.

~ ☾ ~

Without thought, he sat on the bed and lifted her trembling body and held her against him. Shushing her cries, he rubbed her back until she calmed.

Still asleep she clung on to him, her fingers curled around his shirt and her nails dug into his skin.

"Wake up, Emma, it's a nightmare," Cyn whispered to her. Her entire body went limp. Her eyelids fluttered and her head fell back.

Slowly, Emma raised her.head and looked around confused.

Disbelief was foremost in her wide eyes. She searched his face and reached out with a trembling hand to stroke his cheek.

"You're okay. Thank God," Emma studied him closely, as if to ensure he was real.

Being near her was a huge mistake. His heart constricted as yearning for her surged through him.

She'd never looked more beautiful to him.

"Oh God," she buried her face into his neck and wrapped her arms around his waist in a firm hold. "Cyn don't leave, stay for a little bit."

Cyn swallowed hard. He needed to get away from her. She was fine. She wasn't hurt. Why didn't he leave? Her familiar scent enveloped him.

Just for a minute.

When she began to kiss his throat and jaw-line, his treacherous body responded immediately. He couldn't help but moan as her warm kisses left a trail of desire.

With willpower, he didn't know he possessed, Cyn placed his hands on both sides of her face and held her back, so that he could look into her eyes.

He would to tell her to stop. He would get up and leave. But when her gaze met his, it was as if he fell through space unable to grab anything to stop his fall.

"I have to go."

~ ☾ ~

He didn't move.

"Okay." She replied with a breathless whisper.

Both remained frozen in place, their bodies rejoicing in the familiarity of the touch.

Cyn took her lips in a hungry and desperate kiss. Emma responded by opening her mouth and tangling her tongue with his.

His breathing became shallow with want. How he'd missed the taste of her and the feel of her touch as she ran greedy fingers through his hair and down his back. He couldn't stop now if his life depended on it. A small part of him, screamed for self-preservation — to get away from her. But the rest of him, most of him, wanted...no needed her.

Cyn broke the kiss only long enough to pull the oversized t-shirt up over her head and then took her mouth again. His lips trailed lower down her creamy throat to her breasts. Emma clung to him so tightly that her nails scratched his shoulders.

The sensation of flying began as soon as he took her pebbled nipple into his mouth while he caressed her other breast. She fit perfectly in his palm.

She was made for him.

With her hands on his shoulders, she kissed the top of his head before she arched her back to give him more access. "Oh god Cyn, I need you inside me," Emma's words turned to a moan when he complied by pushing her panties aside to slide a finger inside her while his thumb worked its magic.

Her entire body shook as she crested, and cried out his name. He laid her back. She was temptation itself, with her parted lips and half closed eyes. He hurried to remove his clothes and drop everything on the floor in his haste.

He yanked her panties off and joined her in the bed

again.

"You are so damn beautiful," Cyn told her, "I can't hold back, I want you so fucking much." She responded with a heated kiss, her tongue teasing his.

He urged her legs apart and pushed into her heat and into her mouth with his tongue at the same time. He held the back of her head and angled his to better suckle her sweet lips.

Unable to take it slow, he slammed in and out of her and she met him thrust for thrust, digging her fingers into the small of his back.

Cyn was close to cresting, but he didn't want to come yet, so he slowed the pace and rolled over to his back bringing her with him. Emma straddled him and leaned over him so that he could take the tips of her breasts in his mouth as she rocked back and forth. His hardness slid in and out of her at a slow steady rate.

He allowed her to set the tempo, yet just the sight of her on top of him was so sexy, he swelled insider her. When her pace became faster, Cyn lifted his hips, and thrusted into her as she pushed down. Finally, nearing her climax, Emma's movements became frantic until she threw her head back and cried out before collapsing on him.

He rolled her onto her back and lifted her bottom to give him better access. He pumped into her, each time pulling out almost completely, before he thrust back in.

Encouraged by her mews of excitement, his rhythm became faster and faster until he lost all control and came into her already pliant body.

# # #

The sun flickered through a space in the curtains and glistened on the copper streaks in Emma's hair. Cyn had been awake for a long time just watching her sleep.

Upon waking, he'd been shocked to find he'd spent all night with her. Although they made love twice before they finally succumbed to sleep, he felt rested and stress-free for the first time in many years.

Beautiful Emma with her lips pursed in her sleep, clung to his hand. Even in sleep she seemed to fear he'd leave. Her small body, warm and soft, pressed against him. She was vulnerable and in need of his protection. If only things were different.

If only he could trust her.

She snuggled closer and her thigh brushed against his erection. He wanted her again. Why couldn't he get enough of this woman?

It was so right with her tucked into his side, her head resting in the crook of his arm and her leg thrown over his midsection.

He wasn't sure what to expect when she awoke, but he was pretty sure she would not remain in bed with him.

Emma's eyes opened and she yawned. She went to move, but stopped when she felt his presence.

She closed her eyes again and a feline-like smile tugged at her lips.

"Good morning" he told her, and kissed her mouth lightly.

"You stayed," she replied, "I'm glad." Her guarded eyes scanned his face.

Emma's apprehension jabbed him in the chest like an ice pick, piercing his heart.

He wanted to reassure her.

He wanted her period.

How could he want her so much and not trust her at the same time?

"Do you want me?" he asked. "Because I can't believe how much I want right now."

~ ☾ ~

Lost in her unwavering gaze, he sighed when she pressed her breasts against him. Her arms wrapped around him and she pushed her hips against him. He understood her invitation and drove into her ready and waiting body.

Face to face, he placed his hand on her hips and steadied her so he could move in and out of her. She kept her legs together giving him a deeper path, the sensation as he slid between her soft thighs, made it hard to take his time.

For now, reality was a distant concept. They were in what felt like their own private world and he savored each kiss and caress.

Emma began to tremble as she came; her pants of pleasure escaped past her parted lips.

Watching her pushed Cyn over the edge and he joined her.

Thunder rumbled outside as they lay quietly listening to the rainfall.

Her hands cupped his face and she kissed the tip of his nose. "I hope this means you have forgiven me. I know it's too much to ask that you trust me again and it's okay that you don't, Cyn. This whole thing is going to end soon." She pressed her lips against his before continuing. "When it does I want you to know that I won't make it hard for you. I'm going to ask the bank for a transfer and leave Atlanta with or without Briana."

Not sure of what he felt at her statement, he remained quiet.

The shrill of his cell phone made them jump apart. Cyn got out of bed to retrieve it from his pants on the floor and answered it.

"Blue's been taken by Argos," Roderick's voice shook with rage. "The fucking demon grabbed him when the boys stopped for coffee on their way to school."

~ ☾ ~

Cyn grabbed his jeans and jammed them on, by the time he ended the call he was fully dressed. “I have to go,” he told Emma.

Emma must have ascertained something was wrong and had already thrown the t-shirt back on as well as a pair of jeans. She pushed her feet into her shoes and scrambled behind him out of the bedroom.

“What happened?” she asked. “Please tell me.”

“It’s Blue. Argos, his birth father, grabbed him on his way to school. I have to go.” He stormed through the house searching for his sword and jacket.

Emma ran after him shrugging on her jacket. “I’m coming with you.”

Cyn didn’t have the strength to argue.

All he could think of was not losing his son. A mixture of fury and sheer terror battled inside him. He didn’t even bother with the security system as they ran into the garage and got in the truck.

# # #

The rain diminished into a light drizzle by the time they screeched to a stop in front of the coffee shop. Rachel and Roderick stood outside waiting for them. Cyn jumped out of the truck. He noticed Brock sitting in the car looking toward them through the window, his eyes wide with worry.

Roderick relayed everything that Brock told them.

The trail was still fresh. Cyn focused on the direction Argos had taken his son. He could still smell the demon.

He turned back toward Roderick his eyes blazed, “I’m going to kill that son of a bitch. Let’s go. We need to follow the trail before it gets cold.”

He started to move toward the car when he heard Kieran’s voice over his earpiece.

"I've got them. Hurry I can't go in by myself."

"Kieran left to follow the trail, while I waited for you." Roderick explained, his face pinched with anguish. As a father himself, Cyn knew he understood his myriad of emotions.

"Let's go." Cyn replied.

~ ☾ ~

CHAPTER TWENTY ONE

The men ran to Cyn's truck. Emma started to follow, but Rachel stopped her.

"It's best we let them go alone."

Emma watched helplessly as the truck sped away and turned a corner. "I can't just sit back and wait, Rachel."

No sooner had the Protectors drove away than Fallon's Jaguar drove up, a black sedan right behind him. Emma tugged her arm out of Rachel's hand and raced to Fallon's car.

She gave Rachel an apologetic look as she got in and told Fallon where the others headed.

"Call me with any news" Rachel called to them as she walked toward her car.

Fallon waited and watched Rachel get in her car.

Noticing that the sedan followed Rachel as she drove off, Emma gave Fallon a questioning look.

"They are guards," Fallon told her.

They rode in strained silence while Fallon weaved around cars. This time his speed did not bother Emma in the least, she was as anxious as him to find Blue and help Cyn.

They continued south, leaving the city behind them. Tall buildings gave way to houses and then the houses grew farther and farther apart. Fallon turned off the road onto a field, barely slowing. The Jaguar bumped and tilted violently over the rough terrain. Emma gripped the door handle with both hands and held on.

~ ☾ ~

Finally Fallon brought the car to a stop behind a crop of pecan trees and cut off the engine. They waited for a few minutes. Fallon sat motionless, his eyes straight ahead. Emma glanced at him and wished could hear what was coming through his earpiece.

"Stay near me and don't make a sound," Fallon told her when he opened his door and got out of the car.

Emma climbed out and scampered to catch up to him. It surprised her how fast the man could move without making a sound. A snap echoed into the air as she stepped on a thin branch. Fallon glared at her. Another mishap would not be tolerated. She almost yelped when he yanked her down to crouch behind a tree. They waited for a few seconds and listened to ensure no one heard them.

He leaned into her ear and whispered. "Now, please step where I step."

As they continued ahead, Emma couldn't help but notice Fallon's nice butt, strong muscular back, and broad shoulders.

Julian sure knew how to pick them.

Fallon kneeled down behind a thick tree and she knelt beside him. She peered through bushes and saw a small nondescript ranch-style home. With weeds overrunning the front lawn and knee-high grass, it looked abandoned. An old yellow dog barked half-heartedly.

After a moment, voices became audible and Fallon shoved her lower to the ground, both of their eyes trained on the ranch house.

Cyn, Roderick, and Kieran stepped into view. All three Protectors walked backwards. They held their swords in front of them, ready to battle. A group of demons walked toward them. They were followed by an older higher-level demon with a twisted scowl—Argos.

Argos pushed Blue ahead of him. Emma's heart broke

seeing Blue limp and stumble as he struggled to walk.

A demon lariat bound him.

Her heart leaped to her throat. Demon lariats were incredibly painful. They constricted the body with each movement like an anaconda and stung like the devil.

A scorching torrent of fury coursed through Cyn at seeing his son in so much pain.

Argos stopped walking and signaled for the demons to move closer around him and Blue.

Cyn's eyes locked on his son's. He tried to convey a message to him to remain calm. The lariat would tighten if he became too scared or agitated. Blue responded and stood straighter, his face firm. The boy tried hard to be brave. However his wide and shiny eyes told a different story.

"How much Argos? I will pay you whatever amount you want, just let my son go." Cyn shouted at the demon. Argos' accomplices stiffened, their worried glances shifted to Argos.

"Your son?" Argos laughed, "Ah, I see you have developed feelings for my bastard. Of course, you must understand that I won't release the brat until you pay me."

Argos looked at each Protector through narrowed eyes before he continued. "If you or any of your friends make a move against me or my associates, I will invoke the lariat's power and the boy dies." Proud of his plan, Argos' gave him a triumphant look. "I know you are a very wealthy man," Argos continued. "I want ten million dollars cash. You have twenty-four hours." Argos turned to Blue, a cruel smile curved his lips. "Who would have thought you'd be worth so much?"

Roderick spoke under his breath to Cyn. "We have no

choice. Only Argos can uncoil the lariat. Damn it. If a demon other than Argos even tries to free Blue, it will kill them. It's highly doubtful that we'll find a willing volunteer."

Cyn's gut clenched.

Argos tugged the stumbling Blue back toward the house. "The clock is ticking." He yelled over his shoulder.

"Wait! How do I know you will keep your word and not hurt him?" Cyn called out in an attempt to delay him.

Argos stopped and shrugged. "I wouldn't risk losing that amount of money."

Cyn didn't trust the demon and refused to leave Blue alone. "A Protector must remain here. If you harm my son, you will not get a dime." Cyn's hands shook with rage and worry.

"No." Argos dropped his hold on Blue and took a step toward Cyn. "You don't get to make any demands, Protector. You play by my rules. I have the upper hand."

The fluttering of wings filled the air when a flock of birds burst from nearby trees and drew everyone's attention. The next thing Cyn knew, Blue streaked past him toward Roderick and Kieran with several demons right on his tail.

Three Protectors stopped them.

Fallon had arrived.

His face transformed with fury, Argos' hand flew to his sword and he snarled through elongated fangs.

Good, they were in the same mood now.

Without giving Argos a chance to utter a word, Cyn beheaded him.

Argos' body flopped to the ground and then everything began to move in slow motion around him.

Blue ran back toward the house, followed by Roderick.

Someone lay on the ground.

Dead or unconscious, he couldn't tell.

~ ☾ ~

Emma? It was Emma—she lay in the same spot Blue had stood just moments earlier.

Jesus, Emma had sacrificed herself to save Blue.

Cyn whirled around toward Fallon. Rage took over as he stalked toward him. "You fucking bastard. You brought her here to die, didn't you?"

Cyn's fist connected with Fallon's jaw, sending the man flying backwards. Fallon didn't try to defend himself as Cyn fell on him and swung again. Kieran grabbed his arm and stopped him.

His brother struggled to control him, while he spoke to him, "There was no other way to save Blue, Cyn. We all know Argos would have killed him, no matter what we did."

Cyn yanked his arm away from his brother's grasp.

"Did you force her to do this?" he screamed at Fallon. His body shook with barely restrained fury. "Did you fucking force her?" He yelled again.

Fallon's anxious eyes met his. "No, I wouldn't ask her to do that. She got away from me and ran out to the boy before I could stop her. She said she had to do it."

Kieran nudged Cyn and motioned to where Emma lay. Cyn got to his feet.

Blue knelt next to Emma and held her hand as Roderick felt for a pulse. At the image of Emma so still, the ground swayed under him. Kieran's strong grip on his shoulder steadied him.

"She has a pulse, it's weak but she's alive," Roderick called to them with a sigh of relief. "Being half human is the only explanation to how she survived what equates to a lethal electrocution." Roderick picked up her limp body and ran to his car. "But she's still in danger. We need to get her to a hospital fast."

Cyn went to move toward him, but Kieran stopped him. "Let him take her. There's nothing you can do.

~ ☾ ~

Besides, Blue needs you right now."

Cyn noticed that Blue still knelt where Emma had lain with his head bowed.

Emma's pale face disappeared from view as Roderick placed her in the back seat of his truck before taking off.

Cyn went to his son hoping Blue didn't feel responsible for what happened. He lifted the boy by the shoulders and hugged him. "Are you alright son?"

Blue leaned into Cyn. "I'm sorry Dad —I should have been able to defend myself against Argos and those demons." Blue shoved his face into his shoulder, muffling his voice, "and now Emma is going to die, because of me."

Cyn stopped him. "No Blue, they were too strong for you. Even a weaponless, full-grown Protector would have a hard time defending himself against all of them. And Emma will be fine, you'll see."

Grateful, he held on to his son while he tried to convince himself as much as the boy, that Emma would live.

To see her unconscious on the ground had shredded him to pieces.

In that moment, he realized he loved Emma. He loved her with all his being and if she didn't survive, a part of him would die with her.

Torn between the urge to follow Roderick to the hospital and not wanting to expose Blue to any more trauma, Cyn remained in place with his son in his arms.

Blue's shaky voice interrupted his worried thoughts. He asked him to repeat what he had just said.

"When Emma untied me, she told me to tell you that she loved you." Blue blushed, repeating Emma's words to Cyn.

"And she said she loved me too."

~ ☾ ~

CHAPTER TWENTY TWO

It hurt everywhere. Every part of Emma's body ached. Every joint throbbed.

Just turning to her side elicited a pained moaned.

So thirsty.

She licked her parched lips and tried to swallow, but her throat felt like she'd eaten sandpaper.

Her eyelids weighed a ton and she had to force them open. The blurriness began to subside and she made out a man's figure in a chair next to the bed.

Cyn?

She blinked away the haziness and recognized Kieran.

"Hello Emma."

She hid her disappointment and tried to speak, but her words did not get past her parched throat.

Kieran poured some water from a small hospital pitcher into a cup for her. She drank all of it and held the cup out for more. After she downed the second cup, she lay back on her pillows. "Thank you," she croaked.

"How are you feeling?" Kieran asked.

"I'm good, I guess. I'm alive so I shouldn't complain." Still thirsty, she held out the cup again. "How long have I been out of it?"

"This is day three." He told her as he refilled the cup. The Protector leaned back in the chair. It was too small for his large frame, but he still managed to look relaxed.

Three days.

"How is Blue?"

One corner of his lips barely curved upward, Emma wondered if the man ever smiled. “He’s well.”

“Am I to stay with you when I leave here?” Emma asked even though she really wanted to ask if she would go back to Cyn’s.

“We believe Gerard is gone and it seems your sister left with him.” Emma closed her eyes; she didn’t want to cry in front of him. She waited for him to continue. “It should be safe for you here now. You can return to your own home. We’ll continue to keep an eye on you, just to make sure.”

Emma nodded as sadness flooded through her. There was no reason to see Cyn again. She noticed her overnight bag on a chair, in the room. “I planned to move soon anyway, but thank you. The knowledge that you guys are out there will help.”

Kieran reached over and picked up her hand. He surprised her with the gentleness of his action. “I want to personally thank you for saving Blue’s life.” She was touched by the sincerity of his words.

“It’s the least I could do after everything I’ve done. Because of me, Blue almost lost his father.” Emma swallowed past the boulder in her throat. “Is Blue really all right?”

“Yes, he’s fine. He’s barely let Cyn out of his sight the last couple of days.”

“Good, I’m glad. I’m sorry Kieran, I shouldn’t have betrayed your brother.” her throat constricted. “Please forgive me for putting your only family in jeopardy. Well, besides Blue. They’re it for you as Brianna is...was for me.”

“I accept your apology. When a family member is threatened, it’s understandable to go to great lengths to save them.”

Grateful for his forgiveness, Emma remained silent,

~ ☾ ~

not sure what else to say. She wanted to ask him why Cyn wasn't there. It hurt that he had not come to see her, but she understood that his priority was to take care of Blue and ensure his son was all right.

Kieran stood up. "I better go. You have a visitor."

Wendy stood by the door with a small vase of flowers in her hand. Her eyes were wide and her mouth formed an 'O' while she stared at Kieran. She seemed to gain some self-control, but as she walked into the room, she ran right into the bed table. It slammed against Emma's bed with a loud clang.

"Ouch," she cried, bending down to rub her knee, which caused her to spill the flowers and water onto the floor.

Emma saw a slight flicker of recognition cross Kieran's face, but he didn't say a word. He got up and helped Wendy pick up the flowers. Upon noticing Kieran's proximity, Wendy jerked up and they bumped heads.

Emma bit her lip to keep from laughing. If anyone could take her attention away from her troubles, it was Wendy.

"Ow, damn it. Just go sit down. I got this." Wendy mumbled as she waved Kieran back to his chair. To Emma's amazement, the Protector did as Wendy told him. Seeming to forget he was about to leave.

Kieran was the Protector who'd saved Wendy a couple of years earlier. Alarmed, Emma knew she had to figure out a way to salvage the situation before Kieran found out Wendy could remember him.

"I'm glad you're awake to see these," Wendy said when she walked out of the small bathroom after refilling the vase.

She was about to say something else when Emma interrupted her. "Wendy this is Kieran, he's a friend."

~ ☾ ~

An awkward silence followed, Kieran spoke first. "Nice to meet you, Wendy." He held his hand out and Wendy's small hand reached out to shake it.

"We've met before," she told him. She eyed him warily before she walked around him and climbed into the bed with Emma. She reached across the bed and put the vase on the side table.

Kieran's eyes were glued to Wendy's exposed legs.

Ignoring him, Wendy gave Emma a wide-eyed stare. "I'm so glad you're finally awake Emma. I was so worried." Wendy noticed that Kieran stared at her with a frown on his face.

"What's wrong?" Wendy asked him. She studied his face. "Does your head hurt? Are you all right?"

Kieran's mouth opened, but he didn't say anything. He appeared to be at a loss for words for a moment before he regained his composure. "What do you mean we've met before?"

Emma interrupted before Wendy could say anything. If Kieran found out Wendy remembered him, he would erase her memory. "Wendy, I think you're confused. The guy you saw me talking to that time was Cyn, Kieran's brother. They look a lot alike." She held her breath and waited for Wendy's reaction.

Wendy glanced back at Emma and winked, getting the hint. "Oh okay."

"The doctor said you were electrocuted. You were still out of it when I stopped by yesterday. How are you feeling Sweetie?"

Kieran stood up to leave again. "I better go. Good bye Emma." He regarded Wendy with a slight curve to his mouth, otherwise known as a smile for Kieran. "It was nice to meet you Wendy."

"Bye, nice to see you," Wendy replied meeting his eyes longer than necessary. When she turned back to face her,

Emma bit the inside of her cheeks to keep from giggling.

Behind Wendy, Kieran gave them both a perplexed look. Emma stared at him wide-eyed and wondered if he was trying to read Wendy's thoughts.

As soon as he left, closing the door behind him, Wendy sighed, falling dramatically across the bed "Oh my God, he is sooo hot. I want to grab him and shove my tongue down his throat."

Emma's eyebrows rose, but she let Wendy talk.

"I almost blew it. I was so shocked to see him I couldn't think straight," Wendy continued excited. "It's him, the Protector that rescued me from that horrible demon attack. He took me home and stayed with me until I assured him I felt fine. He was so sweet. When he leaned in close to my face, I thought for a minute he was going to kiss me. But sadly he didn't. Instead, he said," Wendy made her voice deep. "You will forget the demon attack, you will forget me and all that transpired tonight."

Although Emma had heard the story many times she still asked. "So what did you do then?"

"I said okay. He seemed satisfied with that, got up and left." Wendy sighed. "I should have kissed him. Have you ever seen such gorgeous green eyes? I haven't been able to get him out of my mind since that night. Just now, I wanted to tell him to stay, but I didn't want to give away that I remembered him." She sighed again and took Emma's hand. "It's like love at first sight."

Wendy's words saddened her. Emma shook her head and picked up her empty glass. "Keep your distance from him Wendy. It's easy to fall in love with them. They are magnificent men. But they can't commit, and you'll end up broken hearted like me."

Wendy became serious and reached out to touch Emma's cheek. "I'm sorry honey. I know you're hurting."

~ ☾ ~

Emma nodded her eyes misting. “Let’s move away Wendy. I need to leave Atlanta.”

Pressing her lips together in thought, Wendy looked like a little girl, sitting cross-legged on the bed. “Savannah, I’ve always wanted to live there. Yeah, let’s move to Savannah!”

“Are you serious, you’ll go with me?” Emma asked already feeling better.

“Why not? I don’t have any family here and my brother lives near Savannah.”

# # #

A day later, Emma sat up in her hospital bed and ran a comb through her wet hair.

Thanks to her demon blood, her recovery was faster than normal. Her speedy recuperation perplexed her doctor who reluctantly agreed to discharge her. She was just waiting for Wendy to pick her up.

The door cracked opened and Blue peered in. Emma brightened and lifted her arms out to him. He gave her a timid look, but came over and hugged her. Behind him, Rachel entered the room.

Emma smiled, welcoming Rachel and motioned for her to sit.

“I’m glad you’re okay,” Blue told her when she held his face between her hands.

“How are you Blue? Were you hurt at all?” When he shook his head, she kissed him on both cheeks.

Blue blushed brightly at the attention from her. “I’m good. We were worried about you though. Dad and I came to see you a couple of times, but you were out of it.”

Cyn came to see her!

He held out a small box. “I got this for you.” When she took it, he added, “With my own money.” He leaned toward her peering closely as she opened it.

It was a crystal angel on a delicate gold chain. Emma stared at it, blinking back tears. “This is so beautiful Blue.” She unclasped it and reached around her neck to put it on.

“Thank you.” She smiled at him and wiped away the moisture in her eyes. “I will treasure it always.”

Blue’s face beamed. “You’re more angel to me than demon.” He told her with a crooked smile. Her throat constricted and Emma could only nod in reply.

“Aunt Rachel, I’m going to grab a soda. I’ll be right outside okay?”

When Rachel agreed, he gave Emma another hug before he walked out of the room. “See you later.”

Rachel waited for Blue to leave before she spoke. “I am so grateful for what you did Emma. You saved his life and he knows it.” Rachel’s eyes became misty and she sniffed. “Well aren’t we just a pair of soppy women today?”

“I couldn’t just stand there and let him die,” Emma replied, fingering the crystal angel that hung between her breasts.

“You love Cyn, don’t you?” Rachel asked her, her eyes sympathetic.

Emma nodded.” I love him with all my heart. And Blue too,” she added. “But I know that it would never work out. There are too many obstacles to overcome.” She sighed before continuing, “Like I told Kieran, I’ve decided to move. I think it would be easier for us both.”

Rachel nodded, “I understand Emma. Protectors take an oath when they are initiated; one part of it is not to marry unless their leader arranges it or they meet their life-mate on their own, which is highly unlikely. A wife or a child is considered a weakness — a vulnerability for them. Julian was furious when he found out that Rod and I were married."

"How did it happen?" Emma asked her

Rachel got a faraway look on her face as she spoke. "I was attacked by a demon and Rod rescued me. I was dying by the time he got me to his house. He should have let me die. Later, he told me that he just physically couldn't let me go. He gave me some of his blood. He studied medicine and got his MD while working as a Protector. He practices medicine now that he is retired. Anyway, he gave me a transfusion with his own blood. When a Protector does that, they lose some of their strength and share their immortality. The transfusion made me immortal."

Rachel sighed. "I didn't know about that at first. I fell in love with him almost immediately during the two weeks it took for me to be well enough to leave."

"What did you do when you found out?"

Rachel held her hand over her heart reminiscing. "I was furious. I wasn't sure how I felt. I was worried about losing my soul and how a prolonged life would affect my life. I refused to see him for two months. Then I found out I was pregnant. Rod demanded I marry him and wouldn't take no for an answer. After the two months of missing him so much it physically hurt, I knew I loved him too much to live without him. I couldn't fathom life apart from him. So we decided to get married. Afterwards, we went to Italy to face Julian." Rachel laughed softly before continuing. "I thought Julian was going to demolish his fancy Italian villa around us. His anger actually made the ground shake.

But when he learned I was pregnant, he calmed down. He told us it has rarely happened. Protectors are sterile unless they are with their life-mate. Julian said maybe it was meant to be, but he insisted that Rod retire from the Protectors as punishment. So for the most part now, he works as a doctor and steps in to help the Protectors when they need him."

Emma was enthralled. "What about Brock? Is he immortal?"

A shadow passed over Rachel's face and Emma wished she hadn't asked.

"We don't know. If there is something I fear the most, it's to see my son age and die while I remain the same." Her brow furrowed and she pushed her long hair back behind her shoulder.

"Julian is convinced that Brock will be a Protector. So I need to hang on to that belief. Otherwise I'll go crazy."

Rachel smiled at Emma and reached over to squeeze her hand. "If you love Cyn, then fight for him Emma. He's been a real grump these past few days. He loves you too, you know?"

"Maybe, but he doesn't trust me."

"Perhaps not before, but you were willing to give your life for Blue. I'm sure he feels differently now."

After Rachel and Blue left, Emma's thoughts tumbled around her head. She wondered if she and Cyn were meant to be. Was their love strong enough to stand up against Julian? Was it possible that she was Cyn's life-mate?

Her betrayal would be a constant hindrance. She didn't hold out much hope for a happy ending like Rachel and Roderick.

As planned, she would move to Savannah.

And try to forget Cyn.

~ ☾ ~

CHAPTER TWENTY THREE

Two Weeks Later.

"Well at least in the spring when we move to Savannah, the weather will be warmer and we can go to the beach. It will be a fresh start in a brand new bank branch." Wendy told Emma while they ate hamburgers and fries, in a downtown diner. "Besides, it gives you plenty of time to sell your townhouse too."

Emma finished her sandwich and eyed Wendy's. Wendy narrowed her eyes and moved the plate back. "Don't even think about it sister. I'm starving."

Emma rolled her shoulders in an attempt to get rid of the tension. "I hoped to leave as soon as possible so I don't run into Cyn."

She reached over and grabbed a fry from Wendy's plate and gobbled it down. "Man, I have been so hungry lately. It's probably all the stress. I'm so worried about Briana. She hasn't contacted me at all."

Wendy slid her plate further away from Emma. "Well I'm not going to avoid Kieran. I'd really love to see him again. I would settle for a one-night stand. Oh just to see him naked once." Wendy closed her eyes and pretended to swoon. When she opened her eyes, she caught Emma snatching more of her fries and gave up. She pushed the plate to the middle of the table, but picked up her sandwich. "You're such a pig."

"You know Wendy, Kieran is kind of intimidating. I don't think the man has an emotional bone in his entire body," Emma told her.

"I'd love to find everything out about his *entire body*," Wending giggled, then her eyes widened.

"Oh-oh," Wendy said under her breath. "Um, Emma, I think you're going to have a little itty bitty problem avoiding Cyn." She took a bite of her sandwich.

"What?"

Wendy pointed toward the door and mumbled with her mouth full. "He just walked in."

Emma felt his presence before seeing him. Her skin prickled and a shiver ran down her spine. When Wendy waved toward the front of the restaurant, Emma wanted to kick her friend under the table.

He came to their table and smiled at her. "Hello Emma." He smirked at Wendy. "Hey."

"Hey Cyn," Wendy chirped.

Upon seeing Cyn, Emma could only stare transfixed. Every time she saw him, he was even more handsome. His hair was shorter, not quite to his shirt collar; it accentuated his strong jaw line. Her eyes traveled over him noting the light blue pullover sweatshirt and jeans he wore.

He surprised her by sliding into the seat next to her.

Wendy placed her elbows on the tabletop and put her chin in her hands. She beamed at Cyn with a wide smile on her lips. "How you been?"

"You two have met?" Emma asked, confused.

"Yeah, he was at the hospital for two days straight while you were out of it. Didn't I tell you?"

"No Wendy, you didn't," Emma replied, annoyed.

When Cyn shifted, his arm brushed against hers. A tingle of awareness made her tense. She was sure her heart pounded audibly. When their thighs grazed, she almost jumped out of her skin. She tried to slide away without him noticing.

~ ☾ ~

She cleared her throat and brushed her hair behind her ear to be able to glance at him out of the corner of her eye. He looked around the café, his pose relaxed.

Wendy slid out of the booth and made a show out of getting her oversized purse on her shoulder. “Well I better go. You two have a lot to talk about, especially with the new development.” She winked at Emma. “I’ll catch you tomorrow and pay my part of the bill.”

Emma glared at Wendy willing her not to leave.

But her friend ignored her look, reached across Cyn and gave her shoulder a quick squeeze. After a sly smile at Cyn, she gave him a peck on the cheek. “I know you’ll do the right thing.”

Cyn turned and gave Emma a puzzled look, his eyes full of questions. Emma didn’t dare look directly at him, but she saw it.

She took deep breaths and tried to get her nerves under control.

Mae walked up and burst into a loud laugh. “Well I never thought I’d see the day. Finally, you got you a lady friend.” She pinched Cyn’s cheek. Emma pressed her lips together to stifle a smile when he blushed.

“Both of ya’ll come in here so often, I’m surprised I haven’t seen you together before.” Mae put down a glass of sweet tea in front of Cyn and gave Emma a stern look, while she pointed at Cyn. “This is a good man. He’s a little too pretty for a man, but he is a decent guy. He’ll do good by you.”

“Mae, thanks for the sales pitch, but can you get me some food please,” Cyn said, but not before Emma saw the muscles in his jaw twitch.

Emma smiled at the interaction between the two. It was good to know that Cyn had other people in his life that cared for him. She wished they could be friends, if nothing else. But it would be impossible for them to try to remain just friends.

Cyn drank his tea and sat in silence next to Emma. He considered how nice it would be to have someone to eat with and share his day-to-day occurrences with. He pictured them going for walks together and taking an actual family vacation. He could get used to something like that. He inhaled her scent and held back the urge to draw her closer.

"How have you been?" He asked breaking the silence.

She shrugged. "Good."

The short one word answer did little to convince him.

When Mae placed his usual Rueben and fries in front of him, he liked the fact that Emma didn't hesitate to take one of his fries. He picked up his sandwich and offered her a bite. She took one and met his eyes momentarily, before she looked away.

"It's really good. Thanks." She told him, her voice shook just enough to tell him she was nervous. He hated how distant she felt from him.

"I can't do it Emma —I'm having a rough time. I can't stop thinking about you." Cyn watched her take another fry from his plate.

The honesty in her reply surprised him. "Me either, that's why I'm moving. Once I'm gone, you will have an easier time concentrating on Blue and your work. Rachel told me you've been a grump lately."

Cyn took her hand. "That's not what I want. Look at me. I can't stay away from you. I want you with me always."

This time when her eyes met his, the depths of her beautiful honey-brown eyes warmed him.

Damn, he was in deep.

Emma stared at him seeming to be at a loss for words.

~ ☾ ~

She merely raised her hand and brushed her fingers down his cheek. She then snuggled into his side.

He continued eating and felt satisfied when he heard her sigh and relax. Tenderness filled him as he looked down at Emma's slight body molded next to him. It felt right. Cyn leaned over and kissed the top of her hair.

Emma finally spoke. "But Cyn, you can't break your oath — Protectors can't marry."

Mae returned to fill his glass and gave them a bright smile. He waited until she walked away before speaking.

"We can marry, but our wife has to be chosen for us or she has to be our life-mate. Most of us are not willing to enter into an arranged marriage. As a result, very few Protectors marry."

"How do you know if someone is your life-mate?" Emma asked.

Cyn shrugged, "Julian says it's very rare, usually someone we will feel a strong connection to right away, and I'm not sure what else. I've never cared enough to ask."

Emma tensed and moved away from him. "Good thing I'm moving because I'd be tempted to kill the woman you end up with." She drank from her beer while her free hand played with the angel hanging between her breasts.

Cyn laughed. "You're who I want to end up with." He told her and kissed her parted lips when she looked up at him with a stunned expression.

Emma responded by laying her head on his arm. He wanted her to remain there forever, didn't want to think about a future or any kind of life without both her and Blue in it.

While he ate, they discussed how Blue was doing. After they could prolong it no longer, they exited the diner and Cyn walked Emma to her car.

Not able to wait any longer, he pulled her to him and

kissed her. His hunger for her would not be denied.

He loved the feel of her lips and the familiar softness of her body against his. He could not allow her to go.

She wasn't moving anywhere.

Emma ran her hands over his shoulders up behind his head, and kissed him back with intensity. That sealed it, being apart from her was not an option. He couldn't bear it.

"Come home with me," Cyn whispered in her ear.

Emma moved back, and put space between them. "There is nothing else in the world I want more than to be with you, but it will only make it harder, later when we are forced to separate. I can't Cyn."

"Emma I mean it, I want you with me." Cyn looked into her eyes and realized he was being an idiot. He was really screwing things up.

He took her hand led her to his truck and leaned against it with her in his arms. The wind blew Emma's hair across her face. He brushed it aside and kissed her again. This time he kept it chaste.

"With Argos' death, I am finally able to legally adopt Blue. He is taking my last name and has decided to change his first name too. In two weeks, he will be Malcolm Fraser. He chose my brother's name."

"Oh Cyn, that is great." Emma hugged him and sniffed, a tear spilling down her cheek. "I am so happy for you and Blue. Er, Malcolm."

"Blue is his nickname, we'll still call him that." Cyn reassured her. "There's something else that's just as important and I hope changes your mind about leaving." He looked into her eyes and held her face between his hands.

"Emma, I love you. Will you marry me?"

~ ☾ ~

"I, I.... we can't do that!" Emma gasped as she threw her arms around his neck, happy beyond belief at his declaration.

Tell him you love him. Her heart demanded.

If only she could reply in kind, but she couldn't, not when she had to walk away from him.

Bowled over by the depth of love for her evident in his expression, she believed him. There wasn't any room for doubt. The man truly loved her. Unfortunately, that wasn't enough.

Exhaling deeply, she rested her forehead on his chest. "If only we could, but you know what I am. Julian would never allow it, and I won't have you go back on your oath for me —for a demon."

With one last lingering look, she turned away and hurried to her car.

~ ☾ ~

CHAPTER TWENTY FOUR

Before she could reach her car, Cyn came up behind her and lifted her into his arms. He ignored her shriek of surprise and carried her back to his truck.

Embarrassed at what the people in the diner witnessed, her cheeks warmed. “Put me down Cyn, people are watching.”

“I don’t care,” he replied, his tone even.

He struggled a bit opening the passenger door but managed it. He sat her in the passenger seat, and buckled her in. Emma could only stare at him. She opened her mouth to protest but found that she was at a loss for words.

“We will finish this conversation at the house.” He told her in a won’t-take-no-for-an-answer tone, his glare daring her to move. The dangerous Protector was back and she did not contradict him.

Torn between elation at knowing he loved her, and fear of the hurt that would come when forced to walk away from him, Emma could only sit and stare straight ahead.

She closed her eyes and tried unsuccessfully to form a cohesive thought.

What happens now?

The longer she stayed around him, the harder it would be to walk away.

When he got into the truck, the ice-blue eyes she loved so much met hers for a moment. She almost caved upon seeing so much emotion in them. He turned away, cranked the engine. He turned up the volume on the radio and let music fill the space around them.

# # #

When they walked into his house, Blue came out of the kitchen with a stack of grilled cheese sandwiches. “Hey Dad.” It was a moment before he noticed Emma.

A broad smile split his face. “Hi Emma. You’re back, that’s awesome.” He turned and shuffled toward his room not looking back.

“Hey, you didn’t eat your dinner. You said you weren’t hungry and now you’re eating a tower of crap.” Cyn called after him.

“You’re cooking sucks, Dad. Sorry!” Blue called back before his bedroom door slammed shut.

Emma smiled at Cyn’s frown. He walked to the hallway entrance and looked toward Blue’s room, as if trying to decide what to do about his son.

“You must have not eaten your dinner either since you ate a sandwich at Mae’s earlier.” Emma reminded him. “Let Blue have his tower of sandwiches. Grilled cheese is not that unhealthy.”

Cyn turned to her, his expression sheepish. “My cooking *is* pretty bad. Do you want something to drink?” He went to the kitchen and took two beers out of the fridge and poured one into a glass for her. “Please sit down.”

There was no way she could resist him, not for long anyway. She loved this man with all her heart and soul. No doubt he would try and convince her to marry him and how could she say no. It was useless to deny the feelings she had for him. If only they could be together without Cyn having to resign from the Protector force.

Being a Protector was his life. She would never let him quit.

She had to be strong.

He held a chair out for her.

She sat, ignoring the beer and steeled herself to what he was about to say.

If he was going to convince her to marry him regardless of the consequences, she didn't know if she could resist.

"I never thought I'd fall in love. I did my best to avoid it at all costs... oh God, this is not the best way to start this discussion." His nervousness was obvious, but his resolve proved stronger. "I'm not good with words Emma. I don't know how to express my feelings. I convinced Wendy to get you to Mae's diner so I could talk to you." He blushed. "Shit sorry, I wasn't supposed to tell you that either."

The little traitor. She'd deal with Wendy later.

Cyn took her hand. "Emma, I want you to understand that I'm willing to do anything not to lose you."

At seeing her fierce Protector so vulnerable, she ached for him. Emma stood and wrapped her arms around his waist and rested her head on his firm chest.

His sigh made her heart constrict, as he relaxed and held her. How could she say no? God help her.

Cyn put his hands on both sides of her face and they looked into each other's eyes for a moment before his mouth fell on hers. The kiss was soft and sweet, his lips brushed feather soft strokes over hers.

Cyn nipped her bottom lip and deepened the kiss while he walked her backwards toward the couch. When the back of her leg touched it, they fell back into the soft suede, never breaking their kiss. Emma scooted over to allow him room to lie next to her.

He removed the clip from her hair and it cascaded to

her shoulders, Cyn buried his face in it. "I love your scent Emma."

Emma rubbed his back, and basked in the feel of his amazing body.

I want to fight for us. I love him. The thought took her by surprise.

"I love you Cyn."

His wide smile warmed her heart. His mouth found hers again and this time his kiss was hard and demanding. Emma ran her hand under his shirt needing to touch his skin. He pushed his hardness into her and she moaned.

The sound of a branch against the window got Emma's attention. She realized what they were doing and she pushed Cyn back. Both were breathing hard.

"Blue could walk in, that wouldn't be good," she told him.

Cyn responded by pulling her in for another kiss before he got up from the couch and held his hand out to help her up. "You're right, it would be rather awkward. No kid wants to see his Dad making out."

Emma gasped in alarm when Cyn grabbed her and threw her behind him. The speed of his movements astounded her. She peered around him and her jaw dropped at the sight of the man who stood in the room.

The male that appeared before them looked as if he'd fallen to earth directly from Mt. Olympus. There were two words that described him, perfection and terrifying. The air sizzled as his shimmering eyes landed first on Emma and then on Cyn.

He had to be Julian.

The man radiated pure power.

Fear seized her, yet she tried to take him in. If Emma thought Cyn and the other Protectors were the most handsome men she'd ever seen, it was because she'd never met Julian.

No male could compare to him.

He looked much younger than she expected, perhaps mid-twenties. His broad shoulders and a sleek, yet muscled, physique were evident under his white collarless shirt and tan slacks. The slight vee gave a glimpse of a light feathering of hair on his chest.

He wore his jet-black hair short and combed back away from his face. Michelangelo himself could not have created more breathtaking features. Long eyelashes and perfectly arched eyebrows framed midnight eyes. His lips were full and sensuous, even now, when he held them in a firm line as he studied them.

Cyn shifted and Emma moved with him instinctively curling her fingers around the material of his shirt. She waited for either man to do or say something.

Julian stepped toward them. His movements reminded Emma of a sleek panther sizing up its prey. She had no doubt that without effort he could overcome Cyn, if he wished to. Still she was glad to be sheltered his large body at that moment.

"Hello Cynden," Julian's voice was deep with a slight accent. "Hello Emma." He nodded to her. After a long lingering look, he looked back at Cyn. "She is lovely."

Emma wondered if Julian knew that she and Cyn had just been making out. Self-conscious, she reached up and smoothed her hair as best she could.

# # #

Julian's words did little to calm Cyn. The Protector in him took over and his fangs elongated, to let Julian know Emma was his.

Cyn tried his best to maintain control, but remained tensed. He didn't like the way Julian sized up Emma, not at all.

“She is to be my wife.” He wrapped his arm around her waist and held her possessively to his side.

After a moment, Julian nodded in understanding and turned away from them. He gripped his hands together behind his back and walked to the oversized windows.

The Roman peered out to the barrier of trees that surrounded Cyn’s house.

“I don’t like this city—it seems to affect Protectors in a peculiar fashion.”

Cyn didn’t reply. Julian continued unfazed. “Two Protectors, taking wives, it has never happened. Not this close together.” With an unreadable expression he turned back to face them. He looked pointedly at Cyn. “We must talk.”

Emma moved in front of him, as if to protect him and his heart leaped in joy at her action. But, it was foolish to allow her to offend Julian in any way. So he gave her a reassuring hug and pushed her toward the bedrooms.

“Go to my bedroom and wait, please.” He could hear Blue’s music blaring. *Good, he shouldn’t come out for a while.*

Emma’s eyes were wide with anxiety and concern as they met his. Although he could sense her reluctance to move, she nodded and glanced once more at Julian before walking away.

Cyn took a deep breath and forced his fangs to retract when Emma left the room.

He respected Julian. He didn’t envy his superior. The man carried the heavy burden of commanding the Protector Army. Julian always proved to be a firm but fair leader, and one who kept himself at a distance from them.

Through the years the Protectors learned bits and pieces about Julian, but for the most part, his past remained a well-guarded secret.

The Roman didn't wait for Cyn to speak. "I already know what you are going to say Cynden. You plan to marry her whether I approve or not."

Cyn nodded, accustomed to Julian's abilities. He was torn between his allegiance to the Protectors and Emma. "Please don't make me choose."

For the second time in his life, Cyn was uncertain of his future.

"And if I do, which will you choose?" Julian asked him.

"I would choose to marry Emma."

"I see." Julian's expression remained blank. "After today, you won't have a decision to make."

"Come, we must go."

~ ☾ ~

CHAPTER TWENTY FIVE

Still fully dressed Emma woke with a start. She must've fallen asleep on Cyn's bed.

She grabbed her cell and saw that it was six in the morning and sat up blinking to fully wake-up.

Cyn wasn't in the bedroom. It looked like he'd never come to bed. She wondered where he was and why he hadn't come to find her last night. Fear filled her and she ran from the bedroom to the living room.

The house was empty. The bed in the spare bedroom wasn't rumpled.

Cyn hadn't slept in there.

Confused and worried, she went to find Blue. She knocked on his bedroom door and heard a mumble. She opened the door and walked over to his bed and shook him gently. Half asleep Blue rolled over and looked up at her.

"Where's Cyn?"

"heeelft anot" Blue mumbled and turned back toward the wall.

"What?" Emma grabbed his arm and shook him harder this time. "Blue! What did you say?"

"He left you a note on the kitchen table." Blue mumbled.

Emma hurried out of the bedroom to the kitchen. His note was propped up in the middle of the table. Dread filled her and with shaky hands, she picked it up.

"Emma,

Everything is fine, don't worry, I'll see you tonight. Your place.
I love you,
Cyn."

She sagged with relief. How was she going to get home? Should she stay there until Cyn returned?

She went back to Cyn's bedroom to find her cell phone. Her car keys were next to her purse on the nightstand along with a small garage door opener. She smiled. He'd had her car brought to her.

After she ensured Blue deactivated the alarm system and she reminded him several times to reactivate it after she left, Emma made her way to the garage.

Her light green VW beetle was indeed there.

Emma went home.

# # #

The thickness of the tension in the room was hard to ignore. Whatever Julian was about to announce could not be good. Cyn leaned against the counter at Kieran's house, his body strung tight with apprehension. Kieran and Julian were already in the room. Kieran sat at the table and drank from his ever-present cup of coffee. Julian stood still as a statue and peered down at a map of the city that had been spread across the table. Fallon and Roderick entered and gave Cyn questioning looks before they sat.

He shrugged.

Julian began to speak without a greeting. "Our numbers are not growing as fast, especially in comparison with the increasing growth of the demon population. I like to keep the Protector force at one for every two hundred demons or so. I've recruited three new Protectors in the last year. The demons on the other hand, have multiplied by hundreds. This means that no Protector can be relieved from his duty and those that have been, will be asked to return to the force." He looked at Roderick. "I have to ask you to resign from your job at the hospital and return to the force."

Roderick nodded his acceptance. Next Julian leveled an intense look at each Protector. "With the number of high-level demons converging in this area, I don't want any of you to patrol alone for the time being. I don't have extra men I can send to help right now." He stared at the map seeming to be lost in thought before he continued. "Fallon and Kieran will work together as partners. Cynden and Roderick, you two are partners."

Kieran and Cyn looked at each other with raised eyebrows. Julian glowered at them. "I can't have brothers as partners. It makes you too vulnerable."

"We've fought alongside each other many times," Kieran began, but stopped when Cyn glared at him in warning. "Fine, whatever." Kieran frowned into his coffee cup.

Cyn didn't like the idea of partnering up; they couldn't cover as much territory that way. By the stoic faces of the others they weren't too keen on the idea either.

Julian cleared his throat and got their attention again. "There will be an influx of demons at the next full moon. The festival of Dionysus will commence. Atlanta will be a popular destination. At that time, Rowe, Thor and I will also come out to help, if needed. Any questions?"

The Protectors spent the next hour discussing how to divide the city, to ensure every area was patrolled, and decided who would patrol where. New high-powered, silent motorcycles would arrive for them in a few days.

"Rachel, Brock, Blue, and now Emma, will have to be placed under protection." Julian told them. Cyn's eyes snapped up, but the leader continued, not looking at him. "I know they may be resistant to the idea of losing their freedom, but it's the only way for your families to be kept safe. I have hired bodyguards for them. The guards are human, but they are trained to battle demons. They have been sworn to secrecy and are trustworthy, skilled men."

Julian sank down on a chair, and for the first time that Cyn could remember, the Roman looked fatigued. "I fear we may be fighting a losing battle at times. But I never wonder about the commitment of the Protectors to keep innocent people safe. I know you will defend humans to your last breath. And, I am just as sure that when I return at the full moon, all of you will be present."

When Julian stood to leave, he motioned for Cyn to follow him outside. The other Protectors remained seated, each deep in thought taking it all in.

Julian walked to a sleek sedan, his face softened as he placed his hand on Cyn's shoulder. "You must observe the Roman ritual to marry Emma. She is your life-mate." Julian hesitated to let the information soak in. "You have succeeded in finding her."

The pull — that's why he'd bitten her the first time they'd made love. And why they'd felt such a strong draw to each other from the beginning. It was her being half-demon that had given him cause for doubt.

Through the fog that took over his brain, he became aware that Julian was still speaking. "She must agree to every part of it in order for your union to be valid and become your mate. You will find the vow scripts and everything else you need in the box I left in your truck." Julian tightened the hold on Cyn's shoulder and Cyn returned the gesture.

"Are you sure?" Cyn didn't know why he asked. His brain no doubt was still addled.

~ ☾ ~

"Yes, I knew it as soon as I saw her. If she is to become your wife, I congratulate you and wish you the best." Julian walked away to his car.

Emotions flooded over Cyn, he leaned against a tree and looked up at the sky.

He was going to get married.

He'd found his life-mate.

Julian's taillights disappeared from view.

A wide smile spread across his face. Cyn let out a loud yell.

The Protectors rushed outside. Kieran held his sword in his hand and sported a large coffee stain on his shirt. They stopped in their tracks at his laughter.

Roderick and Fallon instantly understood the reason for his jubilation. They came over to shake his hand and thump him on the back.

His brother's solemn eyes met his. Kieran nodded his head and went back inside. It was as close to congratulation as he would get from him.

# # #

"Where is he?" Emma wondered aloud going to the front window. She peered out for at least the tenth time. She considered driving back to Cyn's house but someone could follow her, so she discarded the idea, not willing to put Blue in any danger.

Flames from candles swayed in the light breeze from the swirl of the ceiling fan casting an intimate glow about the room. Besides the candles, the dining room table was set with a vase of fresh white tulips and all white china. The tantalizing aroma of rosemary chicken flowed from the kitchen.

Emma pictured Cyn's face when she surprised him with a romantic evening. Emma fought against the impulse to peek out through the blinds again and instead resumed pacing. She glimpsed into a wall mirror and smoothed her hair. She had to admit the extra effort spent on her appearance was well worth it. She'd taken time to apply eye make-up and brush her hair up into a French twist. A knee-length, black dress and matching sling-back sandals completed her look.

A tingle of anticipation ran through her. What would his reaction be to the new black lacy panties and bra she wore?

She wanted at least one last night with Cyn.

Last night, while she fretted over Julian's visit and paced in Cyn's bedroom, Emma had plenty of time to think. She knew that Julian would never agree to their marriage. She had no other choice but to release Cyn from his proposal. It was the right thing to do, but it still tore her to pieces. Every instinct screamed at her to fight for him. Taking a shaky breath, she picked up a glass of wine.

The ding of the doorbell made her jump.

Wendy walked in not waiting for her to open the door. She grabbed the wine out of Emma's hand and gulped it down. "I hate to bother you, but you were so distracted on the phone today...oh!" She stopped when she saw the table set for dinner. "Oh shit did I interrupt? Is he here?" Wendy peered toward the bedroom.

"Not yet, he's coming over. He called earlier." Emma replied. She grabbed her friend's hand. "Wendy, he asked me to marry him."

"Eeeeek!" Wendy jumped up and down clapping. "Wait, was this before or after you told him you were preggers?"

"What the hell are you talking about? I'm not pregnant." Emma snatched the wine glass back. It was empty.

~ ☾ ~

"You shouldn't drink in your condition." Wendy cautioned her and grabbed the glass back. "How can you not know you're pregnant?"

With surprising strength for her petite size, Wendy grabbed Emma by the shoulders and pushed her into a dining room chair. She pointed her finger into Emma's face. "You haven't had a period since the last time you and Mr. Tall, Blonde and Yummy did the mattress mambo. You eat everything in sight." She motioned to Emma's hand, already holding a piece of bread. Emma threw it back into the bowl as if it was poisonous. "And you've been dizzy and have an upset stomach in the mornings. Duh."

"Oh. My. God." Emma sat transfixed and stared wide-eyed at Wendy, as she went over the last few days. "Oh my God Wendy, I can't be pregnant. I mean they are...well you know."

"Who are what? I know what?" Wendy asked her, with a befuddled expression.

"The Protectors are sterile." Emma told her. She reached for the bread again and she took a healthy bite. "Well unless they have sex with their life match, perfect mate or ....some kind of mate," she spoke through a mouth full of bread.

Both women jumped this time when the doorbell rang. Wendy gave Emma a reassuring squeeze before she ran to open the door.

Cyn stood at the door with an intricately carved wooden box in hands. He seemed surprised by Wendy's presence, but smiled politely at her.

When he directed his attention to Emma, his face softened.

Her knees turned to jelly. Love, this is what it felt like.

"Well I better go, just came by to give Emma some...er, news." Wendy headed for the door. She patted

Cyn on the shoulder having to reach up to do it. “Bye.”

Cyn wasn’t dressed in his standard casual attire. He wore a tunic style shirt and loose linen pants. On his feet, he wore sandals. He didn’t speak right away and his expression was no closed and difficult to read. At his silence, Emma tensed. Was something wrong?

He peered past her to the table and his lips curved and she relaxed.

“I made dinner for us,” she told him when he approached. She stood on her toes to kiss his jaw. “Is everything okay?”

Cyn placed the strange box on her coffee table.

Then he came back to her and took her into his arms. When his mouth covered hers, she gave into his kiss and lost herself in the feel of his strong body against hers. God, she could never tire of his kisses.

Cyn lifted his head and looked into her eyes. “Hi. I’m sorry if I’m late, I didn’t know you were cooking. Do you want to eat?”

Emma shook her head. She’d lost her appetite after her talk with Wendy. “I’m not that hungry now, are you?”

Cyn shook his head, “I ate before I left home. Well, I tried to eat. I made spaghetti, but it tasted like crap.” Emma enjoyed the rumble in his chest when he chuckled. “It smells very good. Maybe we can eat later.” Cyn took her hand, “Come sit down, I have some things to explain to you.”

Once they were seated, he regarded her for a long time before he spoke. The sparkle in his eyes helped Emma feel at ease at whatever he was about to tell her.

“Emma, you have to promise to listen to everything I tell you without interrupting me. All right?”

“Okay.” Emma leaned back on the couch and folded her legs beneath her. She waited to hear what he was about to tell her and tried to untie the knots in her stomach.

Cyn took both of her hands in his and frowned for a minute. “Julian won’t allow me to leave the Protectors. And I agree with him.”

Emma felt her heart tear in two. She’d expected this, but the pain still ripped through her upon hearing his choice. It was a good thing she’d promised to listen and not interrupt. If she had to speak right now, there was no way she could get the words past the lump in her throat.

“But he has also agreed to our marriage.” Her eyes widened but she bit her lip to keep quiet. “In order for our marriage to be valid, you must agree to marry me in an ancient ritual that I will explain to you and we must complete it exactly as directed.”

“Ritual?” Emma stammered, “Do I have to kill something?”

Cyn chuckled and shook his head before giving her a stern look. “It’s the only way for you to be with me forever. Now, quiet love, just listen.”

# # #

Her pale pink bedroom was suddenly too frilly. Emma grabbed two fuzzy throw pillows tossed them in her closet. She walked back to the bed, sat on the edge. In her mind she went over everything Cyn explained to her. She’d already agreed to marry him, but he insisted she take at least thirty minutes alone to think about it.

She smiled, at the worried look on his handsome face when she agreed and went to her room. It was almost an hour later and she hadn’t changed her mind, but now that she knew what was ahead for them, she was nervous

Elated.

But, very nervous.

~ ☾ ~

Cyn glanced at the clock on Emma's mantel once again and then back to her closed bedroom door.

She said yes. What had possessed him to tell her to take some time to think it over? What would he do if she changed her mind?

Once again, he went over what had to be done to complete the ritual and ensured it was set up exactly as instructed.

Finally, her door opened.

His heart stopped when she walked out to him. Except for a thin red sheer veil across her shoulders that hung to her ankles, she was completely naked. Her anxious eyes traveled around the room but when they met his, her features relaxed into a smile.

He moved to the couch to undress. Once nude, he took her hands and guided her to the purple velvet cloth spread on the floor.

Emma looked around her, four crimson candles flickered, one set on each corner of a rectangular purple cloth spread on the floor. On the coffee table, a small oil lamp burned and a slender golden vase sat next to it.

On the floor next to the thick cloth lay a glass vial. She knelt as he had instructed her earlier and Cyn knelt before her. His smile was reassuring, but what really calmed her nerves was the deep love reflected in his beautiful eyes.

Without taking breaking eye contact, he picked up the vial and uncorked it. He poured the fragrant oil onto his fingers and traced it down her chest while he recited the ancient vows

"Your heart is mine. My heart is yours." He moistened his fingers again and ran them across her chest. "Your life for my life."

He handed the vial over to Emma. Her hand trembled as she repeated the vows and traced the same pattern over his chest.

Then Cyn lay back on the cloth and waited for her to come over him. It was a sign of submission for him to be on the bottom. By doing so, it symbolized his willingness to die for her.

Careful not to let her veil fall off, Emma straddled him. She peered between his legs—he was erect. She spread her thighs and positioned herself to make access for him easy. He looked at her apologetically before thrusting his hips up and pushed his thick shaft into her without preamble.

Emma stiffened, not quite ready for the intrusion, but her body quickly accommodated his largeness and she relaxed. She lowered onto him so that she could rest on his thighs.

He took her hands, palms touching, fingers interlocked. "Don't let go of my hands no matter what Emma." He told her and then turned his head and gave her access to his throat.

At that moment Emma knew that Cyn offered the most valuable gift he could give.

His immortality.

While she bit into his throat and drank of his blood, he would be mortal. During the time it took her to recite the vows, he would suffer immensely.

"I love you." She reassured him as the unfamiliar feel of her fangs lowering from her incisors told her it was time. Aiming for the main artery, she bit into his neck.

Cyn's jaw clenched and she could tell that he fought to squelch any expression of pain. His body temperature spiked and he instinctively struggled under her, almost bucking Emma off. She strengthened her hold on his hips with her legs. At the same time, his hands flinched around hers. His right hand began to shake, but he didn't seem to notice it, as his entire body convulsed in agony.

After she took from him as much as she could, Emma retracted her fangs from his neck and licked the wound to close it. She cleared her throat and recited her vows. "Where you are Gaius, I am Gaia - Wherever you are Cyn, I Emma will be. I will love you and honor you husband."

Emma resisted every urge to release Cyn's hands and comfort him. Although still too pale, he finally stopped trembling. Once he completed his portion, all his strength would return to him.

She leaned forward and offered him her throat. He nuzzled her neck weakly not seeming to have the energy to bite her. "Go on sweetheart, take from me." Emma urged.

After a moment, he opened his mouth, the snap of his incisors dropping echoed in her ear. A mixture of pain and ecstasy shocked her when his fangs tore into her delicate flesh. It took all her strength not to push her hips forward and take him in deeper when a powerful climax hit her. She wanted to scream as burning sensation seared left hand, but managed to keep it to only a hiss, as the pain left as quickly as it hit.

Cyn's hold on her tightened and he continued to drink her blood and she didn't move, so he could to take what he needed to regain his strength.

Finally, he retracted his incisors from her neck and began his vows, his voice strong. "Where you are Gaia, I am Gaius. Wherever you are Emma, I Cyn will be. I will love you and protect you wife."

His fingers wrapped around her waist and Cyn helped her lift off of him.

They stood, both careful not to step outside the cloth.

~ ☾ ~

When Cyn swayed Emma reached out to steady him. He pushed her hands away gently.

Cyn picked up the oil lamp and the vase and held them to her. “With these elements of water and fire, I vow that I enter this union willingly.”

Emma’s hands shook as she took them from him. “I accept these elements and vow that I enter this union willingly.”

She placed both items down on the table, and then turned to face Cyn who looked at her with a combination of disbelief and awe.

“It’s done wife. ‘Wife’ the one gift I never dared to even fathom to receive.” He took her in his arms. Emma wrapped hers around him in a fierce hug, allowing tears of happiness to fall freely.

She sniffed loudly. “I love you. Are you all right?”

His warm eyes met hers. “I love you too. I feel great.”

Finally they stepped apart and Cyn carried her off the cloth and set her on the couch. She slid the veil away and picked up a towel he’d thoughtfully left on the couch and wrapped it under her arms to cover her nudity.

Cyn wrapped another towel around his waist before he blew out the candles and oil lamp. He folded the cloth and placed everything back into the box.

With that completed, he sat next to Emma. “Look at your left palm”

A circular symbol with an intricate design was imprinted on her palm. It resembled a henna tattoo she’d gotten once. Cyn raised his right hand to show her a mirror image of the symbol on his palm.

“So that’s what the burning was.” Emma said in a hushed voice. “That was extreme Cyn. Are you sure you feel okay?”

He nodded, “I’m all right. I didn’t know what to expect. Julian said it would hurt, but he didn’t tell me how much. It's different for each Protector." He leaned over and kissed her. "I can't be unfaithful to you now."

Emma gave him what she hoped was a seductive look. "I don't plan on you having the energy to even look at another woman."

"How about a toast?" Cyn got up and poured two glasses of wine.

Emma reached for her glass. Without a word, their eyes locked and they clinked their glasses together.

She took a sip and coughed. The wine reminded her of the earlier conversation with Wendy. A gasp left her lips. *Could I be?* She put the glass on the coffee table with a bang.

Cyn gave her a questioning look.

"I have something to tell you." She blurted, her heart thumping in her chest. At a loss for words, she took his hand and placed it over her stomach.

"I think, but I'm not sure. I'm kinda late..."

His eyes widened when he understood what she tried to tell him.

# # #

The next hour was a flurry of activity, Cyn insisted they get dressed immediately and drive to the nearest drugstore for a pregnancy test. Emma blushed with embarrassment when she placed the pregnancy test on the counter and Cyn placed another one next to it.

He shrugged at her. "Just to make sure." He gave the cashier a broad smile and the woman behind the counter nearly swooned at the sight of it.

Emma smiled and elbowed him. "Turn down the vibe Fraser, you're a married man now."

Half an hour later, Cyn knocked again on the bathroom door and asked to come in. But Emma made him wait; she didn't want him watching her pee on a stick. After using both tests, she walked out and handed the sticks to him. He studied them each and compared them to the instructions to be sure.

"Yes!" Cyn's face split into a wide grin.

Tears sprung to her eyes when he picked her up and swung her around.

"I'm going to be a father. Blue is going to be so excited!"

He picked up his cell phone but Emma stopped him. "Maybe we should tell him in person. Do you want to drive over there now?"

Emma watched him ponder her question, his handsome face serious.

Her husband. How much she loved him at this moment.

Cyn shook his head, a crooked smile spread across his face. "I think we can tell him tomorrow. I want to celebrate alone tonight."

His lips covered hers with a softness that melted her entire being. She had to hold on to him to keep her knees from buckling, as the kiss became ardent.

"I want you Emma, I need you." His voice was hoarse with desire.

His hungry mouth took hers and Emma lost the ability to think as fireworks exploded in her head.

Her heart hammered against her chest, yet she managed to step away from him and unzip her dress. The payoff was worth it, Cyn's heated gaze followed her every move as she slid it off her shoulders and let it fall to the floor.

Her purchase proved a wise investment judging from the hungry way Cyn's eyes devoured her as she stood before him in the lacy lingerie and heels.

"Don't move," he instructed. Cyn undressed, the

entire time his attention never wavered from her. Emma could not tear her eyes from him as he revealed every inch of his stunning physique.

And he was all hers.

So this was what total happiness feels like?

Desire rammed into her when Cyn held his hand out to her. "I want to make this a night you'll always remember."

Emma took his hand and he brought her to him. He cradled her head and turned her face up to him. "I love you."

A soft moan escaped past her lips when he feathered soft kissed over her face. She ran her fingers over his strong arms and around his neck. When Cyn picked her up and carried her to the bedroom she felt as if she was floating.

He placed her on the bed and lay next to her on his side. Emma remained on her back without moving allowing him to explore her body. His fingers caressed her breasts, she panted when he circled first one nipple and then the other. When his touch roamed from her breasts to her stomach, he leaned over and kissed the flat surface. Butterflies danced in her stomach. She couldn't help but close her eyes when his hand moved between her legs. Her thighs parted to allow him more access. She went to touch him, but he pushed her hand away. "Let me love you."

"You are so beautiful," Cyn told her, his amazing eyes meeting hers. "Come for me."

Her eyes rolled back and she moaned when his fingers began to strum at her core. The friction of the lace fabric magnified each stroke of his fingers. Emma clutched the blanket and cried out.

~ ☾ ~

Watching Emma's reaction to his touch nearly did him in. She shuddered in release, her beautiful face thrown back. Cyn had always hoped to have a partner that allowed him free reign of her body. He wanted someone who understood his need to watch her reaction to his touch. Emma's boldness fit him perfectly.

Pure heat hit when she pushed him on to his back. "My turn."

Unlike him, she moved faster and was not gentle. Just as he liked it. Her blunt teeth bit his throat, but not hard enough to break his skin. He moaned as she nipped a path down to his chest. Her hot tongue flicked over his nipple sending a wave of heat straight between his legs.

Her fingers traced circles in the most sensitive places. He thrust his hips in response. "Steady love, I'm not done yet," Emma's husky words did not help.

Nips and bites from his chest down his stomach left a heated trail on his skin. Emma pushed his legs open and her hot mouth suckled his inner thigh.

"Fuck." Cyn hissed. "I'm going to lose it Emma."

His breath caught at the sight of her wicked smile. "Do it."

Her lips wrapped around him and she suckled him so hard that he did.

When he stopped shaking, she let him slip from her mouth and moved to lie on his chest.

"I love you Cyn." Emma told. "I never thought I could be so happy."

"I've felt that way for as long as I can remember," Cyn replied. "This is a dream I never dared to have."

They lay for several minutes in silence.

She wrapped her hand around him and began to stroke his length. When he became aroused again, Emma purred. "This time I want you inside me."

~ ☾ ~

A few hours later, the buzz of the cell phone on the nightstand woke Cyn. He reached for it and looked at the display.

It was Roderick.

Something was wrong.

~ ☾ ~

CHAPTER TWENTY SIX

Cyn told Roderick he'd call him right back and hung up. He slid from under Emma, who continued to sleep soundly. He carried his clothes to the living room and got dressed.

Once in his truck, he called Roderick back. The Spartan was tracking a group of high-level demons. A rare occurrence that didn't sit well with Cyn. High-levels never hunted as a group, their bloodthirsty nature made them lone predators.

As he drove into the dark Atlanta night, he couldn't deny a sense of well-being despite the nature of his trip. He still couldn't believe he'd found his life-mate. With Blue and another child on the way, his life couldn't get much better.

He had a lot of reasons to be thankful.

# # #

Cyn arrived to find Roderick leaning on a crumbling brick wall. The Spartan motioned him over.

"Interesting choice of street gear," Roderick scanned over his tunic, linen pants and sandals. "At least you've got your jacket."

"High-levels, I can sense them," Cyn replied, ignoring Roderick's fashion critique.

"Yeah, this doesn't feel right - I watched several go to the empty lot back there. Why would high-level demons hunt together?"

"Bigger prey than usual?" The thought troubled him as he peered into the shadows. He didn't get a chance to ponder further. A blood-curdling scream filled the air.

Swords in hand, they rushed into the darkness.

Cyn stopped dead in his tracks when they came upon four high-level demons with their swords drawn surrounding a human male. The human didn't look hurt or distraught. By expectant look on the man's face, it was obvious he was there of his own free will.

The hair on the back of Cyn's neck rose.

Gerard.

The Master demon stepped from behind the group.

He and Roderick were the prey.

Cyn held back the urge to shove through the demons and attack Gerard. He clenched his jaw and glanced at Roderick. By the tautness in Roderick's stance, it was obvious that he restrained himself as well.

As usual Gerard made an elaborate entrance, he walked between the four demons and stood with his arms relaxed at his sides and smiled at the Protectors. "Again, I have to say, I'm surprised at how easily I can get you two to come to me."

Cyn spit on the ground and glowered at Gerard, barely able to contain his fury. "What the hell do you want this time?"

Gerard let his head fall back as he laughed. "Two things actually — the freedom of our Supreme Ruler and you two dead."

"How about no and no?" Cyn answered with a smirk

No other words were exchanged as the Protectors moved as one and attacked. The ringing of metal clashing against metal echoed into the night.

The demons fought aggressively. Something seemed off. When Cyn had corned one and swung his sword for the killing strike, the demon evaded with extraordinarily quick movements. Their lightning speed gave away the fact that they weren't ordinary high-levels.

They were Warrior demons.

Cyn hadn't seen a Warrior demon in over a hundred years.

"Kill them!" Gerard yelled.

# # #

A buzzing sound startled Emma, in a sleepy haze she tried to figure out what the sound was. She stretched her arm and looked for Cyn but found his side of the bed empty. When her cell phone buzzed again, she reached for it and answered.

The voice on the other end jolted her awake. "Emma, I need you. I'm in trouble." It was Briana. She sounded terrified. "Please hurry. Come and get me." As soon as she gave Emma an address, Briana disconnected.

Emma leaped from the bed and threw on some jeans and a t-shirt, not bothering with underwear.

She ran through the house to look for Cyn. Where could he have gone at this hour? She pushed his number into her cell with shaky fingers. It went straight to voicemail. She left a short message, along with the address that Briana had given her.

Did Briana change her mind? Was she ready to come back? Maybe everything would be perfect now. She would finally have her family complete with Cyn, Blue, the baby, and now Briana.

Car keys in hand, she ran out of the house.

Checking for addresses at night, in an area with few streetlights made for slow progress. Emma drove at a snail's pace until she spotted the correct numbers on a dilapidated mailbox that leaned at an awkward angle. She turned her headlights off and coasted closer.

It was a small abandoned print shop. Through the cracked windows, Emma could see movement inside. She clenched the steering wheel and tried to figure out how to let Briana know she'd arrived. Emma slid out of the car leaving the door open. She didn't want to close it and make any noise, in case someone else was in there with her sister.

At that moment, a door on the side of the building opened. Emma crouched behind the car door and peeked around it to see who it was. A hooded figure stepped out.

Emma heaved a sigh of relief when she recognized Briana in the shadows. Her sister walked toward the car and she motioned for her to hurry.

A cold breeze hit her right before she realized that someone rushed up behind her. Emma turned and kicked at the bulky male when he lunged for her. But he grabbed her around the neck and yanked her off the ground. Emma flailed wildly while being dragged over to the side of the building where Briana and another demon waited.

"Briana what is going on?" Emma stammered, out of breath. She attempted to push away from the demon that held her. He didn't release her, but loosened his hold on her.

"What are you hoping to accomplish?" Emma asked her sister.

Briana ignored her and spoke to the demon beside her. "Where do we take her?"

The demon shrugged. "Gerard told us to stay here and wait for word."

"We can't just wait around here!" Briana hissed at him. "The Protectors could be following her. They will kick our asses."

~ ☾ ~

"Briana, listen to me!" Emma brought Briana's attention back to her. "Please listen to me. Nothing good is going to happen if you stay with Gerard. He's pure evil. Can't you see that he isn't interested in anything other than freeing the Supreme demon?"

"Shut up Emma. You don't know what the hell you are talking about. The Supreme ruler has to be freed. Don't you see? Only then will we be in control. The world will be ours, not the stupid humans' who persecute us and make us feel like monsters."

Gerard's words, Briana was parroting the bastard. Did her sister really believe what she was saying?

"A world of death and desperation is that what you consider a good outcome?" She looked into Briana's black eyes, and didn't see much of the little sister she shared so much with. She almost lost her resolve as an enormous sense of loss overcame her. "Are you even Briana anymore?" She whispered.

"Emma, just shut up. You'll come with us and accept your fate. You are a demon and as such, you will embrace your true self — what you were born to be." Briana looked at her with disdain. "Personally, I would rather leave you with the humans, but for some reason Gerard wants you."

"I can't Briana. I will die first. Please don't do this. I'm going to be a mom."

She wasn't sure, but thought she saw uncertainty flicker in Briana's face but it was gone the next second. "It's already been decided Emma. A child changes nothing."

When another demon arrived, Briana tensed. Her sister's hand went to the hilt of her short sword.

None of them seem to recognize the newcomer. There was something different about the demon. Emma saw Briana send a questioning glance at the demon who held her.

"Warrior," the demon replied. "They are as strong and fast as the Protectors."

The demon's arrival gave Emma a chance to fist the hilt of a small dagger she kept in her jacket. She held it inside the pocket, waiting for an opportunity.

Briana walked toward the Warrior with confidence. "Who sent you?"

"Gerard," the demon grunted back.

"We have to go back before Protectors come. One of them considers my sister his mate." Briana informed him.

The Warrior's eyes were flat and emotionless. "Gerard sent me to kill you. Both of you." He glanced toward Emma.

The energy in the air changed as Briana drew her sword and began to battle the demon.

Emma jerked away from the grasp of the demon holding her and managed to take a few steps before he grabbed her again.

The soft swish of his sword changed very the air around her. In a terror filled motion, Emma stabbed him.

She missed his heart.

Emma managed to back away until she reached the wall of the building.

With desperation, she threw the dagger at the demon.

He grunted and stumbled back grabbing at the dagger planted on the right side of his chest.

Emma's heart plummeted. She'd missed again.

With little effort, he yanked it out. The demon snarled and rushed toward her.

His sword sliced through the air headed straight for her heart.

At that precise moment, Briana fell backwards and

bumped into him, knocking the demon off balance. The Warrior's sword initially aimed at Briana sliced the demon's shoulder.

Her attacker hissed in pain and cursed at the Warrior. "You fucker, you're here to kill them, not me."

Without replying, the Warrior beheaded him.

Taking advantage of the Warrior's distraction, Briana plunged her sword into him, but he was fast and she only managed to cut his arm.

He charged and sliced Briana across the chest.

Briana collapsed onto the ground.

"No!" Emma cried. "Oh my God!"

She ran to her sister, but just as she touched her, Briana evaporated.

Emma's scream pierced the night. "Nooo!"

My baby sister.

Drawing energy from the need to protect her child, Emma grabbed Briana's sword and managed to block the Warrior's next slash. But she was inexperienced with a sword that within seconds, her sword flew out of her hand and clanked heavily on the ground.

Before the Warrior demon could stab again, Emma scrambled away from him. But she soon ran out of options and backed herself into a corner.

He lifted his sword one last time and Emma almost laughed at the irony of it all. Here she was again in the shadows, about to die because she was half-demon.

She crumpled to the ground wrapping her hands protectively over her stomach and waited for the fatal blow.

In those few seconds, she thought of Cyn and their last night together. She ached knowing he'd hurt at the news of her death. She wasn't ready to die, but would face death with bravery, her eyes locked with the Warrior's fixed stare.

~ ☾ ~

The Warrior froze with his sword halfway down. A shocked look came over his face, as he fell onto the ground next to her with a stomach-turning thud. She scurried away from him as he vanished.

A Protector came into view. Kieran.

Lines of distress crossed his face as he reached for her.

In a daze, Emma heard other sounds of swords clashing. Fallon had come too. He was battling another demon that had just arrived. She collapsed against Kieran and tried to contain her sobs.

"Are you hurt lass?" Kieran's soft Scottish burr grounded her. "Let's have a look at you." He held her away from him and assessed her for any injuries.

Emma pushed away from him and ran to where Briana had fallen. She sunk to her knees as a wave of grief struck.

Kieran picked her up. She began shaking uncontrollably as he carried her to his car. Since Fallon was already behind the wheel, Kieran got into the back seat still holding her.

"Cyn, please, I need Cyn."

Kieran stroked her back and assured her they were on their way to him.

~ ☾ ~

CHAPTER TWENTY SEVEN

Cyn's arm muscles quaked.

But he didn't even register any pain when a sword sliced into his side. If anything, he felt a surge of adrenaline. After he forced the Warrior demon to retreat, he turned and stabbed at one behind him. It leaped back surprised.

Cyn noticed that Roderick was having better luck, as he fought just one warrior demon now.

He lifted his sword with both hands and aimed for the demon once more. Unfortunately, the demon blocked him again.

Cyn shoved him and the Warrior stumbled back.

He grabbed a dagger out from his coat. Before he could throw it, he was forced to block a strike from the other warrior.

Hissing between clenched teeth, Cyn forged ahead through sheer willpower. Finally, he had enough room and he let the dagger fly, striking one of his adversaries in the heart.

The angry growl from the other Warrior demon was enough warning to block the sword aimed to cut his head off. Cyn stumbled slightly before regaining his balance. Now he was furious, and losing a lot of blood.

Fueled by his anger, Cyn rushed forward and swung his sword all his strength.

This time he didn't miss.

Injured and bleeding from a deep gash to his

shoulder, the Warrior demon stepped back. He snarled at Cyn and ran away.

Cyn went to follow but stopped. It could be another trap. Roderick's opponent fled as well.

The Warrior demons were gone and so was Gerard. Cyn finally felt the throbbing from the gash on his side. He held a hand over it and applied pressure.

Roderick walked over. "Where the hell did they come from?" He shouted shoving Cyn's hand aside to inspect the wound. Cyn leaned back on an abandoned vehicle and winced as Roderick poked in the wound.

"Shit Roderick, why don't you just stick your entire hand in there while you're at it," Cyn grumbled.

"Don't whine," Roderick said as he tore a strip from the bottom of Cyn's shirt and wrapped it around his torso. "It's not cool for a Protector to whine."

"You want to know what the fuck is totally not cool?" Cyn yelled, taking his anger out on his friend. "Those damn demons ruined my first night with my wife. That's what's not cool! Why didn't Julian warn us about those damn things being back?"

Roderick shook his head as they walked toward Cyn's truck. "That is a question I plan to ask our fearless leader. But first let's ensure Fallon and Kieran know about the newest crap in town."

Once he was seated in the truck next to Cyn, Roderick pushed the button on his earpiece and talked to Fallon for a few minutes.

When he disconnected, Cyn got his attention. "Look, I am going back to Emma's house and wash off the stench of demon. Then I'm going to wake Emma up and make love until I forget all that hurts." He wagged his eyebrows at the Spartan. "You should go home too. However, what you do when you get there is your own damn business. I'll drop you off at your car. It's around the corner. Right?" He let out a weary sigh. "Tomorrow is soon enough to call Julian."

Cyn's gut reacted when Roderick's worried gaze met his.

"Cyn, we need to head to your house."

# # #

The front door burst open crashing against the wall. Cyn rushed through the living room headed to his bedroom plowing past Fallon.

Kieran stepped in front of him to block his path and held his hands up. "Don't go in there scaring her Cyn. She's all right. Everything is fine. Calm down."

"Get the fuck out of my way." Cyn tried to shove him aside, his focus on Emma alone.

"Move out of his way Kieran. I'm surprised he hasn't flattened your ass." Roderick spoke up. "If he hadn't been driving and in a hurry to get here, he would have shoved his sword up mine."

"Fine." Kieran shook his head and stepped aside. "See that's why we shouldn't get married. That's why I can't believe Julian allowed it. Brother, you cannot expect us to ignore the damn rules." He called after Cyn's retreating back.

Cyn raced to the dimly lit room. Emma sat on the bed and rose when she saw him. Satisfied that she was alive and unharmed, Cyn crushed her against his chest. She began to cry and clung to him.

"Calm down Sweetheart, you're safe now. No one is going to hurt you." He pushed her hair back from her face and kissed her teary face until she calmed.

It wasn't until after she finally lay against him, sniffing softly, that he began to feel relief. However, he was so angry with her that he couldn't keep quiet.

~ ☾ ~

"Emma, why did you go out by yourself?" Cyn asked her in a quiet but stern voice. "I explained to you that from now on you should not go anywhere without the body guards. You said you understood and accepted."

"I know. I really am sorry, but when I heard Briana's voice, I didn't think. I tried to call you. I forgot you told me you could only communicate with other Protectors while on duty. Maybe if I hadn't gone out there, Briana would still be alive." Emma began crying again.

"Cyn, she died." Emma choked on the last word. "Please forgive me. I know you're angry, but promise you won't leave."

Cyn gathered her closer and held her face up to him. "I can't leave you love. Not because I am not allowed to, but because I can't live without you. I am angry with you." He kissed her on the lips. "But Emma, I love you too much to ever want to be away from you."

"I can't imagine living without you either," She replied burying her face into his shoulder.

Cyn laid her back onto the pillows and went to get up, but she protested, and clung to his arm. "Please stay a little while longer."

"I'm not going anywhere. Let me take a shower and I will join you okay?"

When Cyn came back out of the shower, he slid under the blankets and drew his sleeping wife to him. She shifted in her sleep and burrowed into his side.

A hundred thoughts had run through his head when Roderick told him that demons attacked Emma.

He'd wondered if she betrayed him again and had found it difficult to breathe.

When he learned that Briana lured her out, he felt a bit better.

Now he wondered if the baby was all right, but that would wait until later. Right now it was enough to have his wife next to him safe and sound.

His eyelids became heavy and he closed his eyes.

~ ☾ ~

CHAPTER TWENTY EIGHT

Julian's fury was loud and clear as it blasted through the speaker in the library at Fallon's house. The room reminded Cyn of the décor during the 1800's with its thick carpeting and plush seating. The Roman's Italian accented voice vibrated, as he responded to the news of the Warrior demons. Cyn's eyebrows lifted, he was glad the man was not there in person.

"You should have contacted me immediately."

Moments later, after he listened to all the Protectors had to say, Julian sounded calmer. "I am surprised to hear Gerard found any Warrior demons willing to support his cause. Warrior demons are unpredictable and disloyal." Julian sounded thoughtful, "They are not willing to die for anyone or anything, including their Supreme Ruler. That's why they will leave a losing battle. Be wary of everything from now on. Gerard and his followers are going to extraordinary measures to free Thames." Julian said.

Kieran stood up and stretched. "I didn't feel a deadly threat from the Warrior demons. It was almost as if they were just toying with us, not willing to get close enough to be killed."

Fallon nodded. "I agree, the bastard I fought turned and ran the first chance he got."

"I want all of you off the streets for a few days. Let's see what they do. I need to know if they are a threat to the humans or just looking to kill Protectors." Julian's voice came across, stilted.

"That doesn't sit well with me." Kieran groaned. "I prefer to go out and face them. Not hide."

Cyn, Roderick and Fallon's eyebrows rose as they waited for Julian's reaction. They were not disappointed. "Follow my damn orders Protector. I didn't ask what you would prefer."

Kieran glared at the others and replied through gritted teeth. "Understood."

"Now," Julian continued. "Remain in secure quarters for the next seven days. Take a break. Spend time with a woman and relax. But keep an eye on things. Gerard returned because he feels at an advantage with the Warrior demons on his side. He is not patient and I'm sure he is formulating some sort of a plan as we speak."

"Is there something you are not telling us Julian?" Roderick asked the man he'd known longer than the others in the room.

Julian's voice came on after a few moments of silence. "The Autumn Solstice is in three weeks. The festival of Dionysus will take place then, it lasts seven days. Things are about to get worse."

Every ten years, Zeus allowed Dionysus to roam the earth for seven days. The god of wine evoked madness and ecstasy when he entered the human realm.

Every decade, the god's appearance caused all types of mayhem and atrocities in the larger cities around the globe.

The room was still as they realized how much worse this year could be with the return of the Warrior demons.

"The chosen cities will have extra Protectors assigned. New Orleans, Rome, New York, Paris and Atlanta."

Julian continued. "I am putting all of you on a forced lockdown, until I see what the Warrior demons do." The grumble of the Protectors filled the room until Julian growled. “Enough.”

“Rowe and Thor will arrive to Atlanta in two weeks. I’m also sending in Logan West. He’s new but very efficient. Fallon, they will be staying with you, as you have the largest home. Sebastian has agreed to provide any needed assistance and is already ensconced within the coven to find out what he can.”

“I don’t trust the incubus,” Cyn told them with a scowl.

“I do.” The men gaped at Kieran, surprised. Kieran didn’t trust anyone.

He shrugged. “What? The guy saved my ass back at the compound. He’s okay.”

“Lockdown can be boring without entertainment.” Fallon arched a brow at Kieran. “So, where does one go about finding a willing woman in this town?”

“It’s going to be a long seven days,” Kieran replied, ignoring his question, “I’m going home.

Cyn and Roderick stood up and prepared to head home.

“Wait,” Fallon stated, “I’m serious. I do not intend to stay locked up for seven days and not have pleasurable company.”

Julian replied, “Kieran, you will remain there with Fallon.”

Kieran’s mouth opened, but he didn’t say anything since he’d already stepped in it earlier. Instead, he glared at Fallon.

“Cyn and Roderick, you will have additional human guards posted at your homes. Additionally, human demon slayers will patrol the city. They are not allowed to confront any of the warriors. I need them to keep a low profile. Under no circumstances will they engage demons in battle. Merely keep surveillance and report back to me.”

~ ☾ ~

When Julian's call ended, Fallon narrowed his eyes at Kieran's enraged expression. "I suppose Julian missed the part of my comment when I requested "pleasurable" female company."

His response was Kieran slamming him to the floor.

Cyn and Roderick watched the men tussle across the room.

"What is Julian thinking?" Cyn said shaking his head. He stood up to leave, Roderick followed.

Cyn took one last look to check on his brother. Kieran and Fallon lay next to each other on the floor panting. He walked out.

"Ow," Kieran bellowed. Fallon must have gotten one last punch in.

# # #

Emma sat still and watched Cyn pace back and forth in front of her. Two days had passed and he was not dealing well with the lack of freedom. Like a caged tiger, he couldn't seem to stay still. And she couldn't keep him busy in bed, since Blue was quarantined with them.

"They are out there, hurting innocent people. Meanwhile, I'm sitting here on my ass, not able to a damn thing." Cyn repeated for the umpteenth time. "What the hell is Julian thinking, locking us up?" He grunted. "The human slayers are not even allowed to come to engage any of the demons. What good is that?"

She ached for him and placed her hand on his arm. "I have an idea. You said Blue's awesome with computers, that he and Kieran are masters in the Cyber world. Why don't you ask them to break into Atlanta's traffic-cam system? You won't be able to see every single street, but you should be able to see most of the city. Maybe you can call and get help for victims when you spot a demon attack."

"That idea has definite merit, Mrs. Fraser," Cyn hurried to their bedroom, no doubt to call Kieran.

In five days, the Protectors would be back out on patrol. Emma wasn't sure she was ready for it, especially with the upcoming "festival". Not exactly a fun time for many. Especially those who would become victims of the altered emotions Dionysus would bring about.

Her phone rang and snapped her out of her thoughts. It was Wendy.

"I'm almost done packing. I'm going to visit my brother in Savannah next week. Although, I really don't think it's necessary Emma. I'm sure I'd be safe and sound as long as I stay in my apartment for those seven days." Wendy sighed. "Maybe you can arrange for a certain Protector to come and check on me. Regularly."

Emma's eyes darted down the hallway to ensure Cyn was out of earshot. Without him knowing, she'd warned Wendy to leave town. She wanted her friend to be safe.

She darted to the spare bedroom and sat on the bed. "It's not a joke Wendy," Emma whispered, "I would feel much better if you leave town."

"Okay, I'll leave. I'm only doing this because you don't need any more stress in your condition."

"Good, I love you," Emma smiled relieved. "If it helps, Kieran is locked up too, and next week they'll be incredibly busy."

"Oh God. Maybe I need to stay. What if something dreadful happens to him?" Wendy said.

Great. Why did she have to open her big mouth?

"Nothing is going to happen to him. Just promise me, you will go to Guiles' house."

"Okay," reluctance was evident in her friend's voice, "but promise to call me immediately, if anything happens."

~ ☾ ~

After she hung up, Emma felt somewhat reassured. She hoped Wendy would follow through. She had enough to worry about the following week, with Cyn facing off against the Warrior demons and all the mayhem that was expected.

The next morning, Blue sat at the kitchen table with his chin in his hands he watched Emma cook breakfast. "Can I wake Dad up now?" He asked once again. "I'm starving and if we wait until he gets up, everything will be cold."

His expression was sincere— Emma had to give her handsome stepson that. It surprised her how smoothly their life had slipped into a family routine.

A framed picture of her and Brianna with their arms around each other caught her eye. It would take time for her to accept that her sister was gone. Brianna would in all probability have become more evil over time after being turned by Gerard, but Emma couldn't help but wish she still lived.

She turned the last pancake and smiled at Blue. "I'll go wake Cyn. He still hasn't adjusted to being home at night and has trouble sleeping. I'm shocked the smell of food hasn't woken him. One thing about you and your Dad, food is of the utmost importance. It's given me incentive to expand my culinary repertoire. Go ahead and dig in."

# # #

A noise machine filled the peaceful room with the simulated sound of waves crashing on a shoreline.

Not able to help herself, Emma paused beside the bed and looked down at her husband. Cyn's soft snore made her smile as her eyes feasted on his parted lips. He was fast asleep, with one arm over his eyes and other stretched over her pillow. At the handsome sight, she lost all willpower and leaned over to press her lips on his.

Quick as lightning, he hauled her onto the bed and kissed her soundly, not releasing her until she moaned.

His sleepy, crooked smile enticed her to snuggle into his arms and stay.

A slight frown marred Cyn's perfect features. "Do I smell breakfast? What time is it?" He sat up and swung his legs to the side of the bed.

Emma laughed at his quick change of mood.

He gave her a puzzled look. "What?"

"Nothing, just that it's time for breakfast my sleepy prince. But you better hurry Blue is in there alone with a stack of pancakes. He won't give them a chance to get cold."

Cyn smiled widely "Yum." He looked into her eyes, and his expression became solemn. "Thank you Emma." He reached for her hand and kissed her knuckles softly.

Emma shrugged. "It's just pancakes."

"Not just for that. Thank you for making my life complete." Cyn lay on his side and faced her, without speaking he took her in his arms and his mouth covered hers.

At that moment Emma felt more treasured than ever.

How she loved this man. The comfort of his arms was heaven.

In a few days, the Protectors would be out in full force, to protect innocents, and uphold their oath to the force.

But for now, she would relish these moments.

When his hardness rubbed against her thigh, all thoughts disappeared and Emma melted into her husband's embrace.

"You are my dream come true." Emma murmured against his lips.

# # #

~ ☾ ~

The pancakes were indeed cold by the time they made it into the kitchen.

Those that were left anyway.

~ ☾ ~

Acknowledgements

Thanks to my husband, Kurt, who does so much around the house, allowing me time to write, without a complaint. You Rock Babe! I love you.

My greatest appreciation to my critique partner Ciara Knight, for her gentle encouragement. To the Georgia Romance Writers, for teaching me everything I know. The best RWA chapter ever! To my staunchest supporters, who cheered me on every step of the way. My dear friends, Beth Hockey, Cindy Boyer, Julisa Nixon, Kathy Gray, Masie Hendrix, Patti Little, Rob Smith, Stephanie Pettis, Stacey Warner, Susie Donnelly and Tonya Bieda, I love you all so much!

Lastly, a very sincere thank you to my wonderful and hardworking editor, Donna O'Brien.

Hildie McQueen

Hildie was born in Mexico, and grew up in Sunny San Diego. After a jaunt in the Army, living in Texas, Germany and Hawaii, she settled in Augusta, Georgia. She lives with her wonderful computer whiz, hubby Kurt, and two tiny dogs (Pancho & Pepito) as well as a scaredy-cat named Dyson that she hardly ever sees.

Writing has always been a part of Hildie's life. However, a couple years ago, when a friend grabbed her and forced her to attend a Georgia Romance Writers, she decided to polish her skills and get serious about it. Now the characters won't shut up and she's always itching to get home and onto the laptop to write.

Amongst her hobbies, travel, reading, watching romantic comedies and occasionally scrap booking.

Stop by Hildie's website and check out her blog to see what she's up to lately.

www.hildiemcqueen.com

CPSIA information can be obtained at www.ICGtesting.com
Printed in the USA
LVOW081225071011
249535LV00001B/3/P